Changeling EXILE

MARINA FINLAYSON

FINESSE SOLUTIONS

Cover design by Karri Klawiter
Editing by Larks & Katydids
Formatting by Polgarus Studio

Published by Finesse Solutions Pty Ltd
2018/08
ISBN: 9781925607024

Author's note: This book was written and produced in Australia and uses British/Australian spelling conventions, such as "colour" instead of "color", and "-ise" endings instead of "-ize" on words like "realise".

A catalogue record for this book is available from the National Library of Australia

My earliest memory is of hiding: a note of panic in my mother's voice urging me through dark spaces, the salt smell of her fear. Nice fae ladies don't sweat, and I never knew her to do so, even after a day of working in our small cottage garden, yet the memory feels so real I can't believe I imagined the whole thing. She says I did; just one more fault to lay at the feet of her disappointing changeling daughter. No wonder she was so keen to get rid of me.

Now, I was hiding again, though it was no nameless terror that had me lurking in the tiny ladies' bathroom of The Drunken Irishman at ten o'clock on a Monday night. Just good old stage fright.

I jumped at a sharp rap on the door.

"I know you're in there, Al." The voice belonged to my friend, Rowan, and it was tinged with frustration. This wasn't the first time he had knocked. He played the drums in our small band, and I played the fiddle. Or guitar. Or anything with strings, really. But I didn't *sing*. "We're on in five minutes, and if you don't come out right now, I'll sic Willow onto you. She's already pissed enough that she's lost her voice. Don't make me tell her you've chickened out."

Five minutes. Shit. My stomach, already seething with nerves, tied itself into a giant knot of terror. For a moment, I seriously contemplated climbing out the tiny bathroom window. But I'd probably end up face first in a pile of stinking rubbish in the alley behind the pub if I did—and Willow would still make me take her place as lead singer for the night.

The door swung open and Rowan's dark eyes peered around it, making sure I was alone in the tiny bathroom. With the door open, the bass thump of the music upstairs was more noticeable. It sounded like Queen's "Another One Bites the Dust". The musical tastes of Randall, the pub's owner, were firmly rooted in the previous century. That worked in our favour, since not many other venues were prepared to give a gig to our kind of Celtic-influenced sound. I'd barely been born when The Corrs were popular. Now the drumbeat invaded my body and my heart thudded even louder.

I opened my mouth to speak, but my throat was too dry to produce more than a raspy squawk. I swallowed hard and tried again. "I don't think I can do it, Ro."

"Of course you can." His long hair was loose tonight, making him look something like a cross between Thor and Captain Jack Sparrow. He usually wore it out when he was performing, and the girls went wild when he whipped it around like a seventies head banger. His open shirt showed his iron ward, a silver amulet on a chain around his neck. "You've got a great voice. I've heard you singing in the shower—and you sing harmonies all the time."

"That's not the same as being lead singer. Everyone will be looking at me."

"Everyone will be looking at you anyway. You're young, hot, breathing—every guy in the place will be imagining putting his—"

Hastily I cut him off. "No one even notices I'm there when Willow's on lead vocals." Willow drew attention wherever she went. It wasn't just the mane of ginger curls and the curvaceous body. There was something about her that simply commanded attention. She walked like a queen and bestowed attention as if it were a royal favour. Growing up a favoured daughter of the Spring Court had a lot to do with it—she'd been pampered from birth, and took adoration as her due, but it was more than that. She was a born performer.

And, of course, being fae didn't hurt. Men had been bewitched by fairy women since Moses was a boy.

"Then I'll do it," he said.

Even in my panic, the thought of Rowan on lead vocals made me smile. "Drummers don't make good singers."

"Phil Collins would beg to differ."

"Rowan, I love you like a brother, but you can't sing for shit."

"So you'll do it?" He cocked his head and put on his most appealing smile.

I knew I'd been played, but I nodded helplessly. Sage, our bass guitarist, didn't know the words to half our songs. Rowan sounded like a frog with a bad sore throat at the best of times—and Willow actually did have a sore throat. So sore, in fact, that she'd barely been able to whisper a greeting when she'd showed up half an hour ago.

"Good. The show must go on, you know. In less than two minutes, in fact, so let's get moving."

Resigned to my fate, I let him pull me out the door and up the steep, cramped stairs from the basement to the main floor of the pub, my legs shaking already. It wasn't that I didn't like singing. My mother had forbidden me to sing around the house, but once she'd thrown me out, I had sung wherever and whenever I wanted to. I just didn't want to sing *here*, with all eyes on me. Playing the fiddle or the guitar, safely anonymous behind Willow's mesmerising performance, I felt free to lose myself in the music. It didn't even feel like performing. I was just rocking out with my friends.

Sage met us at the top of the stairs, wearing dark jeans and a white singlet at least two sizes too small that showed off her assets and the considerable muscles of her upper arms and shoulders. Her black hair was cropped short, leaving the long, powerful lines of her neck exposed. Sage only had two hobbies—music and working out—and she was very good at both. "I was starting to think you'd fallen in. We're on in two minutes."

"I know."

"You'll have to sing."

This time it came out more like a whimper. "I know."

She took my arm and hustled me through the packed tables toward the corner where the band was set up. "Sage is the smartest and most attractive of all my friends."

I blinked at her, momentarily startled out of my panic.

She grinned, teeth flashing white in the darkness of the room. "I was shooting for another 'I know'. Relax! You'll be fine. Willow says to pick one face in the crowd to focus on and forget the rest."

Standing on the tiny stage with the spotlight blinding me a moment later, I couldn't remember ever feeling so nervous as Rowan shoved the microphone into my hand and gave me a comforting pat on the shoulder.

"Hi," I said, then winced as the mic squealed. I moved it further from my mouth and tried again. "Hi, I'm Allegra, and we are The Outcasts."

There was barely a dint in the noise levels. Randall had turned off the jukebox, but the roar of conversation continued unabated, liberally sprinkled with the clinking of glasses. The cavernous room smelled of sour beer and stale sweat, and the mic in my hand began to shake. Willow only had to open her mouth to have the crowd hushed, hanging on her words, yet in that whole sea of faces hardly any were turned my way. I knew I would be crap at this. Why had Rowan made me do it? I threw a desperate glance at Willow, standing behind me in a tight black dress with guitar in hand, red hair piled up in a messy yet still elegant bun. She made an impatient "get on with it" motion.

Okay, no small talk tonight. "Our first song is called

'Wake the Fire', written by our own drummer, Rowan Hart."

Rowan launched straight into the intro and I blew out a shaky breath, trying not to squint against the glare of the spotlights. A slowly revolving disco ball over the dance floor directly beneath our tiny stage threw blue and green speckles of light across the faces of the crowd. The dark pits of their eyes stared expectantly at me. Those who were watching, anyway. Many still talked among themselves. I couldn't hear them anymore with the music behind me, but I could see their mouths moving.

Usually we started with "The Devil Came Down to Georgia", just to get the blood pumping and the crowd revved up, but Willow was no fiddler, so that was out. Hopefully, Rowan's song would still get a good response.

"Al!" Sage's fierce whisper broke into my thoughts, and I realised with a thrill of horror that I'd just missed my cue.

I cleared my throat nervously—right into the mic, of course—and waited while my friends repeated the intro. *Come on, Al, how hard can it be? Just pick one person and sing to them.*

Naturally, my boyfriend, Adam, wasn't here tonight. Seeing him leaning on the bar might have calmed me, but he'd been coming to our gigs less and less frequently lately. Desperately, my gaze roved over the crowd until it was arrested by a pair of eyes staring straight back at me.

Their owner stood at the back, near the doors, arms folded across his chest. He wore a black T-shirt, and both the arms and the chest were so bulging with muscle that for a moment I forgot my nerves, forgot all about the music—forgot everything in rapt appreciation of his sculpted form.

When I finally dragged my gaze back to his face, his lips were curved into a sardonic smile, as if he knew what I'd been thinking. Hastily, I looked away, a flush warming my cheeks.

I managed to catch my cue this time, and launched into the first verse, filling the room with Rowan's heartache over his ex. My voice was as good as Willow's even if my stage presence wasn't, and the conversations in the room began to die, more of the pale faces in the dark turning toward me. I could do this. Not that Willow needed to fear for her job. I'd much rather be back there on that guitar. I winced as she hit a wrong note. Yes, we both had our areas of expertise.

When I sneaked another look at him, the dark-haired guy was no longer staring at me, which allowed me to admire him a little more. The coloured lights played across his hair, bringing out green and purple highlights. I was used to seeing gorgeous men—everyone in the Realms looked like a supermodel, and Adam was pretty good-looking for a human—but this guy had something else, a brooding quality that wouldn't allow me to look away. Something about the way his dark brows drew together, or how his short beard caressed his square jaw, made him look deeply serious, yet his full lips suggested he knew how to play, too.

His eyes met mine again, and a spark leapt between us. Or maybe that was just me. I stumbled, lost the thread of the music, and recovered it again, heart racing. This was no time to be fantasising about Mr Dark and Brooding. I had a job to do—not to mention a boyfriend waiting at home. Resolutely, I turned my attention away before I embarrassed myself by forgetting all the words to the damn song.

A guy about my age, twenty-one or twenty-two, sat at the bar with a couple of mates, but they were chatting to each other across him while he stared down into his beer as if it was the most fascinating thing he'd seen all day. He was kind of cute in profile. I had the feeling that I'd seen him somewhere before, especially when he smiled suddenly at something one of his mates had said. I could *almost* picture that smile on another face, but I couldn't quite place it. Maybe I'd point him out to Sage, who was currently unattached. He looked more approachable than Mr Dark and Brooding.

We made it through the song and received a smattering of applause. Gradually, the knot in my stomach began to unwind. I was nearly finished the next song before my maddeningly familiar friend at the bar looked up from his beer again. I was looking straight at him, so I saw his flinch, so big and dramatic it looked as though he were trying out for a part as the villain in a kids' pantomime. Then he grabbed the arm of the guy sitting next to him and shouted into his ear, gesturing wildly toward the stage as he did so.

At me? I still couldn't figure out why I felt as though I should know who he was—had he recognised *me*? I nearly lost the thread of what I was singing again. This looking at the audience thing sucked big time. How did Willow manage to concentrate? I shifted my focus to a point on the back wall instead, but I could still see the guy out of the corner of my eye. When the last chords of that song sounded, I could hear him, too, yelling over the low rumble of conversation.

"Horns! He's got horns! Look—can't you see? Are you blind? Look at him!"

Okay, he wasn't waving at me. Heads started to turn in the audience and I sneaked a glance over my shoulder at Rowan, just to be sure he hadn't flared accidently. In his fae form, he sported an impressive set of antlers.

Of course he hadn't. And antlers weren't horns, anyway. Ro frowned at me as Sage began the next song, and his hands moved automatically over the drums even as his attention was diverted by the growing noise out front. He still looked completely human. If I'd watched him out of the corner of my eye for long enough, I might have glimpsed that other self, shimmering under the surface, but I was a changeling. I'd spent my whole childhood in the fae Realms, and I could see things that regular humans couldn't. Fae like Rowan had the ability to hide their true nature from mortal eyes, putting on a convincing human front whenever they needed to. No one but other fae—and the odd changeling—should be able to sense his true form beneath the human façade.

I stumbled my way into the next song, more than half my attention on the guy. Was he drunk? He slid off his stool and started weaving through the crowd. One of his mates followed, grabbing at his arm, but he shook him off. Where was Randall? This was taking a turn I didn't like.

But the publican, who was also fae, was nowhere to be seen. Only Cathy, as human as they came, stood gaping behind the bar, watching the guy's unsteady progress across the room. He stumbled as he hit the crowd on the dance floor, and a woman fell against her partner. His friend, who was still following him, tried to stop him again, but he was waving his arms in the air as though he was having some kind of fit. A small space opened up around him as people became aware of the crazy guy in their midst and tried to shuffle out of the way.

We got to a softer moment in the song, and I could hear him again, still yelling about horns. Demons, too, this time. I couldn't tear my eyes away. What could I do but keep singing? A quick glance showed me that the others were aware of him; Willow was giving him a death glare, and Sage watched him with narrowed eyes, almost daring him to get any closer. If he did, we'd have to do something. We couldn't have the audience climbing up on stage attacking the band members.

Because I was pretty sure that was what he wanted to do. Green and purple lights swirled across his face, which was screwed up into an expression of intense hatred. His other friend came to help the first, one of them grabbing each arm, but there was no stopping him. His fury gave him strength, enough to shove one into a crowd of girls.

The girls squealed as their drinks went flying, and a couple of them stumbled in their high heels. There was nothing for it; I'd have to get down there and take him on myself. I was confident I'd be more than a match for some drunk guy who couldn't even see straight, but I had a feeling Randall wouldn't be too impressed at me decking one of his customers.

As if thinking of him had summoned him, Randall appeared at last, with his son Tony in tow. Randall had some troll blood back in the family tree somewhere for sure. He and Tony were both built like ambulatory mountains, with legs the size of tree trunks and biceps too big for me to get my hands around. Okay, I had smallish hands, but they were massive.

Tony grabbed one arm and Randall grabbed the other, and they lifted the guy off the ground as if he were a child. He kicked and flailed, but the crowd made room and they bore him towards the doors and out into the night. A few moments later, they came back inside, and the guy and his friends didn't. Randall must have cast an Aversion on them.

I relaxed back into the music and we finished the set with no further disturbances. I squeezed my way through the crowd once we were on a break, gratefully accepting a glass of water from Cathy. My mouth felt drier than the Sahara.

"Where did Randall go?" I asked her. I wanted to find out what the guy had been saying, and whether he really could see through Rowan's Glamour.

"Don't know," she said. "It's pretty busy for a Monday night. You guys were great!"

"Thanks." I took my drink and pushed through to the

door. Sure enough, Tony was outside in the cooler air, like some giant guardian statue. His dad employed him as a bouncer and, consequently, The Drunken Irishman was the only pub in the area that didn't have the police turning up at least once a week.

"Nice singing," he said. "What happened to Willow?"

"Thanks. She's lost her voice, so I'm filling in tonight. What was with that guy you threw out?"

He shrugged his massive shoulders. "I reckon he was on something before he came. Probably ice. I've seen some angry drunks before, but that was something else."

"He seemed to be … hallucinating, right?"

His eyes were the colour of granite, but shadowed with worry. "I hope so, Al. I hope so."

2

"Maybe he was a changeling," Sage said as we hoisted the last of our equipment into the back of Willow's four-wheel drive later that night. Or, rather, early the next morning. It was only a little after twelve—normally, we hung around much longer after a gig, chatting and drinking, but Willow felt like shit and we'd all been thrown by the strange incident with the crazy guy. No one was in the mood for socialising. "That could explain it."

It could. It wasn't uncommon for changelings to turn to drugs after they were booted from the Realms, as they inevitably were. Fairies loved stealing human babies, but once those babies grew up they lost their appeal, and the fickle foster parents wasted no time sending them back. Some barely made it to their teens, others lasted almost to adulthood, but no one got to stay in the Realms forever. The king of the Realms had seen to that when he'd issued an edict that fae parents had to gift some of their own power to their stolen offspring, making those children fae themselves, in order for them to stay.

I'd been seventeen when I'd landed back in sunny Sydney, abandoned to fend for myself. The human world seemed so flat and colourless after a childhood growing up surrounded by magic. Maybe our DNA was human, but our hearts were fae. A lot of people had trouble adjusting.

"We would have heard if another one was coming through," Rowan said. The fae community here had a bit of a network set up through the city, so that no one would be left on the street. "But he looked a little old."

"Tony said he thought the guy was on ice," I said. None of the others had thought the guy looked familiar. He probably just reminded me of someone I'd seen on TV.

Sage perked up at that. "I knew a guy once who got high on ice and thought his mother was the devil. He was all ready to stab her when the cops arrived."

"Nice."

"Did you see the knight?" she added, changing tack in a typical Sage move. She had the attention span of a five-day-old kitten.

"No," I said, intrigued. There was a knight there? Fae knights were rarely seen outside the Realms. Rarely seen *inside* the Realms, for that matter, especially since the king had disappeared. There were only a handful of them, sworn servants of the king. Even among a rather warlike people, their fighting skills were legendary. "Which one?"

"The Hawk," Willow said, in a gravelly voice quite unlike her usual sweet tones. She was more familiar with fae nobility than the rest of us, since she belonged to it herself.

"Thought they were all dead," Rowan said. He didn't keep up with fae politics at all, having long ago decided he preferred the human world. "Didn't they die when the king did?"

"Only the Bear died," Willow said, "and if the king's dead, the Hawk has been wasting his time all these years looking for him."

"That would be sad," Sage said. "It's kind of romantic, though, isn't it? How nobly he's devoted his life to the search?"

"Romantic?" Rowan echoed in a scornful tone. "A hopeless quest looking for a guy no one will ever find because he's been dead for twenty years? That's not what I'd call it. I remember now—this guy is the laughing stock of the Court. I thought he'd given up looking years ago."

"I don't know why I'm even talking to you," she said. "You haven't got a romantic bone in your body." She sighed. "He was really hot, though. He was at the back near the doors when we started the first set, but I got distracted by the crazy guy and lost sight of him after that."

Hmm. "Did he have dark hair and a beard? Dressed all in black?"

"Yes! You did see him. Hotter than Papa Bear's porridge."

Rowan gave a shout of laughter, but Willow only rolled her eyes, which showed how sick she was. Normally, a new piece of slang got a much bigger reaction from her. She and Sage competed to find the most outrageous examples they could; they called it their assimilation project, as nothing marked you as odd more than swearing by a goddess that no human had ever heard of.

Mr Dark and Brooding had been hard to miss. We certainly hadn't been the only two women in the pub watching him. But I hadn't realised he was a knight. No wonder he'd looked at the happy, half-drunken crowd as if they were beneath his notice.

Willow slammed the back door, her normally vivid green eyes dull and shadowed with illness. "Coming?" she croaked.

"You look shocking," I said, firmly putting aside visions of getting up close and personal with the knight. As if a knight would ever look twice at a lowly changeling. "Go home and get some sleep. Rowan and I can walk."

Rowan's people came from the great forests of Autumn, and his night vision was as sharp as any owl's. Once, I'd roamed those same forests, and while my night vision couldn't match his, it was far better than any normal human's. At least Faerie didn't take back all its gifts when it renounced its changeling children.

She and Sage got into the car and drove away, and I stood in the grimy car park, watching their red tail lights disappear around the corner. A powerful reek drifted on the night air from the dumpster against the back wall of the pub, and snatches of laughter and voices raised in drunken song floated from the street out front.

"Somebody liked us," Rowan commented as the unseen singer launched into "Forgiven, Not Forgotten" by The Corrs, which had been part of our final set.

"We were pretty good," I said, slipping my arm companionably through his as we left the car park. "All things considered."

"I told you you'd be fine," he said, smiling down at me with obvious pride at his own powers of prediction. "You seemed to get over your nerves pretty fast."

"Except for when that guy was going off. He looked like he wanted to rip your head right off your shoulders."

"He could have tried." The supreme indifference of a being that knows itself superior coloured his voice. Even after all this time in the human world, Rowan could be very fae at times. It was easy, looking at his unlined face, to forget he was over a hundred years old. That was still young by fae standards, but he certainly had a few years on the rest of us. He patted my hand where it curled around his arm. "I'm sure you would have stopped him before he got that far."

"Don't be patronising."

"I'm not. I've seen you fight." He studied my face for a moment by the anaemic white light of a streetlamp. We had the pavement to ourselves, the only sound our footsteps against the background hum of distant traffic on the main road. "You're worried about it, aren't you?"

"It sounded like he could see you. How can that be?"

"Maybe Sage is right, and he's a changeling."

"I know you don't believe that."

He sighed and patted my hand again. "Let's not borrow trouble, Al. If it becomes a problem, we'll deal with it."

"Are you sure you're not being patronising?"

He grinned. "I swear it by the Silver Tree. Let's talk about something else. It's been a long week."

"But it's only Monday." I glanced at my watch and corrected myself. "Tuesday."

Almost twelve-thirty in the morning, in fact, and I was tired, despite the fact that it was a relatively early night for me. Many fae, like Rowan, preferred the night, but between picking up a few shifts at the local service station in the day time and performing in the band at night, I'd managed to completely screw my schedule. My body clock was permanently out of whack, and only coffee kept me functioning.

I had the rest of the morning off, but I was due at work from two until ten. I had a place to live now, thanks to Rowan, who let me rent the converted garage of his house for a nominal amount. Which was just as well, because nominal was all I could afford. It was hard to find a decent job without a proper education or any kind of qualifications and, even after four years, I was still finding my feet in the mortal world. It had been a little easier since Adam had moved in, but he was studying journalism at uni and had even less money than I did.

My education in the Realms had prepared me for life in the forests of Autumn. I could do things with herbs that would shock your average pharmacist, I could recite the Lay of the Silver Tree and the history of the House of Autumn back to Giseult and the planting of the Forest. I could hunt and trap, fight barehanded and with knives, but I was no digital whiz, though I could manage the register at work. Willow had taught me to drive, but I didn't have a licence.

Thank the Lady for TV—or "thank God", I should say. If I sounded like a native, it was only because of the hours I'd spent in front of the television, absorbing the culture and picking up the way modern humans spoke.

We turned a corner onto a quiet residential street lined with old-fashioned terrace houses. Built in the previous century, they huddled close to the street, separated only by ornate iron fences from the public footpath. Home was only a few blocks away, faster if we took the shortcut across the park. Up ahead, a streetlight flickered lazily, as if it was as tired as I was.

Behind us, a tiny scraping sound caught my ear. It was my only warning.

I was half-turned toward the sound, head cocked to one side, when a man came flying around the corner at us. I leapt aside, but a shoulder slammed into mine as the figure passed, and I staggered. Rowan shoved the man violently, but that only seemed to enrage him more.

"Demon spawn!" he shouted. It was our crazy friend from the pub; I knew him as soon as I heard his voice again. "Get back to hell where you belong!"

They grappled together, swaying. I wasn't in the habit of bringing weapons to gigs, so I had no knife, but I dropped and swept his legs out from under him. His head hit the pavement with a crack that made me wince, and he lay still.

Shakily, I got up. Though I often sparred with Sage, it had been a long time since I'd had to fight anyone in earnest.

"You okay?" I asked Rowan.

He shrugged himself back into his leather jacket, which the guy had half ripped off, and straightened his iron ward. "Of course. Is he dead?"

I could see the man's chest rising and falling even without bending down. "No. He's probably got concussion, though. He's a persistent bastard—what's his problem? Is he using?"

"I'd check his pupils, but he's unconscious. See if he's sweating."

I crouched beside the body and lifted an arm, enough to check the underarm of his shirt. There were no wet patches. His skin felt warm, but not unusually so. I leaned closer, peering at his face. "What's this around his mouth?"

Rowan bent down. "Where?"

"Here, in the corners." Something sparkled there like glitter.

"No idea. Haven't seen that one before." He straightened and looked up and down the deserted street. "Come on, let's get moving before someone comes along and wonders why we're standing over an unconscious body."

I rose, but hesitated. "We can't just leave him here."

"Why not?"

I paused. Why not, indeed? To a fae, it was a perfectly reasonable question. The man, whoever he was, had shown himself to be an enemy by attacking us, and the fae really didn't grasp the concept of mercy for enemies.

But he was just a guy, under the influence of some drug or other. He might be perfectly nice under normal circumstances. Regardless, he was now a guy with a serious concussion, lying defenceless in the empty street. It didn't seem right to just walk away.

I pulled out my phone. It was the most basic sort available, and it didn't do anything but make phone calls and send texts, but that was enough. I dialled the emergency number and began to report an unconscious man lying in the street. Rowan rolled his eyes and leaned against the brick wall behind him while I gave the street name and a rough summary of the man's injuries. I hung up when the operator asked for my name.

"Happy now, Miss Samaritan?"

"They'll be here in five minutes," I said, resisting the urge to point out that the Good Samaritan hadn't done the beating up himself. I'd read the Bible cover to cover several times, so I knew my stuff; human spirituality fascinated me.

I refused to leave until I saw the ambulance turn into the street. We waited further down, shrouded in shadows, until the paramedics got out, then continued our walk home in silence. Hopefully, that was the last we heard of that guy.

I should have known not to jinx myself like that.

I said goodnight to Rowan and headed down the driveway to my tiny home at the back. The light over my door was on, but no lights showed through the window, so I was very quiet as I slid my key into the lock. Closing the door carefully behind me so as not to wake Adam, I slipped off my shoes and carried them in my hand as I crossed the small lounge room.

A faint scent hung in the air that I couldn't identify, something sweet and floral. I left my keys and phone on the kitchen bench, next to his, then headed for the bedroom. The door was closed, but I heard a murmur on the other side. Damn. I thought I'd been quiet enough, but I must have woken him.

And then I heard a giggle. I froze, a chill sweeping through my body from head to toe. That was a woman's voice.

I held my breath, waiting—I don't know what for. Some other sound that might convince me that I'd misheard? Some other explanation to occur to me as to why there was a woman in my bedroom in the middle of the night? Some innocent, rational explanation other than the painfully, horribly obvious?

I'd be waiting a long time. No wonder we'd been fighting so much lately. No wonder he hardly ever came to watch the band perform anymore. I gave the handle a vicious twist and flung the door open.

A woman shrieked in surprise. The curtains were drawn, and it was dark in the tiny bedroom, but my enhanced night vision showed me the scene clearly enough. The sheets were rumpled, carelessly flung aside, and my boyfriend lay sprawled on his back. A dark-haired woman straddled him.

I flicked on the light, which elicited another little scream from the naked woman. The whole thing seemed even more tawdry in the glare of the electric light. I felt like I'd kicked over a rock and found nasty, scuttling things underneath it as the woman scrabbled for something to cover herself.

Adam sat up, blinking in the sudden light, as his partner slid off the bed, not meeting my eyes as she hurried to shrug herself back into a too-tight dress. "Al! You're home early."

Rage built inside me as I fought to control my trembling. "That's the best you can do? *You're home early*? Not even 'I swear I've never done this before' or 'I'm sorry I'm such a cheating scum'?"

"I haven't! I mean—I'm sorry. So, so sorry." He got off the bed, too, on the other side from the frantically dressing girl. The bed took up so much of the small space that there was barely room to stand on either side. He made to move towards me, still naked.

"Put your clothes on and get out." Did he think I was stupid? "I don't care if it's the first time or the hundred and first—we are done."

"Please, baby, I'm sorry. I know you're angry, but we can talk about this, huh?" He zipped his jeans so fast it was a wonder he didn't catch anything in the zipper. Not that that would have been a great loss. "I love you. You're the only one for me, you know that."

The girl snatched her shoes off the floor and approached the door, hesitating. She looked like she wanted to be anywhere else but here but wasn't sure it was safe to get too close to me. One strap slipped off her shoulder and she hitched it up nervously.

"Did he pay you?" I snapped at her.

Her eyes widened with indignation. "I'm not a prostitute."

I knew that; I just wanted to hurt her. I clenched my fists and moved to let her pass. She wasn't the person I should be taking my anger out on. He'd probably picked her up in some pub and brought her home without ever mentioning that there was a girlfriend on the scene. She fled down the hall, and the front door slammed shut behind her.

I turned my attention back to my boyfriend. My suddenly *ex*-boyfriend. "I'm the only one for you? It sure doesn't look like that from where I'm standing."

"I'll make it up to you, I swear." His light brown hair was tousled in that way I used to think looked sexy. Now it made me feel sick, knowing how it had got like that. Some other woman had been running her fingers through it, touching him. *Riding* him. In my own goddamn bed. And if I hadn't come home early, I would have gone to sleep in that bed, right there, where he'd been screwing someone else hours before. It made me want to heave.

And then I realised—I'd probably done that before. Many times. I'd probably even had sex with him myself, with someone else's sweat and God knows what else on his skin. I shut my eyes for a moment. My body wasn't big enough to contain the rage and pain swelling inside me. Any minute now, I would shatter into a million pieces of bottled-up agony. I couldn't look at him a moment longer.

"You have to leave." I sounded calm. Controlled. Like a normal person. What a joke.

My tone must have made him think he had a chance to talk me around, to somehow excuse his behaviour. He moved closer, arms outstretched. "Babe, let me—"

My hand flew out and slammed him in the centre of his chest, sending him staggering back onto the bed. "Don't. Touch. Me."

A red mark bloomed on his chest where I'd struck him, and a new wariness showed in his eyes. He scrambled awkwardly to his feet and held out his hands in a placating gesture, the way you do when you're dealing with an aggressive dog.

Ha. He thought that was bad? Wait until I really got started.

"Of course, of course," he said, inching closer. "Whatever you want, babe. Just let me explain."

I ground my teeth. "Despite your apparent opinion of my IQ, no explanations are required. The only thing I need from you now is your absence."

I stepped into the hall and moved aside so he wouldn't brush against me as he passed.

"But, babe, it's the middle of the night. Where am I gonna go? Why don't I just sleep on the couch out here and we can talk about it in the morning?" A wheedling note had entered his voice. How many times had I heard that before? Usually, it worked on me, but not this time.

"I swear, if you don't leave this house right now, you won't live to *see* the morning." I spun on my heel, marched into the kitchen, and grabbed one of the knives from the block.

"Hey, hey, no need for that," he said, stepping back in alarm. "What the hell is wrong with you? Calm your shit down."

I stalked toward him, brandishing the knife. "The only thing that's wrong with me is that *you are still here!*" My voice rose with each word until I was shouting in his face. "Get the fuck out of my house *right now* and don't come back! We are *over*."

He snatched his car keys off the kitchen bench and backed up, much faster than before. "Okay, okay, I'm going. I'll ring you tomorrow." He pulled the front door open.

"Don't bother. I won't be taking your calls."

The door slammed behind him, and I stood there for a moment, shaking with rage. Then I dropped the knife and let the tears come, hot and angry.

I was still standing there long after the noise of his car's engine had faded away.

Not surprisingly, I barely slept, finally falling into an exhausted sleep only an hour before the alarm went off. I considered calling in sick and just staying in bed, but all the crying had given me a towering headache, and I knew I needed food and painkillers, so I dragged myself out of bed. The bathroom mirror assured me that this was a bad idea—my eyes were bloodshot and puffy, and the circles underneath were almost as blue as the eyes themselves. I ran my fingers through my short blonde hair and called it good. No amount of makeup was going to fix this, and I couldn't be bothered anyway. A girl was entitled to a couple of days of wallowing after a break-up before she had to straighten her shoulders and move on. I splashed water on my face, then inhaled my asthma preventer—I took two puffs, morning and night, and hadn't had an attack in years—and wrinkled my nose as the taste hit the back of my throat.

In the kitchen, I boiled the kettle and added two large spoonfuls of instant coffee to my favourite mug. I needed the wake-up if I was going to get through this day. The box of painkillers was nearly empty—I'd have to add those to the shopping list. I downed a couple and looked out the window, which overlooked Rowan's small back garden, while I waited for my bread to toast.

Two ravens perched expectantly on the low stone wall that separated my tiny "courtyard" space from the rest of the yard. I called them Thing One and Thing Two, not because they were destructive, but because I'd been a fan of Dr Seuss stories since I'd first arrived in the city, frightened and cold, and had discovered that libraries were wonderful, warm places to while away a winter's day.

Things One and Two visited me most mornings, and I bought a small stick of cabanossi when I did the groceries every week just for them. I cut a couple of slices, then slathered peanut butter on my toast and grabbed the coffee. Juggling it all, I nudged the door open with my elbow and headed outside.

Thing Two hopped sideways along the wall as I approached, giving me the side-eye from one black and white orb. Australian ravens had the weirdest eyes, so different from the black-eyed ravens I'd been used to seeing in the forests of Autumn: their white irises looked like little buttons, with the pupil in the centre the black thread that was holding it on. Thing One was braver, and held his ground. Actually, I had no idea what gender they were, but I figured they were a mated pair, so had randomly assigned Thing One as a boy and his partner in crime as a girl. Thing One was missing an eye, so it was easy to tell them apart. I laid the two pieces of cabanossi on top of the warm stone, then retreated to my plastic table and chair with my breakfast, glad for the ravens' company. My thoughts had been going round and round in painful circles all night—I could do with a distraction.

Thing One took his snack up to the branches of the giant gum tree that dominated the small yard. Thing Two hopped over to claim her share, then joined her companion on the branch.

"Cheers," I said, raising my coffee cup in salute. Ravens never had to deal with cheating partners, the lucky little bastards. They mated for life.

Their jet-black feathers had a purplish tinge to them in the morning sun that reminded me of Mr Dark and Brooding's hair. The Hawk's hair. Why had he been there? What possible interest could a pub in the human world hold for a fae knight like him?

Sure, it was something of a gathering place for the local fae and their outcast changeling friends. But he wouldn't find the lost king hiding among us, if he really was still looking after all this time. I doubted the king had ever been to the mortal world in all his long life.

I wondered if the Hawk had ever cheated on anyone. Probably—fae weren't exactly renowned for their faithfulness, although everyone seemed to think the knights held themselves to higher standards than other fae. His bearded face, with those intense eyes, floated in my mind's eye. He was certainly gorgeous. It wasn't hard to imagine a procession of women throwing themselves at him. Maybe being with him would be worth the pain of the inevitable betrayal.

A raven's harsh cry broke into my thoughts. Thing One

was back on the low wall, just a short hop away, fluffing his feathers huffily at me.

"What's wrong? Didn't I give you enough?" Greedy little devil. Maybe one day he'd feed from my hand. He looked about ready to flutter over to my table to make his point. "Sorry, but I'm not buying more than one stick of cabanossi a week. That shit's expensive, you know."

He croaked mournfully.

"Besides, think of your figure. You'd never be able to get your fat arse off the ground if I let you eat all you wanted."

I stood up and tossed the last piece of peanut butter toast on the ground. That probably wasn't ideal bird food—hell, it wasn't even ideal people food—but I wasn't hungry this morning. I'd have to look up what ravens ate next time I was at the library.

I had a few errands to run before I started my shift at the service station, so I chucked the dirty plate and cup in the sink and headed out. If I'd had a computer—or even a smartphone—I could Google it, but my budget didn't run to either of those things. Maybe I could get some time on one of the library computers if I couldn't find a book on it. You had to be lucky to find a free library computer, though. In the mornings, they were monopolised by pensioners, and in the afternoons, the school kids descended on them.

My phone rang as I was locking the front door behind me.

I fished it out of the back pocket of my jeans, ready to reject the call if it was Adam, but it wasn't his number. "Hello?"

"Is this Allegra Brooks?"

I rolled my eyes as the familiar deep voice carefully enunciated each word, as if there was a prize for clear diction. "Who else would be answering my phone, Dorset?"

Dorset was attached to the Court of Eldric, Lord of Autumn. I'd never been quite sure what his official role was; I suspected Dorset wasn't sure, either. He seemed to do everything from running minor errands to organising Court visits to walking Lord Eldric's dog. One of his duties, apparently, was being a pain in my backside.

A familiar exasperation entered his voice. Dorset was frequently exasperated in his dealings with me. That only seemed fair, since he drove me crazy. "How should I know who this ridiculous piece of plastic will summon?"

"You make me sound like a demon. I've told you before, there's no magic involved, it's just technology." That was funny—me, the least tech-savvy person I knew, talking about technology as if I had a clue how any of it worked— but compared to Dorset, I was a guru. "If you dial my number, you will be connected to me and no one else. That's how phones work."

One day, I would have to get someone else to pick up when he rang, just to mess with him. The thought lightened my black mood. Unfortunately, he didn't call often. Only when Lord Eldric needed something from the human world and remembered that I existed.

Some fae made it a point of pride that they had never left the Realms in all their long lives. Others weren't quite as rigid, but most preferred not to enter the mortal world unless they absolutely had to, and the older and more powerful they were, the stronger that preference became—which was why it had been so odd to see one of the king's fabled knights at the pub. Fae of his standing found it physically painful to be in an atmosphere so full of iron. The more power a fae had, the worse the pain.

Sure, they could ward against iron by wearing something Charmed to resist it, but that made it much harder to access their magic. Minor spells weren't too draining, but using magic that required any decent amount of power became exhausting. As a result, if something needed to be done in the mortal world, or fetched from there, powerful fae called on their flunkies. Even the flunkies had flunkies, which was where I came in. Eldric gave tasks to Dorset, and Dorset passed them on to me.

"I'm not interested in how phones work," he said frostily.

I started down the driveway to the street, mentally reviewing the list of things I had to do before work: pick up Rowan's dry cleaning, visit the library, grab some more milk and something quick I could eat for dinner tonight on my break. Only half my attention was on Dorset and whatever inconvenient task he was about to give me. He sounded testy, but that was nothing unusual. Maybe he always sounded so peeved when he called because he had to leave the Realms, however briefly, to get a signal.

"What I *am* interested in," he continued, "is ensuring that you attend the Hall tonight. Lord Eldric wishes to speak to you."

I stopped dead in the street, my heart pounding, all thoughts of love and betrayal forgotten. I hardly heard the end of his sentence, with those magical words ringing in my ears. Attend the Hall.

He wanted me to go back into the Realms. To go home to Autumn.

I started walking again, more slowly. Usually, Dorset passed on his Lord's instructions over the phone. This was the first time I'd been summoned to Eldric's presence. What could it be about? Not that I really cared. If I was invited into the Realms again, I was going.

"Allegra? Are you there?"

I realised I'd been silent for too long. "Yes, I'm here. I'll be there."

"Good. Make sure you wear something suitable for Court. Jaxen will meet you at the Fold."

"No jeans. Yep, got it." There weren't too many other options in my wardrobe, but I'd find something. "See you tonight."

"Yes," he said, in a tone that implied he was not looking forward to it. But what did I care? I had an invitation to Autumn.

Autumn, my childhood home, the one place in both worlds I most wanted to be. The place that was closed to me forever.

My shift on the checkouts at work was one long procession of increasingly tired-looking faces. Customers waited for their items to be scanned, or paid for their petrol, with no more life in them than robots going through the motions. Most did no more than grunt when I said hello, but I felt surprisingly upbeat, considering the mood I'd started the day in. But not even my break-up with Adam mattered, compared to going home to Autumn. Every time I caught myself dwelling on the scene last night, I only had to redirect my thoughts to what was happening tonight to instantly feel better. Besides, I'd spent the day rejecting his calls and ignoring his increasingly pleading texts, which had given me immense satisfaction.

I'd brought a change of clothes with me and, as soon as my shift was over, I darted into the toilets to shrug out of my work clothes and put on something that Dorset might consider appropriate for an audience with Lord Eldric.

Ricky had the night shift; he whistled when I came out

of the toilets. "You going to a fancy dress party, Al? 'Cause you sure look fancy." He laughed, a wheezing sound that ended in a coughing fit, as usual. He was completely bald, with a grizzled beard, and old enough to be my father. Possibly even my grandfather. He often took the night shift because the money was good, and he said he was too old to sleep much anyway. His naked scalp gleamed under the fluorescent lights as he grinned at me. "You're gonna knock them boys dead tonight. You found one to marry yet?"

Despite having married and divorced three wives, Ricky was a big fan of marriage—for other people, at least.

"Nah, Ricky, I'm still waiting for you to propose." I'd never expected to end up with Adam. But I hadn't imagined it would end the way it did.

He laughed another of his wheezy laughs. "I reckon if I was twenty years younger, I would, too. But I can't afford any more ex-wives—why do you think an old geezer like me's working so hard? At my age, I should be out playing golf, enjoying the life of a retiree. Goddamn child support payments are killing me."

I smoothed my dress over my hips. It was red velvet, tight and short. Apart from all the leg I was showing, it was reasonably modest, with long sleeves and a high neckline. "I need to impress my old boss," I said. Eldric wasn't really a "boss" so much as a liege lord, but that wasn't something I could explain to Ricky. "Do you think this looks okay?"

"Okay?" Ricky snorted. "If the man's got a heartbeat, he'll think it's a lot better than *okay*. But why do you need to impress him? You're not gonna change jobs and walk out on me, are you?"

"And leave all this?" I waved my hand around at the sterile shelves of junk food under the harsh white lights, at the lino floor with the inexplicable stain by the door, and the bank of fridges humming and leaking away on the back wall. "Of course not. This is more of a social thing."

Working at the service station wasn't the greatest job, but the hours were flexible, which was handy, since Eldric seemed to want something at least once a month that involved me disappearing for days at a time. Last month, I'd only had to hook the court up with a new coffee supplier, but back in January, I'd had to track down a kobold who'd gone on a bender in Melbourne and disappeared. It had meant my first plane ride, which was fun, but I'd been gone for over a week. I couldn't pull a stunt like that with most jobs, but my manager had just shrugged and reassigned my shifts to someone else.

"Well, you be careful walking around the streets looking like that."

"Always am."

I strode out the automatic doors and across the brightly lit concrete past the fuel pumps. The service station was on the corner of a busy road, and cars whizzed by, even at nine o'clock at night. Three guys in a van called out to me as I waited at the crossing for the lights to change, but I ignored them. My phone buzzed with another call from Adam, and I ignored that, too. At least the calls were getting further apart—maybe he would eventually get the hint that I had no intention of ever speaking to him again, much less taking him back.

The train station was two blocks down the road, and I only had to wait a couple of minutes for the next train. Peak hour was long over, but there were still plenty of people on board: a few office workers sprinkled among girls in high heels and short skirts and their partners, heading into the city to hit the bars and night clubs. I looked like one of them.

Sage called while I was watching the dark city fly past beyond the windows. I hesitated for a moment before taking the call, knowing I'd have to tell her about Adam.

"What are you up to?" she asked. "Do you want to come to a midnight screening of *Rocky Horror*?" Despite having lived in the mortal world longer than I had, Sage still kept a mostly nocturnal schedule. Probably because she lived with Willow. "Willow's curled up in bed moaning like she's got the black plague instead of a common cold, so I've got a spare ticket."

I smiled at this description of Willow. She took every sniffle as a personal insult. Illness was the one thing she hated about the mortal world. "Sorry, I'm on my way to see Lord Eldric."

There was a pause, and when she spoke again it was in a guarded tone. "To see him where?" She knew as well as I did how unlikely Eldric would be to leave the Realms. "Not in Autumn?"

"Yep."

"He must want something big, then. Don't let the

bastard sucker you." Sage's opinion of the Lords of Faerie was not complimentary. She was a half-breed, offspring of a not-exactly-forbidden-but-definitely-frowned-upon   union between a fae noble and a human woman. Her father belonged to the Spring Court, but the only thing truly noble about him was his ancestral line. He had a bad reputation, even among fae, and Sage's childhood had therefore been a lonely one, with no one wanting anything to do with the half-breed child until Willow had taken her under her wing. As a result, she'd developed a rather jaded view of the high fae, and once you lost her good opinion, that was it.

"I'll be fine. He probably just wants me to locate another lost lamb." Memories of the drunken kobold made me shudder. He'd covered everything I was wearing in spew— it even got into my boots. "Although, if it's like the last one, I'll ask for danger money to cover my dry-cleaning." I forced a laugh, but even to me, it sounded false.

"Is something wrong?" she asked. "You sound kind of tense. Are you nervous?"

She'd find out soon enough. I might as well tell her and get it over with. I just felt so stupid—it was such a cliché. "No, I'm not nervous, I just—I broke up with Adam last night."

"You're kidding!"

"Yeah, it was a surprise to me, too."

"What do you mean? Did he dump you?"

"Nothing that classy. I found him in bed with someone else when I got home."

"Shit. Want me to kill him for you?"

I laughed, and this time it was genuine. "Sure, why not?"

"Consider it done. You want torture with that, too—something nice and slow?"

"Sounds good to me."

"I can't believe he did that to you. What an arsehole. Wait until I tell Willow—she never liked him, you know."

"Yeah, I know. Maybe I should get her to vet my next boyfriend. Obviously, I have a habit of picking losers."

"No, you don't. That Josh guy was nice."

"Okay, so one out of four. Not a great success rate."

"Everyone makes mistakes. Adam's no loss, anyway. You'll be better off without him."

"Yeah, I'm sure you're right."

She made a little noise of frustration. "Now I'm worried about you. You sound so down. Want to meet up for coffee later?"

"I don't know how long this thing with Eldric is going to take. Don't worry about me; I'll be fine. You go enjoy your show."

I got off at St James and headed into the darkness of Hyde Park. There was a night market up one end, which meant there were more than the usual number of drunks around, but I headed for a quieter spot toward the middle and slipped into the darkness under the trees.

"You took your time," growled a voice, and a figure stepped out from behind a massive fig tree.

"Hello, Jaxen. Nice to see you again."

Jaxen was a Jumper, a rare kind of fae with the ability to gate directly in and out of the Realms, rather than having to walk the Greenways through the Wilds like everyone else. He was also Eldric's younger brother, and occasionally—and begrudgingly—ran errands for him. In return, Eldric kept him in style, which didn't seem like much of a deal for Eldric, but I guess you had to ensure a certain level of comfort for your heir, even if it meant he spent most of his time lazing around your hall drinking your cellars dry. Fortunately, it wasn't my problem. Jaxen wasn't one of my favourite people, but I rarely had to put up with him.

"I'd say the same," he said, stepping forward so that the moonlight shone on his huge tawny-gold eyes. At least his wings were out of sight, but no one seeing that face would think he was human. He obviously wasn't planning on staying long. "But I'd be lying."

"I was," I replied coolly. "It's called making polite conversation. But let's not play games. You don't like me, I don't like you. I assume you're here to take me to Autumn, so let's get it over with."

His lip curled into a sneer. "You know what they say about assuming. No, Eldric sent me to give you this. He knows I wouldn't sully my hands with a changeling."

He tossed something that glinted in the moonlight as it arced through the air, trailing a silver chain behind it. I caught it reflexively. It was an amulet made of many different strands of silver, woven into an intricate pattern like the world's most complicated Celtic knot, an emerald nestled in the centre. A whiff of magic clung to it.

"Is this a gate glyph?" I'd heard of them, but I'd never

thought to hold one in my hand. My heart began to beat a little faster. With this, I could open a gate to the Wilds and navigate the dangerous Greenways. The Realms would be open to me.

"Well, it ain't a Christmas present, sweetheart," Jaxen said. "You're to keep it until you finish the job. Don't lose it or Eldric will skin you alive."

Why on earth was Eldric entrusting me with one of these? There were only a few in existence. Since fae could manage their movements between worlds without one, they were only used by changelings or the odd visiting human. The secret of making them had been lost, and none of the full-bloods cared enough to bother trying to rediscover it, so the handful that were left were valuable. Was it possible I was being granted access to the Realms on a permanent basis?

My heart soared, but I reminded myself I'd thought that the first time Dorset had contacted me with a task, too. Best not to get too excited until I heard what Eldric wanted of me. Most likely, he was merely expecting I would need to make several crossings between worlds to complete the task, whatever it was.

Jaxen faded from sight, and a wind disturbed the leaves on the ground and buffeted the branches of the fig as the sound of massive wings beat the air, then abruptly cut out. He had Jumped back to the Realms, leaving me to take the slower and more dangerous route. I closed my fist around the glyph, the chain swinging from my hand.

It was a risk I was more than happy to take.

The Realms were a separate world—or dimension—to the mortal one, existing alongside it but somehow elsewhere. Mostly, that separateness was complete, but there were places where the two worlds came very close to each other, almost touching, and these were called Folds by the fae, who never used a scientific explanation when an imaginative one would do. According to their legends, when Agar Brenfell, the first king, created the Realms from the stuff of magic, he'd thrown his cloak down between them and the mortal world to shield them from human eyes. In some places, the cloak fell into folds, and there, the magic leaked through, creating weak spots in the fabric. In these places, it was easier to cross from one side to the other.

Easier, but not exactly easy.

Scared of losing it, I slipped the chain over my neck, though I still clutched the gate glyph in my fist like some superstitious kid with a lucky charm. A large Fold ran halfway across Sydney, but it was particularly weak here in the middle of the park, which meant a safer crossing was more likely. The gate glyph needed a threshold to work with. Doors, gateways, or even windows were best, but of course there were none of those to be found in the middle of Hyde Park. I looked around for a likely spot, and chose a place where two trees leaned close together, as if whispering secrets, their branches intertwined like lovers' arms.

Dammit. I was *not* spoiling this moment by thinking about lovers. Adam was in the past, and I'd be thinking *very* carefully before letting anyone else into my bed or my heart.

I might be a little slow to learn, but I pretty much had the lesson down pat now—no more picking guys on their looks.

The trees protected a dark, shadowy area behind them, hemmed in by bushes. As I called on the magic clutched in my fist, the darkness pulsed, and a mist curled around my ankles. A thrill of excitement shot through me as I passed beneath the leafy arch.

Long, ghostly stems of grasses that I couldn't see brushed my legs, and the scent of rosemary and lavender rose all around me. The glyph in my hand throbbed with power, heating my skin as a forest grew in my peripheral vision, leaves rustling overhead as the neatly planted trees of the park faded away. An owl hooted, and something small and terrified scuttled in the darkness beneath mighty oaks, and suddenly I was there, in the wild places between the worlds.

I stood in a small, moonlit clearing. Three overgrown paths stretched away into the darkness under the trees. I turned and found another behind me. Ringing the clearing was a circle of birch trees, their slender trunks shining silver in the moonlight. The Silver Circlet. Good. There were few recognisable landmarks in the Wilds, but this one was close to the fae side, which suggested the gate glyph was a powerful one. It should stand me in good stead against the confusing magics of the Wilds.

Still, my heart hammered uncomfortably in my chest as I chose the left-hand path at random. It didn't matter which one I picked—all of them could lead anywhere, or nowhere. It all depended on the power of the traveller. Last time I'd been through here, my mother had been taking me to the mortal world, and I had left the navigation to her. Now, it was up to me.

My destination—the silken Hall of Giseult—firmly in mind, I moved under the trees, treading lightly on the soft earth. Though it was dark, my enhanced night vision allowed me to see where I was going. There was no way I wanted to lose this path. The Greenways didn't obey the laws of physics, but they were the only safe route through the Wilds. If my will, or the glyph's magic, failed, I could end up on the other side of the Realms entirely, in the frigid mountains of Winter, or even in the dark Realm of Night. That was best case scenario. Worst case was that I would wander the Wilds until I died, irretrievably lost.

Or until I stepped off the path and something killed me, I guess.

That was not a happy thought. I realised that my steps had slowed, and forced myself to lengthen my stride again, moving forward with at least the pretence of confidence. Just because there were rustlings in the bushes, it didn't mean something was waiting to pounce on me. I'd grown up in a forest; I knew all about the constant rustlings and squeakings, the creaking of branches as they swayed in the wind, and the strange calls and coughs of nocturnal animals going about their business.

An owl hooted again somewhere off to the right, closer than before. The familiar sound reminded me of the forests around the cottage where I'd grown up, and the tight knot of apprehension in my chest eased a little. People came through the Wilds all the time, even lesser fae whose magic wasn't as strong as the magic of the gate glyph. As long as you kept to the path and focused on your goal, there was nothing to fear. I strode onward more confidently.

The path narrowed until it was barely wide enough for both my feet to fit on it and had become overgrown with whispering grass stems that nodded in the light breeze rustling through the forest. The glyph pulsed in my hand, and I knew that my destination wasn't far now. Stones turned under my feet as the trees arched over the narrowing path, blocking out the moon's feeble light. Something thrashed in the bushes on my right, and I shied instinctively left, one foot leaving the path.

Horrified, I stopped. Only the toe of my right boot was still on the path. Deliberately I lifted my other foot, heart pounding, and placed it carefully back onto the path.

I laid one hand on the rough bark of a tree trunk, listening, but there was no more sound, only an oppressive weight to the air, as if the whole forest was holding its breath. Instinctively, my free hand crept to my waist, but no knife hung on a belt there. Shit. I'd left my knife at home, of course. Lord Eldric would take it as a personal insult if I brought an iron weapon into his presence.

The back of my neck prickled with the horrible insistence that something or someone was watching me. I looked around, steadying my breathing, checking the shadows, but if something was there, it was well hidden. Best to keep moving.

It was an effort to keep from running. These were not the gentle, sunlit woods of my childhood, and the feeling of being watched persisted. I moved as quickly as I dared, without losing the path among the tree roots and undergrowth, trusting to the gate glyph's power to lead me in the right direction. On either side, the trees pressed close, their twiggy fingers snatching at my velvet sleeves as I passed. Mist swirled between their trunks and shapes moved in my peripheral vision, though when I looked directly, there was nothing there. Behind me, the path closed up again as I passed.

At last, I burst out of the forest, into a meadow where long grasses and wildflowers bobbed and swayed in the night breeze. Before me, a small stream chattered over rocks, winding its way across the meadow. Mist rose from the dark water, obscuring the other side, but a wooden bridge arched over the water, its far side lost in swirling white.

My steps quickened. The path here was wide and smooth, bordered in white stones that gleamed in the moonlight. With the forest at my back, I flew down the path and onto the bridge, my footsteps loud on the wood. Mist slid around me, its tendrils caressing me as I passed, until it cleared abruptly and I stepped down off the bridge onto the soft grass of Autumn.

Home at last.

I stood in a green forest clearing, before a vast hall made from living trees. Their great trunks formed the walls of the hall, and their branches interwove to create a roof of sorts, though I knew from experience that large chunks of sky were still visible from within. Silken hangings formed doors to close off the inside from the clearing, and more silk hung in the surrounding trees, in colours of red, orange, and gold that blended in with the fiery autumn foliage of the trees themselves. Some of the silk hung in banners, and other, larger pieces formed privacy screens for platforms built into the canopy above.

Behind me, the wooden bridge still crossed a stream, but there was no sign of the mist I'd just walked through, or of the foreboding forest of the Wilds. All around me stood the forest of Autumn, where giant red trunks stretched straight and tall into the night sky. At their feet, soft grass formed a carpet starred with white flowers and scattered with autumn leaves, while above, their mighty heads were crowned in red and gold. A gentle breeze ruffled the leaves and set the silken banners rippling.

I felt a great urge to kick off my shoes and run barefoot through the soft grass, as I had as a child. Instead, I straightened my dress, picking a few burrs out of the velvet sleeves, before marching confidently toward the entrance to the Hall of Giseult, ancestral seat of the Lords of Autumn.

The two guards who stood before the silk-hung entry were new to me. Even four years ago, before my mother had sent me away, I hadn't known everyone in Eldric's household. Mostly, we kept to ourselves, in our cottage by the rushing River Ivon. I'd been too young, then, to understand that she was ashamed of her changeling child and wanted to keep me away from the eyes of other full-bloods.

The female guard had arms almost as well-muscled as Sage's and was about my height, which was to say, not very tall. Nevertheless, she drew herself up at my approach, an expression of disdain crossing her beautiful face. Her companion stared straight ahead, acting as if he couldn't see me at all.

"Hi," I said. "I'm Allegra Brooks. I'm here to see Lord Eldric."

"Lord Eldric is expecting you," she said, turning to the silken hangings behind her. Patterned with autumn leaves of many shapes and colours, they rippled gently in the breeze. They seemed so insubstantial, but I knew they were spelled to be as impassable as any fortress gate of iron if the guards refused entry.

She drew back the silk curtain and held it aside for me to pass through. A soft current of air brushed the back of my neck as it whispered shut behind me, and I paused as I took in the vast space.

At the far end of the hall was a dais bearing a long table. The remains of a meal for twenty or more people littered it, though only five still lingered there. Above them, orange and gold lengths of silk swooped and draped. On either side, the red trunks of the forest giants rose, solid and strong. Between them stood archways formed by their branches. Some of these were open, others closed by yet more silken hangings, and wooden staircases on both sides spiralled up to other levels where private chambers nestled among the branches. Far overhead, stars peeped through openings in the interlaced branches, their light competing with the glow of lamps that floated high over the hall. A croak that sounded oddly like a raven drifted down to me as something rustled among the leaves. At this time of night, I would have expected owls.

The hall had been created with magic, coaxed out of the forest, part organic and part constructed. The fluttering silks everywhere gave it a feeling of impermanence, as if the Autumn Court had only set up camp here temporarily, and at any moment could take down their hangings and move on.

A young fae sat on one of the spiral staircases, playing a lilting melody on a silver flute. He broke off his tune at the sight of me, and the man at the head of the table looked up.

"Allegra," the man said. "Come in."

"Lord Eldric," I replied, bowing my head before accepting his invitation and crossing the soft, grassy floor of the hall. Scents of mint and jasmine rose as my feet crushed the soft grasses, which sprang back as I passed.

He lounged back in his chair, one elegant white hand hanging over the ornately carved arm, watching me thoughtfully. He wore a traditional fae robe in red and gold, with the whirling leaves of Autumn's sigil picked out in gold thread on his breast. His russet hair was tied back in a careless ponytail, and he wore no jewellery other than a fiery ruby on the hand draped over his chair.

On his left, an empty chair stood between him and Dorset, who was dressed in more modern garb than his Lord: brown trousers with a loose, caramel-coloured shirt. Jaxen sat beside Dorset, and a man with long silver hair opposite him. The fifth man at the table had his back to me, but he was dressed all in black, in stark contrast to the autumnal tonings of everyone else. Even I had been careful to choose a dress colour that would please the Lord of Autumn.

Eldric motioned impatiently to me as I hesitated at the dais, so I stepped up onto the platform. As I did, the man in black turned around and my steps faltered in surprise.

It was the knight from the pub—the Hawk.

He looked even better up close than he had across the crowded pub. His black shirt was long-sleeved, but still moulded to his body, and it was open at the neck, showing tanned skin. His dark hair, now that I could see it clearly, sported red-gold streaks almost the same colour as Eldric's hair, and his eyes were the colour of honey, warm and otherworldly. Hurriedly, I refocused on the Lord of Autumn, before I fell into that liquid gaze and lost myself staring at him again. I had to stay on my toes until I found out why Eldric had summoned me.

"Sit down," Eldric said, indicating the empty chair on his left, which put me opposite the silver-haired man and next to Dorset, who moved his chair ever so slightly away, as if protesting being made to share space with a mere changeling. "Would you like a drink?"

"Allow me, my lord," said the Hawk, before I could answer. He reached for the flagon and poured golden liquid into a spare glass, which he handed across the table to me with a small bow. "I heard you singing last night. You have a lovely voice."

"Thank you."

His fingers brushed mine as I took it, and I shivered, raising the glass to my lips to cover the movement. The sweet liquid burned its way down my throat, and I set it down hastily, clamping my lips around the cough that threatened to burst forth.

"Ah, Hawk—ever the gentleman, I see," said the silver-haired man, tapping his cigarette into an ashtray. If fae smoked at all, it was usually pipes—either this guy spent a lot of time in the mortal world, or he had a gofer like me to keep him supplied. He wasn't old, despite his hair colour, and could have easily got a job as an elven extra in a *Lord of the Rings* movie. Beautiful in the way of all fae men, there was a sneer in his tone that caused me to take an immediate dislike to him.

The Hawk sat down again, completely unruffled, as if the other man hadn't even spoken.

"Dansen, this is our changeling friend," Eldric said to him. "It's good to see you again, Allegra. I trust you've been well?"

Much you care, I thought, returning his smile with one just as fake. As if the Lord of Autumn had wasted one second on thoughts of me since I'd last seen him. "Very well, thank you."

"We have visitors from the palace tonight," Eldric said. "Dansen Arbre of Summer. He's practically Lord Kellith's right-hand man."

He smiled at the silver-haired man, who blew smoke, then formed it into the shape of a dragon. The tiny dragon flew at me until the Hawk made an abrupt gesture and a wind blew the smoke away.

Eldric continued, "And the Hawk, Knight of the Realms. We have a task that requires your unique skill set."

My unique skill set? What the hell did that mean? And what on earth did the Lord of Summer's right-hand man and a Knight of the Realms have to do with me? "Yes, my lord?"

"Do you know what this is?" Eldric handed me a scrap of jewelled fabric. It was green, but it shimmered like mother of pearl, changing hues as I turned it in my hand. The scrap was no bigger than a matchbox, with torn edges, as if it had been ripped from a larger cloth. In its centre, a clear jewel winked, catching the light of the lamps and throwing it back scattered with other colours.

"A diamond?"

"No." Eldric took it back and stared at the jewel, rubbing his thumb absently across it. "It is far more precious than a mere diamond. It's a piece from the skin of a rainbow drake."

Whoa. Okay, I'd heard of those. They were rare, elusive creatures, kind of like a cross between a lizard and a small dragon. They started off their life cycle as small, water-dwelling lizards. They shed their jewel-covered skins as they grew, and a shed skin was worth a small fortune. Eventually, the growing drake developed wings, left the water, and took to the trees, which was why it was hard to find the adult skins. Even a piece as small as this was more money than I made in a year, but a complete skin, particularly from a larger drake, was the province only of Lords. No one else could afford it.

"This particular piece was part of a larger skin that had been made into a cloak," Eldric continued. "That cloak was the jewel in my lady's wardrobe. Two nights ago, it was stolen. The thief was surprised in the act, and made his escape out the window of my lady's chamber, tearing the cloak on a branch as he did so. This piece is all that's left."

Well, someone had balls, stealing from a Lord of the Realms. That kind of thing usually ended in torment and death for the perpetrator. But I was still hazy on what any of that had to do with me.

"This is not the only such theft," Dansen Arbre said. He'd finished his cigarette and was now toying with a very expensive-looking dagger. If I was not mistaken, that was a black opal set into its hilt. "A jewelled garment belonging to the queen has also gone missing. She has tasked the Hawk with finding it." He cut a sideways glance at the knight. "Let us hope that he is more successful with this search than he usually is."

Jaxen laughed—of course—but Dorset actually sucked in a breath at this reference to the Hawk's long quest for the missing king, and even Eldric looked uncomfortable. Dansen moved up a few notches on my list of Arseholes to Avoid in Future.

The Hawk said nothing, merely gazing steadily at the Summer fae until the silver-haired man dropped his eyes.

"When we heard of this theft," Eldric said, quickly steering the conversation back on track, "Dorset suggested that you might team up with the Hawk, since it seems likely that whoever stole the queen's dress was also responsible for the theft of my lady's cloak."

I glanced at Dorset, confused. I still didn't see how I fit into this picture. He stared back, his thin lips pressed into the usual disapproving line.

"We have reason to believe that the thief fled into the mortal world," he said. "Lord Eldric would like you to assist the Hawk in recovering the stolen items."

"I—" Where would I even start? Did I look like someone who dealt in stolen goods? A command from Eldric was hardly something I could refuse, though perhaps I could turn it to my advantage. "Of course, my lord. Though it sounds like it could be dangerous."

Certainly more trouble than hunting down missing kobolds in Melbourne. Dorset made a scoffing sound.

I glanced at the Hawk, but he watched me impassively as I turned back to Eldric. "Will you be offering a reward?" I could hardly believe my own daring. Not that I was interested in Eldric's riches. No, it was something far more specific I had in mind.

"You should be grateful to be of use to your Lord," Dorset protested, his displeasure evident in the black scowl on his face.

Eldric held up a hand before he could say more. "Every changeling wants the same thing, Dorset. You can hardly blame her for asking."

The Hawk seemed to, though. There was a look of disdain on his face that almost matched the sneer on Dansen Arbre's.

"I make no promises, Allegra," Eldric continued. "But it could indeed prove challenging. Let us see if you can manage this successfully, and then we will talk—as long as the Hawk gives a good report of you."

The Hawk still looked as though he'd swallowed a lemon. Probably horrified at being forced into close proximity with a changeling. "I don't suppose you'll be much use, but you can meet me tomorrow night at The Drunken Irishman, and we'll begin."

And with that, I was dismissed.

6

Okay, so maybe he was good to look at—extraordinarily good to look at, in fact—but Mr Dark and Brooding seemed to have the same attitude problem as Dansen Arbre and most of the older fae. They looked down on us short-lived mortals something fierce. Being a knight, he was probably hundreds of years old, but I hadn't appreciated being reminded of that elitist attitude.

By the time I'd finished telling Sage all about the meeting in Autumn and my new "partner", I was almost dreading seeing the Hawk again. I'd have to keep him happy to have any chance of earning Eldric's vague reward, and it seemed as though that might be an impossible task, judging by the way he'd looked at me when I'd brought up the subject of one. But whatever. We didn't all have the luxury of devoting our lives to an ideal.

"Did he say what time he's meeting you?" Sage asked.

We were sitting at the bar in The Drunken Irishman at eight o'clock the next night. Late enough to be dark outside, but not yet late enough for the pub to be packed. Sage was drinking beer, but I'd decided to steer clear of alcohol for the moment. Who knew what I might have to do once the Hawk arrived?

"Not really. Just 'after dark'." Most fae could understand the human timekeeping system, but generally, they were more laidback about the passing of time, since they had so much of it to spare, and didn't bother with such strict segmenting of their days. "After dark" could mean any time from now until midnight, so here I was, waiting on the Hawk's pleasure. At least I had Sage for company. She had thrown herself into distracting me from thinking about Adam.

"I don't understand why he's involved in the search for a missing piece of clothing," she said, her eyes flicking past my shoulder to check the door yet again. She seemed more eager to see the tardy knight again than I was, after the attitude he'd given me the previous night. *I don't suppose you'll be much use.* Not that I expected to become besties with the man, but if I had to work with him, a little respect would be nice. "I thought he was supposed to be searching for King Rothbold?"

I rolled my eyes. "After twenty years, I'm sure he's figured out by now that he's dead."

"Who's dead?" Randall asked as he stopped in front of us to draw a beer for another customer. A pleasant hum of conversation rose around us, the noise shielding our conversation from the other people in the room.

"The king."

"That's not exactly news," Randall said.

"But no one's ever found a body," Sage objected. "He could still be alive."

"Nonsense," said Randall. "If he was still alive, the curse of the Brenfells wouldn't have fallen on Illusion."

"The curse of the Brenfells?" I raised an eyebrow at Sage, but she just rolled her eyes. Guess she wasn't a believer.

Randall delivered the beer, then came back, shaking his big head. "I forget how young you are. You've never heard of the curse of the Brenfells?"

"Never." I knew that Brenfell was the family name of the fae royal family, and Illusion was one of the thirteen Realms. Well, originally, there'd been thirteen. I'd learned the original roll call as a child: Spring, Summer, Autumn, Winter, Day, Night, Dusk, and Dawn, and the elemental Realms of Fire, Ocean, Earth, and Air. Plus the odd one out—Illusion, lucky number thirteen. They were down to nine, now, through conquest and intermarriage. Dusk, Dawn, and Illusion had fallen, and Earth had first been renamed Flowers, then swallowed up by Spring.

"Old wives' tale," Sage said dismissively.

"Don't be so hasty there, young lady. Everyone should know this story. But I'll need a beer myself if it's stories we're telling."

Trolls loved stories. Whenever you heard of a troll who'd been caught out by the sun and turned to stone, it was usually because he or she had become so caught up in a story that they'd lost track of time. Clearly, even part-trolls like Randall shared the genetic weakness.

Randall poured himself a beer and raised his glass in

salute before downing half of it in one gulp. Trolls were also pretty keen on liquor, but fortunately, they had the head for it. "You know, of course, that our first king, good King Agar, created the Realms and everything in them?"

"Yes, of course." I might not know everything about fae history, but that was like asking a Christian if they knew that God had created the earth and all its creatures. There were many stories of this first, legendary king and his fabulous deeds. He sounded more like a god than a fae: even the most powerful of them had nothing like the skills or strength of this greatest of kings. "And he and Queen Merissa had fourteen children, who became the first Lords and Ladies of the Realms. I know that much, Randall. Get to the good stuff."

"No one appreciates a good story anymore," he grumbled.

"None of us are going to live as long as you, either," Sage said, grinning. "Have pity on the poor mortal and give her the abbreviated version."

"Well, if the poor puny mortal has heard all this, I'm surprised she hasn't heard of the curse as well. Did she miss that day in school?"

"Must have slipped my mother's mind," I said.

"I missed as much school as I could possibly get away with," Sage boasted. "You don't get a body like this by sitting at a desk doing sums all day." She flexed one bare arm, showing an impressive bulge of bicep.

Randall snorted. "Call that a muscle?" He pushed his sleeve up and flexed his own bicep, which was easily bigger than my head.

I laughed. "God, Randall, put that thing away before you kill someone with it." I took a sip from my glass. "And could we please get back on topic?"

He rolled his sleeve back down, looking pleased with himself. "Well, then, to give you the abbreviated version …" He grinned at Sage. "Good King Agar ruled for three centuries, and with his prodigious number of children, the peace of the Realms seemed secured, but Queen Merissa's brother, Delamore, watched each birth with growing dismay. He had hoped that if the royal couple proved childless, as so many fae do, *he* might be the next ruler of the Realms. After all, he was the queen's eldest brother, and the king's right-hand man. If not him, then who?"

"This is the abbreviated version?" Sage cut in. "Let me help: Delamore killed the king and made it look like a hunting accident."

A brief flash of annoyance at having his story stolen crossed Randall's face. "That's right. And then he declared himself regent and schemed to steal the kingdom right out from under young Prince Ordrin's nose. But before two months had passed, a great fire took hold of his home while he was away in Whitehaven, and his wife and two children perished."

"Ooh, nasty," I said, giving Sage a warning look. Randall looked as though he needed some appreciation of his storytelling abilities. "And what happened to Delamore?"

"Before another month was out, he was dead, too. Another hunting accident, if you can believe that, only this time a real one. A boar ripped him open from navel to collarbone, in front of a whole hunting party, and there was nothing to be done. After he died and some documents came to light that put a very different slant on the story he'd been spinning, people realised what had really happened to the king. And so, the story of the curse began: Delamore had killed one of the Brenfells, and his whole line was wiped out as a result."

"So, I've always wondered," said Sage, "does killing any old Brenfell count, or does it have to be the king?"

Randall rolled his eyes. "I get the feeling you're not taking this seriously. But look what happened to Illusion—gone from the face of the earth, and their Lord responsible for the death of a Brenfell. That's not a coincidence. That's the curse in action."

"Didn't the Lord of Illusion disappear around the same time as the king?" I asked. "How do you know he was responsible for the king's death?"

"It stands to reason, doesn't it? Not three months later, his whole realm was destroyed. He must have been guilty."

"Or you're getting cause and effect mixed up," Sage said. "I still say the king's alive."

Randall rested an elbow on the bar and leaned in closer. "And if he was, where has he been for the last twenty years? Nah, the man's as dead as a dodo."

"If that's King Rothbold you're discussing, I'll thank you to show a little more respect," a deep voice cut in.

I'd been so caught up in Randall's story that I hadn't noticed the Hawk enter the pub, and now he was looming behind Sage, fixing Randall with a death glare.

"Sorry, sir." Randall bobbed his massive head in a funny little half-bow. "No disrespect meant. Can I get you something to drink, on the house?"

"I haven't come here to drink," the Hawk said curtly, and Randall took the hint and found another customer to busy himself with, as far down the length of the bar as he could get.

"So, you *are* still searching for the king?" Sage asked, a rapt expression on her face. "You haven't given up hope?"

He raked her with his tawny glare. "At the moment, I'm searching for a damn dress." Frustration boiled in his tone. "But when I find it, I'll return to the search, as long as the queen doesn't find any more ridiculous tasks for me."

His hands formed fists at his sides. This guy was intense. Tonight, he wore a dark blue T-shirt that stretched tight across the hard planes of his chest, and a pair of denim jeans. Despite the attempt to blend in, no one could ever mistake him for an ordinary man. He would be turning heads everywhere he went, with that body and those astonishing eyes, golden like the hawk he was named for. He was gorgeous, but I wasn't so blinded by his beauty that I missed the danger lurking beneath. It was like admiring the sleek lines of a panther, watching the light glint off its smooth coat. You didn't forget that at any minute the beast could spring, its whole body a weapon.

"It's not just any old dress, though, is it?" I could understand the queen being distressed at its loss, and I refused to be cowed by the lethal aura of the man before me. If we were going to work together, I wouldn't be cowering every time he glowered at me. "That thing's probably worth half of Whitehaven." I'd never seen it, but I'd heard the king's city was a wonder of the Realms.

The Hawk transferred his glare to me. "However much it is worth, the king's life is worth more."

Ooh, boy, this was one guy who was seriously pissed with his current assignment. Lucky me, getting to work with him. "Good point. So, let's find this thing, so you can go back to your … quest." And I could go back to my quiet mortal life, though hopefully with added perks. The gift of the gate glyph had made me optimistic that I would be allowed further access to Autumn. Lords didn't hand those things out lightly. As far as I knew, Eldric only had the one. And if the Hawk gave a good enough report of me, maybe a permanent return wasn't out of the question. A girl could dream.

"Do you have a plan?" Sage asked.

I turned to him expectantly. The mortal world was large—far larger than the Realms. If we had to search the whole thing, I'd be stuck with Mr Tall and Ragey forever. My eyes were drawn again to the strong line of his jaw under the neat beard. There were probably worse ways to spend a life.

Focus, you idiot. Even if he was interested, you don't want to get tangled up with fae politics. Get the job done, in and out, quick. Mmmm. In and out … No, definitely not thinking about that now. I felt a blush sweep up my face and took a long, cold gulp of my soft drink to give me an excuse to turn away before he noticed, furious at myself. At least imagining the Hawk in bed made a change from reliving the memory of walking in on that girl astride my boyfriend's body. My *ex*-boyfriend's body.

But why was I thinking about this at all? Did I have to start drooling just because he was hot? I'd made my decision: no more relationships for me. It was clear my choices couldn't be trusted. This girl would be rocking the single life from now on.

"The thief is either a fae or a changeling," he said. "No one else has access to the Realms. I've already checked out most of the fae in this area, but there are a few more I need to speak to. It will be your job to cover the changelings."

"What about the fae *in* the Realms? Why do you think the thief is in the mortal world?"

"Because when he was disturbed, the guards chased him. He fled the Realms and they lost him in this city."

Well, that was something, at least. We wouldn't have to search the entire world.

"But he might have gone back," Sage pointed out.

The Hawk shook his dark head, russet highlights shining in the soft glow of the overhead lights. *Stop staring at him, dammit.* "No. Watchers are guarding the Greenways. No one can pass through the Wilds unseen."

No wonder I'd felt as if I was being watched in the dark forest between the worlds. Nice to know I wasn't just being paranoid.

"Report back to me here tomorrow night with anything you have discovered," he said, then turned around and walked back out into the night before I could say anything.

Nice. Who did he think he was, giving me orders as if I was his slave? I was so over men acting like my feelings didn't matter. I sighed. At least it was easier to resist him when he was being a shit.

Sage grinned at the look on my face. "I guess 'working together' means something different where he comes from, eh?"

The next day started bad and got worse. There weren't many changelings in Sydney—only about a dozen, and I knew them all—but what the hell was I supposed to do? Tall, Dark, and Grumpy had been distressingly vague on that point. Only one thing was sure—whatever I did, he'd be unhappy with.

I started with a Summer changeling named Edgar Woodbine. He'd been one of my first friends when I arrived, shell-shocked and ignorant, lending me books and feeding me dinner more often than not.

Changelings usually fell into one of two camps after they were expelled from the Realms: either they longed to return and did whatever they could to ingratiate themselves with the fae in the hopes of being allowed back in, or they bitterly resented their expulsion and came to hate and despise those responsible. Edgar was definitely in the latter camp. I was a bit of both, but if I was honest with myself, I leaned toward the former.

He beamed as he opened the door to me. "Allegra! I haven't seen you in weeks."

I felt a twinge of guilt as I followed him down the hallway to his kitchen at the back of the house. I always *meant* to drop in and see how he was getting on, but somehow the days got away from me. He moved slowly, shuffling his slipper-clad feet, no longer the hale and hearty gardener I'd first met. He still cared for his potted plants, but it had been a couple of years since he'd been up to mowing his own front lawn.

As usual, he insisted on making tea. I watched him fumble with the kettle for a moment, his old hands knotted with arthritis, then gently nudged him out of the way.

"Here, let me." I'd certainly done it enough times over the years to know where he kept everything.

He subsided gratefully into a chair at the kitchen table. At least he wasn't using his walking stick today. This must be one of his better days. The stick, with its ornate head carved in the shape of an eagle, leaned against the bench by the back door, just by the window where Kel sunned himself. The ginger cat was named after Kellith, Lord of Summer, as a petty kind of revenge for being ejected from his lands. Edgar said it made him happy to boss him around, though I was sure Edgar loved the cat more than he'd ever cared for Lord Kellith.

I brought the tea, with milk and sugar added just the way he liked it, to the table and took a seat. We chatted happily for a few moments, but when I mentioned the reason for my visit, I realised how hopelessly out of my depth I was.

"Why are you asking me?" he snapped, setting down his cup with a clatter. "Are you accusing me of stealing from the Lord of Autumn?"

"No, of course not." Kel stared balefully at me from his place on the sunny windowsill between the floral curtains. I already knew *he* didn't like me; I didn't want to add his owner as an enemy. Edgar had always been good to me. "I just wondered if you'd heard anything."

"And where would I hear something? We haven't had a new changeling in years. You and Sage are the only outcasts I talk to these days. Oh, and that boyfriend of yours, but he's not really one of us, is he?" He gazed at me suspiciously, clearly still feeling personally attacked, and it occurred to me that everyone I approached was going to react this way. I mean, what did I think would happen? That the thief would say, *Oh, yes, actually, that was me, stealing priceless items out from under the noses of fae nobility. I wasn't going to mention it, but since you ask …*

Surely this wasn't what the Hawk had meant me to do. But what had he expected? That I would break into people's homes and ransack them, looking for clues? That I would follow people around the city, hoping to catch them doing something dodgy? This whole thing was stupid.

"He's not my boyfriend anymore," I said, glad to divert the conversation away from the touchy topic of thieves and stolen goods. "I kicked him out."

"Good. You can do better than Adam Harris." That surprised me, as I'd always thought Edgar liked Adam. "Did you catch him cheating on you?"

Emotions boiled inside me: surprise, anger, pain, regret. For a moment, I couldn't speak, and drew a deep breath. "Why?" I was proud of the fact that there was only a faint tremor in my voice. "Did you *know*?" If he had known and hadn't told me, we weren't going to be friends much longer.

"No, but I've seen his type before. Too cocky by half. Always thought himself a lady-killer, I'm sure. I'm surprised it took him this long to stray."

Yes, well. I drew another deep breath in through my nose and let it out slowly through my mouth. More likely, it hadn't taken him this long—it's just that this was the first time I'd actually caught him at it. I'd been obsessing over the idea ever since, going back over every memory, looking for signs that I'd been too blind to notice at the time. Every time I'd been on stage with the band, and he'd been sitting at the bar, chatting, what had he really been saying? Did he really have as many female friends as it seemed, or were some of them more than friends? While he smiled and applauded, and I gazed into his eyes, so proud and thrilled to see him there, feeling supported and loved, had he actually been setting up dates with other women? Or was it just sex? How many women had he slept with in sweaty, stolen moments before coming home to me? Or worse, in my own goddamn bed?

I didn't stay long after that. Ed didn't want to talk about the thefts, and I didn't want to discuss my shambolic love life any further, which left very few safe areas, considering how large those two topics loomed in my life at the moment. I said my goodbyes and caught the train to another part of town.

All the way there, I tried to think of a better way to broach the subject, or some more subtle way to find out what the Hawk wanted to know, but my brain didn't do subtle at the best of times, and this was most certainly *not* the best of times.

The second interview didn't go much better than the first. At this rate, I was going to end up with no friends left in the changeling community.

By late afternoon, I'd only covered half my list, but I was well and truly over it. Telling myself that I really needed to get to the pharmacy before it shut, I decided to call it quits for the day and start again tomorrow. Maybe tonight, when I saw him, I could pin the Hawk down on some more sensible strategy for approaching the problem. Surely if one of the changelings *was* the culprit, going around interviewing them all was only going to alert the thief, who'd be even more on their guard than before.

Jamison's Pharmacy was all glass and bright lights, with neatly stocked shelves in clean white, a thoroughly modern store. I walked past makeup displays and down aisles full of baby care products and cold and flu relief to the back of the store where a large sign saying "Prescriptions" glowed neon-bright over the dispensary area. This was also fitted out with neat rows of crisp white shelving, but at the back, an unobtrusive door opened into a very different kind of apothecary. Here, Jamison himself prepared medicines suitable for fae, using a mixture of traditional herbs and modern chemical ingredients.

Most human medicines were safe for changelings, since we'd all started as humans, but we all had some small magics that clung to us from our time in the Realms, like our night vision and the true Sight that allowed us to glimpse fae forms lurking under human disguises. If we didn't want to lose them, there were some human medicines that we couldn't take and, apparently, asthma treatments were among them. In the Realms, my mother had mixed up a concoction to keep my asthma under control, but here in the modern world, I came to Jamison when my asthma puffers were running low.

Jamison caught sight of me from where he was working behind the counter and came forward with a smile on his face. He was an older fae, old enough that he looked like a sixty-year-old man, with greying hair turning white, and so short he made even me feel tall. Unusually, for such an old fae, he was very comfortable in the human world, and had made it his home long ago, aided by a beautiful iron ward in the form of a silver ring. The knotwork on the ring reminded me a little of the gate glyph I wore under my shirt. Willow said that he had fallen in love with a changeling woman and followed her when she was expelled from the Realms. Whether or not this was true, he was always very pleasant to his changeling customers.

"Allegra, how lovely." Unlike most people, Jamison never called me Al. His manners were precise and courtly. "What can I do for you today?"

"Hi, Jamison." No doubt he had a first name, but I'd never heard anyone use it. "My preventer's running low. Can I get a refill?"

"Of course. Come through."

I followed him past shelves laden with medication to the door at the back. A small label on it read "Private". When one of the human staff opened this door, it led to a small kitchenette area where they could make tea and coffee, with boxes of extra stock piled haphazardly against the walls. But when Jamison turned the handle, the door opened into somewhere very different.

I followed him through the door, feeling the shiver of threshold magic brush my skin. We were no longer in the mortal world, but we weren't in the Realms, either—if only crossing to the Realms was that easy! Jamison lived in a sith—a little bubble of the Realms that had been broken away to form a private estate, totally isolated from both worlds.

We entered a rustic wooden cottage where bunches of herbs hung drying from the rafters, giving the room the feel of a hanging garden. Live herbs in pots covered the length of the wide windowsill and, through the window, a tumble of green, growing things filled his extensive garden.

A large wooden table, pitted and scratched from centuries of use, dominated the centre of the room. Rows of shelves against the wall opposite the window housed glass bottles and jars in all shapes and sizes. They held an array of powders and pastes, and a few held more disturbing shapes that I didn't look too closely at in case they gave me nightmares.

"Would you like a cup of tea?" Jamison asked, crossing to the kettle that hung from a hook by the fireplace. A fire crackled cheerfully in the hearth, and the room was pleasantly warm.

"No, thanks, I don't want to hold you up."

He took down a mortar and pestle from a shelf, and began assembling ingredients at a rapid pace. He didn't even look, just reached for things, as if he knew exactly where everything was. They'd probably all been in the same position for centuries, so it wasn't surprising. "This won't take a minute. How have you been?"

"Ah … busy. With the band, and everything." He didn't need to hear about my ex's infidelities, and he probably already knew about the investigation into the missing rainbow drake skins. Jamison had his finger on the pulse of the magic community. "I had to sing the other night, because Willow lost her voice."

He nodded without looking up from his work. "Yes, she came in for some medicine. I told her there was no cure for the common cold, in this world or any other, and she wasn't best pleased." He laughed. I could well imagine. Willow expected the world and everything in it to arrange itself to please her. "I gave her something to soothe her throat instead."

"It was quite a night, actually. There was a guy there who just went crazy—started yelling that Rowan was a demon, tried to get up on stage and attack him."

His brow furrowed, and his busy hands stilled. "A demon? Why? What did he say, exactly?"

"I don't remember the details. It was kind of a shock. But it was something like, 'Can't you see he's a demon?

Look at his horns!' Crazy stuff. I wondered if—" I broke off. No, that was silly. Although, if he was a changeling …

"If what? If he could see Rowan's fae self?"

"Yes. Do you think that's possible?"

"Shouldn't be. Humans with the Sight are vanishingly rare these days." He rubbed at his chin, a troubled look on his face. "But I tell you, it's not the first such case I've heard of lately."

"Really?"

"Yes. I'm starting to think there must be a new drug on the streets, something that gives the user true Sight. I heard of two men chasing a kitsune down the street, calling him an animal. A poor, wee kobold woman down in Coogee barely escaped death when a human attacked her on her way home one night last week. He was screaming about blue devils."

Kobolds in their natural form were the size of a five-year-old child. The poor woman must have been terrified. They were also blue—but how would a human have known that, unless he could see through the outer form? This did not sound good.

One changeling I had somehow missed hearing about was one thing, but two or three or even more? Not possible. The fae at least had the decency to send their cast-off children to the magic community here. They didn't just dump them on the street and run. But if these young men weren't changelings, how could they see a fae's true form?

"If it is a drug, it's making these people very aggressive," I said. "Why couldn't it be something that just blissed them out?"

Jamison shrugged. "It's possible that it only affects some people that way. Or maybe it's such a high that the users don't care about the other side effects."

"Could it be a new type of ice?"

He laid his pestle down and held his hands over the mixture in the mortar. A soft blue light rose from under his cupped hands and I sighed. I loved seeing magic being worked. It reminded me of home, and my life in a cottage rather like this one.

From a box on the shelf behind him, he took a plastic inhaler. It looked incongruous in such a setting. With a wave of his hand, he directed the blue magic into the top of the inhaler. Magic drugs, personalised just for me.

He glanced at me from under thick eyebrows. "It would be nice if we could think so. The aggression certainly fits. But I'm afraid the details are a little too accurate to be hallucinations. Something else is afoot."

I had to agree with him. I shoved the new inhaler into my back pocket, glad that it wasn't my problem—I had enough of them already.

❧

I had spent longer chatting to Jamison than I'd meant to. By the time I finished with him, then stopped on the way home to grab some noodles for dinner, it was almost dark when I turned into my street. Starlings whistled and squeaked and rustled in the big old pine in my neighbour's back yard, and a long, croaking call suggested that Thing One and Thing Two were close by as well. Rowan's house was dark, since he was away for a couple of days, but when I turned into the driveway, I saw a light glowing inside my tiny house out the back and a familiar car parked in the driveway in front of it.

I sighed. Just what I needed: another confrontation with Adam.

I squeezed past his car, resisting the urge to run my keys along its side. The front door of the little converted garage was unlocked, and I threw it open so that it bounced against the wall. I wanted this guy out of my life: hadn't my day been bad enough already without having to come home to more drama? I should have made the bastard give back his key, but somehow, it had slipped my mind in the heat of the moment. One thing was for sure: he wouldn't be leaving with it.

Three cardboard boxes sat in the middle of the lounge room, full of DVDs and books. I stalked into the kitchen and dropped my keys and dinner on the bench. He was in the bedroom.

"What are you doing?" I stood in the doorway, arms folded.

He had a suitcase open on the bed, half-full of his clothes. He popped his head out of the wardrobe and scowled. "Isn't it obvious? I'm getting my things."

"You didn't ask me if you could enter my house."

"You wouldn't take my calls. And anyway, I won't be here long."

That was true. Nearly everything in the house belonged to me. All he owned were his clothes and a few personal possessions like books and DVDs. It wouldn't take long to pack up every trace of our shared life. At least he seemed to have given up on the idea of trying to wheedle his way back into my good graces. Maybe when someone comes at you with a knife, you realise they're not kidding.

"Where are your keys?"

"What do you want them for?"

"I want the key to the front door."

His scowl deepened, but he pulled his key ring from his pocket and tossed it to me. I caught it and started working the house key off the ring. A grim silence fell as he continued to fill the suitcase.

I slipped the freed key into the back pocket of my jeans and dropped his key ring onto the bed next to his suitcase.

He eyed me sideways as he folded the long sleeves of his shirts into the bag. "Are you just going to stand there and watch me?"

"Well, I wasn't planning on helping you," I said, poisonously sweet. "You're on your own now, mate."

"Don't act like this is all my fault," he muttered, and I had to clamp down hard on the urge to punch him right in his cheating face. "If you weren't always off playing at being a rock star, it would never have happened."

"Right, so the fact that you can't keep it in your pants is *my* fault?"

"I was *lonely*, Al. You were never here." He slammed the suitcase lid and zipped it closed, then marched into the lounge room. "Give us a hand out to the car, would you?"

I breathed in, swallowing a sharp retort. Anything to get

him out of the house. It was too soon to see him again—the hurt was too fresh. I clung to my rage like a shield, but underneath, I wanted to cry. So I picked up a couple of cardboard boxes and followed him out to the car, waiting while he opened the boot and loaded his suitcase and the other box into it.

He took the boxes from me and put them in, too. "Well. See you round, I guess."

Not if I could possibly avoid it. I said nothing, merely stepped back and waited while he backed his car out, as if I had to make sure he was really gone. I wasn't sure who I was more furious with—him for being such an arsehole, or me for not realising it sooner.

Why did I make the same mistake over and over again? I should have known. Willow had never liked him, and she was a damn good judge of character. She was too much of a diva herself to put up with anyone else's bullshit. Even Rowan, who was pretty laidback, had always seemed to have other places to be when I suggested the five of us hang out.

I hugged my arms around myself while I watched his car head down the street and make the turn at the corner. At least I wouldn't have to see him again. He wasn't fae or even a changeling, so he had no reason to hang in the same circles that I did anymore.

"Well, that was fun," I said to the last flash of red of his brake lights before he disappeared. The starlings were still fussing in the big pine next door, but they were quieter. Soon, it would be full dark.

And I was due at The Drunken Irishman, to report the dismal results of my day to the Hawk. Maybe he'd had better luck. It would be nice to have one bit of good news today.

I headed for the house. I might get changed and freshen up my makeup before I left. I needed a little bit of a boost before I faced the knight's criticism. He was bound to be disappointed in my efforts so far.

Something hurtled at me from above, and I flinched away, too surprised to even understand what it was—until it turned and came in for another try.

I held my arms up to protect my head as Thing One swooped at me again.

"What the hell is your problem?" I shouted at him, stung by the betrayal. As if it wasn't bad enough for my boyfriend to let me down, now even my bird friends were doing it? "Leave me alone, you daft bird!"

Surely they weren't nesting at this time of year? And why would he attack me, anyway? I fed him every damn day, the ungrateful little shit.

I ran for the house, head tucked into my raised arms for protection, and he let out a piercing cry. Thing Two joined him, fluttering right in front of my face, beating at me with huge, black wings. Her beak was so close. My heart thundered. She could have my eye out in a second.

I retreated down the driveway instead, cowering before the feathered onslaught. I had no weapon on me, but even if I had, how could I hurt them? They were like pets to me. They didn't stop until I was all the way to the front gate.

Thing One landed on the letterbox, flapping and fussing, still watching me with his mad, white eye, as if daring me to move. At least they were no longer attacking. I stood panting at the bottom of my own driveway, driven out into the street by a pair of birds I thought were my friends.

And then my house exploded.

Holy *shit*. I stared, open-mouthed, flinching as the windows blew out and the roof shattered, tiles leaping into the dark sky then raining down in an infernal clattering. I ducked instinctively, but none of them reached me. A few landed on the roof of Rowan's house, and I flinched again at the thought of the damage they would inflict. Flames appeared as if from nowhere, consuming my tiny home. For the longest moment, all I could do was stare.

Thing One croaked at me, then took off in a great flapping of wings. The movement jolted me out of my trance, and I pulled my phone out of my back pocket with shaking hands and dialled the emergency number.

"Which service do you need?" a calm voice on the other end asked. "Police, Fire, or Ambulance?"

"Fire, please. My—my house is on fire." I gave the address and hung up, shoving my phone back into my pocket before I dropped it. My whole body was shaking, now.

Shouts and running footsteps came from behind me, and the man from the house across the road joined me. "Are you all right, love? What happened?"

"I don't know." Goose bumps suddenly blossomed on my arms, and I hugged myself tightly. What the *hell* was going on?

"I'll call the fire brigade."

"I just called them. They're on the way." Not that they would be able to save my home, but at least they could stop the flames spreading to Rowan's.

Other neighbours joined us. Someone driving down the street pulled over to watch. Someone else got out Rowan's garden hose, but the thin trickle of water had no effect on the roaring blaze. The wail of a siren broke through my fog, and soon, the fire engine was pulling up.

The neighbours and onlookers scattered before the firemen's businesslike movements as black hoses snaked up the driveway and water blasted into the flames. Everything was noise and light and confusion. People shouted questions at each other, their faces lit by flames, and one serious-looking fireman, having been told I was the resident, took my arm and asked me if there was anyone inside.

"Do you need an ambulance? Are you hurt?"

I shook my head mutely.

"How did the fire start?"

"I don't know. My boyfriend was leaving—my ex-boyfriend—with his stuff. I was helping him carry it out, and then, before I could go back inside, the house just … exploded."

"Exploded?" The fireman raised his eyebrows, then turned to call another, older, man over. "Jim, this lady says the house exploded."

Jim's eyebrows performed the same upward manoeuvre.

"Right after her ex-boyfriend had been inside," the first guy added, and Jim blinked.

"Any heaters on?" Jim asked.

At this time of year? "No."

"How old is the wiring, do you know?"

I shrugged. "I think Rowan—the owner—only converted the garage about five years ago, so not very old."

"How well do you and your ex-boyfriend get on?"

My turn to blink. "Wait a minute—do you think my ex had something to do with this?"

"Houses don't just explode in an instant without some kind of explosive involved. Did your ex leave anything unusual inside before he left?"

"No. At least …"

He could have. The house was tiny, and I'd walked through the lounge area, past the kitchen, into the bedroom. The only room I hadn't actually seen was the bathroom—but would I have noticed if there was something unusual behind the lounge, for instance, or inside a kitchen cupboard? I hadn't really been focused on my surroundings—I'd been too busy being angry at Adam.

"I'm not sure." I rubbed a hand across my face. Why would Adam do something like that? It didn't seem likely that he would even know how. A man who had trouble operating a washing machine didn't strike me as the kind to be an explosives expert. And was he really angry enough about the break-up to try to kill me? He'd never struck me as the possessive psycho type. "But I really don't think he had anything to do with it."

"Well, that's for the police to decide. They'll want to speak to both of you. We'll know more after the arson investigators have been through." He glanced at the main house. "Is the owner home?"

"No, he's out of town for a couple of days."

He looked thoughtful, and I had the sinking feeling that Rowan was now a suspect, too. They probably saw quite a few cases of people destroying their own property so they could claim the insurance. I rubbed my face again.

"You're shaking. Are you sure you're all right? Do you have somewhere to stay tonight?"

Good question, Jim. Edgar would take me in, but Kel would probably lie on my face and try to smother me in the night. "Ah … yeah. I'll just ring a friend."

He nodded and moved off toward the truck to make some calls of his own. I fished my mobile out again and dialled Willow's number. Thank the Lady I'd had it on me. No—thank God. Whoever. Thank both of them. I wasn't particularly religious, but this was the kind of experience to bring out the religion in anyone. If the birds hadn't stopped me going inside …

My worldly possessions now consisted of my phone, my wallet, one asthma inhaler, and a gate glyph. "Um, hi! Can I stay at your place tonight? There's been a bit of a problem here."

"I could have caught the train," I said, as I got into Willow's car twenty minutes later. I sank into the leather seat with a sigh, letting my head fall back against the head rest.

She gave me a withering look. "Sure you could. I always let my friends stagger around on public transport when they're in shock from having their homes destroyed and narrowly escaping being killed." Her voice was huskier than normal, but at least she could talk again.

"It wasn't quite that bad," I said, though the fact that I was still shaking made the protest less than convincing.

"Which part? Did your home get completely destroyed?"

"Yes, but—"

"And did it or did it not blow up just as you were about to walk back into it?" I said nothing, and she snorted. "So, you almost died. Of course you're in shock. You've had a shitty night, and I'm taking you home for a nice, long bath and a good, stiff drink. Probably several drinks, in fact."

"Sounds good to me." I shut my eyes, exhausted. What a day. They popped open again as a thought occurred to me. "Oh. We'd better stop on the way. I don't even have a toothbrush. All I have is an asthma puffer." Everything else I owned was gone, my home destroyed. It hadn't been fancy, but it had been *mine*. I still remembered the joy of moving into it, gradually furnishing it as I saved the money to buy new things. Until I'd caught Adam bonking someone else in our bed, the place had held nothing but happy memories.

"Already taken care of," Willow said. "It's late night shopping, so I sent Sage out to get you a few bits and pieces, and you're always welcome to borrow my clothes."

"Thanks." What would I do without my friends? I would be forever grateful to Rowan for letting me move in. He'd been one of my first friends, and through him, I'd met Willow and Sage. And now his generosity was repaid with ashes and the suspicion of the arson squad. "And thanks for letting me stay. It won't be for long, just until I get something sorted out."

"Don't be ridiculous," she said. "I have plenty of spare rooms—why would you need to find something else? Now that Adam the A-hole is out of the picture, you can move in with us permanently. It'll be fun. Like sleepovers every night."

Tired as I was, that still gave me a laugh. "When did you ever have a sleepover? Maybe they did things differently in that palace of yours, but I never heard of sleepovers until I came to the mortal world."

"So? I know what they are. We can drink too much and tell each other all our secrets."

"You already know all mine. Although I like the sound of the drinking part."

She grinned across at me when we pulled up at the next set of lights and flicked her red curls back from her face. "I could do with a few drinks myself. I tell you, it nearly scared the magic out of me when you said that your place had blown up right in front of you. What if you'd been inside? You were so lucky."

"Actually, luck had nothing to do with it."

"Oh?" She arched one perfectly shaped eyebrow at me. "What do you mean?"

"I mean I would have been inside, except that Thing One and Thing Two stopped me."

"Thing One and Thing Two? Who on earth are they?"

"You know, the ravens I feed. I'm sure I've told you about them." She continued to look mystified, and I shrugged. "Anyway, Adam had just driven off and I was heading up the driveway to go back inside, when Thing One came out of nowhere, just flew straight at my head. Scared the crap out of me."

"Ravens can be very territorial."

"Yeah, but he's never done anything like that before. He knows I'm not a threat—I feed them both every day. It's not as though I'm a stranger on their turf, we practically live together. Anyway, I tried to run inside to get away from him, and then Thing Two joined in—"

"Why do these birds have such bizarre names?"

I ignored her interruption. "And they're both flapping and screeching, and ravens have such big flipping beaks when you see them up close like that, so I ran down the driveway to the street, and then ..."

"And then the house blew up?"

"Yeah."

Yep, that wasn't suspicious at all. There had to be magic involved. Silence fell, broken only by the sound of Willow's index finger tapping on the steering wheel as she drove. We pulled up outside a nondescript house whose overgrown front yard was separated from the street by a waist-high wall. Willow switched off the engine and we got out, the double thud of the two doors closing loud in the empty street.

"The only question, then," she said as she led the way to the gate, "is whose birds are they?"

I spread my hands helplessly. "But I always thought they were just normal birds. They've never done anything before that seemed odd. It took months before they would even come down to take the food while I was still there."

She paused with her hand on the gate. "Well, they've blown their cover now, haven't they? It doesn't get much odder than stopping you from entering a house that's about to blow up. How did they know?"

We stepped through the gate and into a different world, the familiar shiver of magic stroking my skin as we passed over the threshold. No rundown suburban house stood before us now, but a sprawling mansion. It stood in the middle of a meadow dotted with wildflowers. Willow's home was a sith, just like Jamison's secret room in the pharmacy. Only the lucky few granted access by Willow could open that gate and find themselves here—even other fae needed permission, and uninvited mortals would enter the front yard of the shabby house in the suburbs, if they even got that far. Most such places had a strong Aversion on them, and mortal eyes glided straight over them. From the street, it looked as though Willow lived in a rundown rental, but in reality, she hadn't given up the princess lifestyle at all.

Not that she was literally a princess, of course, but being a daughter of the ruling House of Spring was almost the same thing. And as a late-in-life, longed-for baby, she was the apple of her parents' eye, which was why, when she'd announced she was leaving the Realms for the mortal world, they'd begged her not to go. When it became clear she wouldn't change her mind, they'd set her up with all the comforts of home instead, including servants. No doubt part of the servants' responsibilities was to report to the Spring Court, but Willow blithely ignored that fact, since the arrangement suited her otherwise.

We walked up the path, which was made of some kind of crushed rock that was so white it positively glowed in the moonlight. The mansion was a typical style of Spring architecture, according to Willow, though I'd never been to Spring to see any—very open to the outdoors, with lots of pillars holding up high, airy roofs. A series of interconnected pavilions gathered around a central pool full of water lilies and fountains. We stepped into the first and biggest of these, which was the main living area of the house, boasting a dining room with a table big enough to hold a banquet, and several lounging areas, one with a massive fireplace. Currently, this was decorated with fresh flower arrangements, since it was too warm for a fire.

All of which was way surplus to requirements, of course, since Sage and Willow—plus the three servants Willow's family had insisted on supplying—were the only people who lived here. My tiny, cramped home would have fit into the dining room alone two or three times over. But, hey, I wasn't complaining. It beat sleeping on the street, or breaking into Rowan's house to find a place to lay my head.

An owl hooted overhead, reminding me of what we'd been talking about. "But why would anyone from the Realms be watching me? Who'd be interested in the life of a service station attendant?"

Willow flashed me a grin. "Maybe they're fans of your singing."

"Yeah, right. That must be it." I rolled my eyes at her back as I followed her through the garden, around the pond, and toward the sleeping pavilion. "But seriously, who would?"

"I can't see why anyone would, really. No offence, but it would make more sense if someone was watching me."

I couldn't argue with that. Willow was a lot more closely connected to the politics of the Realms than I was. We walked down a hallway formed by ivy-clad pillars and stopped in an archway. The smell of roses was strong, though I couldn't see any. Beyond the archway lay a room with a large bed draped with green coverlets and cushions. On the other side of the bed, the room opened to a private courtyard filled with a riot of greenery.

"This is your room," Willow said. "Do you like it?"

"It's beautiful." And also the size of my whole place before, though the acres of empty tiled floor made it feel even bigger.

"Bathroom's through here," she added, opening a door I hadn't noticed before to show me a glimpse of a bath sunken into the floor, and more plants—on shelves, hanging from the roof, and on the floor. It probably felt like you were bathing in a jungle pool.

Sage came in, carrying an armful of clothes, which she dumped on the beautiful bed. One of the cushions toppled to the floor, and she casually kicked it underneath the bed. Once her arms were free, she gave me a hug.

"Are you okay?" She held me at arm's length, looking me over for signs of damage.

"Fine, yeah. A little shook up, though." At least I'd finally stopped shaking, though I still felt hollowed out and empty.

"I can understand that. What a terrible thing to happen! You've lost everything." She released me and gestured at the bed. "I got you some clothes."

I looked more closely and realised everything still had the price tags attached. "You *bought* all these?" Willow had said Sage was out getting me a few things, but I'd assumed she meant a toothbrush and some new underwear, not half a wardrobe full of brand-new clothes. There were jeans, tops, bras and underpants, as well as a leather jacket and a couple of silk scarves. "A leather jacket? I don't know if I've got enough in the bank for all this ..."

"Don't worry about that," Willow said. "Consider it an early birthday present. I never know what to get you anyway."

"But, this—"

"Don't argue, doofus. You need help, and I've got lots of money, so let me help you. That's what friends are for."

"Doofus?" Sage eyed her doubtfully. They were always

trying to outdo each other in their "assimilation project", and they took the competition seriously. "Is that a real word?"

"Of course it is. Do you think I'd cheat? It's an affectionate way of calling someone stupid."

"I like it." She turned to me. "I've got a couple more bags of stuff, too. Shoes and socks and other things."

I shook my head. There were already almost as many clothes lying on the bed as I'd owned before. "Any ball gowns? Seriously, Sage—silk scarves? When have I ever worn a silk scarf in my life? You know I'm pretty casual."

"Pretty boring, you mean," Willow said. "This is the perfect opportunity for us to introduce some variety into your wardrobe. If I had to see that Led Zeppelin T-shirt of yours one more time I'd probably have set fire to it myself."

The mention of the fire sobered the mood, which was starting to get that sleepover vibe—judging by the movies I'd seen. Like the other two, I'd never experienced a sleepover in real life.

"Do you think it could have been an accident?" Sage asked. "The fire, I mean. Something funny with the wiring?"

"Not according to one of the firemen I spoke to. And honestly, Sage, it didn't feel very accidental. It wasn't like a little fire started in the wiring and then gradually took hold. It was just—one minute, fine, and then, boom! It was like a bomb went off. The place just blew apart."

Sage glanced at Willow. "Then I'm guessing the police will never find out how the fire started. Magic, right?"

"That's not even the best part," Willow said. "Tell her about the ravens."

"The ravens? Not Thing One and Thing Two?"

I shot a triumphant glance at Willow. I knew I'd talked about them before. Sage was just a better listener. "Yeah. They attacked me to stop me going inside, right before it blew. It was as if they knew what was going to happen."

"Whoa. That's not suss at all."

"I know, right? So who is spying on me?"

She looked at me as if she thought I wasn't quite right in the head. "A better question would be: who is trying to *kill* you?"

9

I woke next morning to the trilling of birdsong, and it took me a moment to remember where I was. Outside, a beautiful day was dawning, blue sky over the perfumed garden. I searched the trees for the singer as I padded across the warm tiles to the bathroom, but couldn't see it. My usual avian alarm clock was the harsh cawing of ravens, and I kind of missed it. Not as much as Thing One and Thing Two would miss their morning cabanossi, of course.

Or would they even still be there? If someone was using them to watch me, there was no point leaving them in Rowan's backyard when I had gone. Were they even Australian ravens at all, or ravens from the Realms, disguised with those freaky white eyes? They needn't have bothered for my sake; I would have much preferred the beady black raven eyes I was used to, and it would never have occurred to me that they were out of place if seeing Thing One and Thing Two always hanging around with their blank white irises hadn't made me check out Australian native birds in the library.

After showering in the beautiful, green-tiled bathroom, I took my morning dose of asthma medicine—thank goodness that hadn't gone up in smoke with all my other belongings—and considered my clothing options. The clothes I'd been wearing the night before reeked of smoke, so I left them on the bathroom floor, wondering what the etiquette was for getting clothes washed around here. I had the feeling Willow's staff wouldn't allow me anywhere near a washing machine.

I'd taken the time to fold my new clothes into the wardrobe before I went to bed, and now I stood before the colourful shelves, feeling a little weird. It was a good weird, but I wasn't used to all the colours. Normally, I just bought everything in black or neutrals like denim so everything went together and I didn't have to fuss about it. No one expected catwalk looks from the girl behind the counter at the service station, and my collection of concert T-shirts suited my other role in the band.

My hand went instinctively to a T-shirt in a warm, russet brown that reminded me of the colour of Lord Eldric's hair. A nice, safe Autumn colour. I bit the tag off with my teeth and shrugged into the shirt. Sage had chosen well: it fit perfectly, with just the right amount of cling, not too baggy but not too tight. I put on a pair of brand-new jeans with fashionable rips at the knees and called it good. My stomach was busy reminding me that a late-night snack before I fell into bed wasn't the same as a real dinner, and it was time for breakfast.

"Looking good!" Sage said as I walked into the vast dining room. She and Willow were seated together at one end of the long dining table, with a big pot of tea between them. I almost panicked before I noticed a coffee plunger on the sideboard. "I knew that colour would suit you. You should wear more warm colours."

Willow nodded and spoke around a mouthful of toast. "Yeah, you look less like a dead thing. No one with skin as pale as yours should be wearing black."

"Duly noted." I slid into the seat next to Sage and started helping myself from a platter of fresh fruit. I could get used to eating like this every day. It sure beat peanut butter on toast. "So, what's everyone doing today?"

"Working," said Sage. She had a job as a part-time receptionist in a real estate agent's office.

"Don't know yet," Willow said. "More to the point, what are *you* doing today?"

I sighed. "I still have more changelings to see for—"

"Surely you're not still going to do that?" Willow broke in.

"Are you kidding? Of course I am. I'm not exactly in a position to say no to the Lord of Autumn."

"But surely you see there must be a connection between what happened last night and this job for Eldric," Willow said impatiently. "Someone doesn't want Eldric finding out who stole his stupid cloak, and they've decided the easiest way to make sure he doesn't is to take you out of the picture."

"Just because the two things happened at the same time,

it doesn't prove they're connected. Why would taking me out make a difference? Eldric would just give the job to someone else. Besides, the Hawk is on the job, too." And I'd completely forgotten about meeting him at the pub last night in all the excitement. Shit. He must have been *so* impressed when I didn't show.

"Yes, but can you think of any other reason someone would blow up your house?" Sage countered, a worried look on her face. "It seems awfully suspicious that it happens now, right when you've taken this job on."

"Exactly," Willow said. "Tell Eldric what happened and pull out. He'd understand."

Easy for Willow to say—she wasn't the one who was homeless and adrift, forever denied the one place in both worlds she most wanted to be. My longing for Autumn was like an ache that never went away. Nothing would stop me from seizing this chance to return, however slim, with both hands—it might be the only one I got.

I snorted. "He'd understand? What's in that tea you're drinking? He's a Lord of the Realms. He doesn't *do* understanding. And besides, he gave me a *gate glyph*, guys."

Sage's dark eyes widened. "You never told me that! Can I see it?"

I was still wearing it around my neck—thank the Silver Tree, or I would have lost it in the fire, too. I pulled it over my head and held it out for her inspection. She leaned closer and took it almost with reverence.

Willow looked away, busying herself with topping up her tea. I understood her discomfort. The gift of a gate glyph offered hope that I might be invited to return home. But no one from Spring would be asking Sage to return, despite her father's noble birth, and her having grown up almost as a sister to Willow. The half-breed child of Fallon Domani wasn't welcome in the Spring Court these days, and no other Realm could offer her a home without risking the ire of the Lord of Spring. And so, while not technically exiled from the Realms, the mortal world was Sage's only practical option. That was why Willow was here. In typical Willow fashion, she'd announced that if Sage had to leave the Realms, then she was going with her. Her parents' entreaties that she return had so far fallen on deaf ears.

Sage handed it back and I lifted it over my head, tucking it safely away inside the russet shirt again. "That does put a different slant on things," she said.

"No, it doesn't," Willow insisted. "Not if her life's at risk."

Sage and I shared a glance. Willow was free to return to the Realms at any time; she couldn't really understand how it felt to be banished forever. To people like us, going home could be worth any risk. "Maybe Al has a point: there's no proof that the two things are related. Correlation is not causation."

Willow threw her hands up. "What, you see a gate glyph, and suddenly you're changing your mind? I thought we agreed this was too dangerous."

"It doesn't matter what you agreed," I cut in, before Willow and Sage started fighting. "It's my decision. I'm only talking to a handful of changelings—people you've known for years. I'll be perfectly safe. The idea that any of them would want to kill me is ludicrous."

Willow's expression was troubled. "Maybe I should come with you today."

"You're overreacting. Probably because you're out of bed so early today. Don't you usually sleep until after lunch?"

"I'm trying to be a polite hostess." Willow rolled her eyes. "I can see I needn't have bothered. Ungrateful bloody mortals."

Later that day, I was beginning to wish I hadn't refused Willow's offer of help. At least she would have been company as I traipsed around the city, talking to changelings. None of them had any useful information for me. Most of them looked at me with less than their usual friendliness once they realised why I was asking, though I tried to make it seem as though I was wondering if they'd heard anything on the grapevine, rather than actually accusing them. Changelings were nothing if not paranoid. No one wanted to do anything to upset the Lords of the Realms, and they didn't like feeling that they were under suspicion. Guess who they took their displeasure out on? By the time I was finished this job, I'd have no friends left in this town.

I had no way to contact the Hawk. I really needed to get his phone number, assuming he even had one. I'd have to hope that he would be waiting at The Drunken Irishman again tonight.

It took a while—I blamed the stress of the night before—but eventually, it occurred to me that he might have left a message for me, so I hotfooted it across town to the pub. I arrived mid-afternoon, when the lunch crowd had thinned out but before the after-work patrons hit, so Randall wasn't too busy. Gratefully, I hoisted my butt onto a bar stool and ordered a beer.

"Did you happen to notice if the Hawk came in last night?" I asked as he set the foaming glass in front of me.

"Ah … he might have. I was a little distracted last night." He shook his head. "Had another drunk come over all peculiar on us—he was laying into the crowd, landed a few good blows before Tony and I could get ahold of him. Someone called the cops."

"Really?" Well, there was a first time for everything.

He groaned. "And then I had to spend half the night talking to them, dealing with the injured, calming the whole place down. I tell you, Santa Claus himself could have shown up last night and I might not have noticed."

"Santa Claus? Look at you, talking like a mortal!"

"I've been running this pub for nearly seventy years, lass. If I didn't speak the local lingo by now, it would be a sad thing."

"Sounds like a bad night."

I almost told him about my own bad night, but decided to keep that to myself for now. He would probably hear about it eventually, but it would be better to break the news to Rowan myself rather than him hearing it from someone else. I'd left a message for him to call me, but so far, he hadn't called back. He'd said he was only heading out to Dubbo to look at a drum kit he was thinking of buying, but perhaps he'd decided to detour via the Realms on the way home. He did occasionally drop in on a couple of friends there.

"This guy that went crazy—was it the same one who tried to attack Rowan the other night?"

He chuckled. "You think I'd let him back into my pub after that? No, this was someone else. About the same age, a young feller." He frowned. "I've seen some bar fights in my time. Hell, I've started a few myself. But these men are too angry. It's not normal." He rested an elbow on the bar and leaned closer. "I keep hearing about a drug called shim—I can't help but wonder if that's the problem."

"Jamison said something about a new drug on the market last time I was talking to him. What's this shim do?"

"Just the usual, I suppose, but it causes serious hallucinations in some people. And anger management issues, I'm guessing."

Another customer called him away, and I stared morosely into my beer. I should have asked him what kind of "hallucinations" last night's crazy guy had had. If he had also been seeing through fae disguises to their true forms, then Jamison was right, and we had a bigger problem than simple "hallucinations". I sighed. Was there any chance that these guys were all changelings I didn't know about? Maybe they were visiting from interstate.

I really needed to find out. My enquiries had to be thorough enough to dazzle the Hawk if I was going to wheedle my way back into the Realms. And I already had a black mark against me for not showing up to meet him last night.

I would have to make up for that by giving him something to work with tonight. But what could I do? Track down the guy who'd attacked us and find out if he really was a changeling? How? I knew what he looked like, but I didn't have a name.

But maybe someone else did. I downed the rest of my beer, keen to get on with the search, and slid off my stool. "That crazy guy the other night, the one who was yelling at Rowan," I said to Randall as soon as he was free, "do you know anything about him?"

"Know his face, but that's it. He's only been in here a couple of times before. Why?"

"I think I need to talk to him." Randall's eyebrows shot up, and I quickly added: "He might be able to help me with something I'm working on."

"Well, as I say, I couldn't tell you the first thing about *him*, but one of the fellers with him the other night works around the corner at Dominion Tyres. Name of Matt. You could try asking him."

"Thanks, I will."

"You want me to tell that knight you were looking for him if I see him again?"

"I'll be in tonight. Hopefully, I'll be able to tell him myself."

I headed back out into the afternoon sunshine. My stomach rumbled, reminding me that the beer was the only thing I'd had to eat or drink since leaving Willow's place that morning.

I knew the tyre place Randall was talking about—it truly was just around the corner, on the main road. It was grimy and a little rundown, as such places often were. Anywhere that involved cars and grease and spilled fuel and dirt quickly started to look less than its best unless the owner was absolutely fanatical about cleanliness, which this one clearly wasn't. I mean, we did our best at the service station where I worked, but the battle against dirt was relentless, and we were always on the losing side. And that was just in the checkout area. The workshop was worse.

The concrete apron of Dominion Tyres was painted black, probably in an attempt to hide the rubber marks that crisscrossed it. I walked straight across it and poked my head into the workshop. "Hi! Is Matt here?"

A man in blue overalls turned around and eyed me up and down. "Who wants to know?"

"My name's Allegra."

"Allegra. Pretty name for a pretty lady."

"Thanks." He didn't seem in any hurry to find Matt for me, so I stood on tiptoe and peered over the cars in the workshop. A couple of younger guys were working on a red Mazda together. They both had their backs to me, but I said, "Oh, I think I see him," and marched right on over.

"Are you Matt?" I asked, addressing the air between them.

They both turned around, but the taller one said, "Yes. Can I help you?"

I liked him better than the guy out front already. He looked vaguely familiar from that night in the pub, though of course he hadn't been wearing overalls then. He wiped his forehead, leaving a smear of something dark across it— grease, probably.

"I hope so. Can we talk for a minute?"

"Come into the kitchen." He led me into a tiny space that was just big enough for a sink, a fridge, and a microwave perched next to the sink. It was hot inside with the door shut, but at least it was private.

"It's about that guy you were with at the pub on Monday night."

His face, which had been politely attentive, closed down in an instant. "Are you with the drug squad?"

"No, I—"

"'Cause I already told the police everything I know."

"No—what?" Did I *look* like I was with the drug squad? I mean, hey, my new shirt was several levels up from my usual level of grungy T-shirt, but I doubted the drug squad even took twenty-two-year-olds. "No, I'm just …"

Just what, Allegra? It might have been a good idea to come up with a story before I got here, but I'd been so focused on finding the guy, that little detail had slipped my mind. I could hardly say I was looking for him in connection with a robbery in the fae Realms, because I thought he might be a changeling, could I?

"I'm … looking for something. I thought he might be able to help me find it."

He scowled at me. "You're looking for shim, aren't you?

Goddamn druggies." He wrenched the door open. "Get out. I don't want your type around here. I *told* him not to take it."

"No, really, I just want to talk to him."

"That's gonna be pretty hard, then, isn't it? Considering that he's dead."

10

"Dead?" I stared at the bitter expression on the guy's sweaty face in confusion. I'd seen his friend on Monday night, and he'd been pretty damn lively then. Surely he couldn't be dead? But Matt didn't look as though he was joking.

A horrible thought struck me: was this my fault? I'd knocked him out and left him lying unconscious on the ground. But the ambulance had come straight away. He should have been fine.

"I'm … I'm so sorry. How did he die?"

"Overdose."

A wave of relief washed over me: I hadn't killed him. And then I felt guilty—the poor bastard was still dead.

"You need to leave; I have to get back to work."

He still thought I was a junkie. "I'm not looking for drugs, I promise. I'm with the band—we were playing that night. I was singing when your friend started shouting." I was babbling, trying to convince him not to throw me out before I found out what I needed to know. If his friend *was* a changeling, and he'd been involved in the thefts, maybe his death hadn't been an overdose at all, but only made to look like one. The timing certainly seemed suspicious.

"Oh." He looked more closely at me, and his frown eased. "Sorry, I thought you were … Yeah, I thought you looked familiar."

"I'm so sorry about—what was your friend's name?"

"Peter. Peter de Gruner. Known him for years—we went to the same high school. Shared a house for the last three years." He shook his head. "I can't believe I'm going to his funeral on Monday."

"That's awful," I said, feeling inadequate and more than a little guilty. Was this how reporters felt when they were pumping the bereaved, trying to get a good story? But I really did need to know. There was more at stake here than selling newspapers.

"That damn shim ruined him. He only started using it a couple of months ago, and he promised me that he was gonna quit. But it was too late."

"I've never heard of this shim," I said. "Is it like ice?"

"Worse, I reckon. I mean, two months and now he's dead." His eyes were suspiciously bright when he looked up at me. "What did you want to talk to him about?"

"I wanted to find out what his beef was with our drummer. I was afraid he might follow us to our next gig and cause another scene."

"That was the drug talking. He was the nicest guy when he was clean, not an aggressive bone in his body. But he used to see all sorts of weird shit when he was using, and it terrified him. Convinced it was real, of course." He sighed. "Guess you don't need to worry about it anymore."

"No. I guess I don't."

Awkwardly, I said my goodbyes and left, my thoughts churning. What was this shim, and where had it come from? Maybe Peter de Gruner was just a regular guy who'd had a bad experience with drugs, and his death was the accident it seemed. I fervently hoped that was the case, but I had a bad feeling there was more to it. His hallucination had seemed uncannily accurate the night I'd seen him, accurate enough to make him a changeling on a high—and if he was now dead, right when I wanted to question him about the thefts, that seemed rather a large coincidence to swallow.

Which left the question of who had wanted him silenced. Was it the same person who had tried to kill me last night?

On the way back to the pub that night, I finally got a call from Rowan.

"Hey," he said. "It's me. What's up?"

"Umm …" What was the best way to put this? I stalled for time. "How's your trip going?"

I could tell he wasn't home yet, or he wouldn't be asking so cheerily.

"Fine." Suspicion entered his voice. "You sounded upset in your message. Is something wrong?"

"Yeah."

"Spit it out, then. Did you break up with your boyfriend?"

"Yeah, actually, I did."

"Oh, is that all?" He sounded relieved. "I mean, I get that you're upset, but I didn't think he was right for you anyway."

"That's not all. Did … did the police call you?"

"The police? Why would they be calling me? What have you done?"

"Oh, I like how you immediately assume it's something *I've* done."

"Sorry, sorry. Look, just tell me, would you? You're making me nervous!"

"Your garage. It, um. It blew up."

There was a short silence. I could almost hear his eyebrows shooting up in surprise. "It … blew up? You mean there was a fire? An electrical fault? Shit, are you all right?"

"I'm fine. But the garage—there's nothing left."

"When did this happen?"

"Last night. I called you straight away, but I couldn't get hold of you. The fireman said the police would probably want to talk to you, but maybe they're waiting for the arson inspector's report."

"So they think it was arson? What in the name of the Tree is going on? Who would want to burn down my damn garage?"

"I don't know."

"Were you home at the time?"

"Sure was. It was pretty scary. The roof blew off, the glass in all the windows exploded—it all happened so quickly. It was like a bomb blast."

"Shit. Thank the Lady you weren't hurt."

"It was a close thing. I'd probably be dead now, except I'd gone outside just before it happened, and the ravens wouldn't let me go back in."

There was a much longer silence this time, as he digested that. The streetlights were just starting to come on, so it was probably still too early for the Hawk, but I could grab something to eat while I waited. I didn't want to go back to Willow's for dinner and risk keeping him waiting. I needed to stay on the knight's good side—I wanted him singing my praises to Lord Eldric.

"Those ravens you feed?" Rowan finally asked. "I thought they were just normal birds."

"Me, too, but I guess we were wrong."

"Then whose are they? And why are they protecting you?"

I sighed. "There's no use asking me, Rowan; I have no more idea than you do. I'm sorry about your garage, though."

"I'm sorry about all your stuff. Wait—where are you staying? Did you find the spare key for the house?"

"I'm staying at Willow's for now. Don't worry about me."

He snorted. "You can't tell me someone's trying to kill you and then in the next breath tell me not to worry about you, Al. That's not how it works."

"Right." I really didn't want to worry him further, but I was still so shocked I was desperate to tell someone. "And speaking of being killed …"

"Lady save me, Al. I leave you alone for a few days and everything goes to shit. Someone's been *killed*?"

"Yeah. You know that crazy guy who was going off at the gig who attacked us?"

"He's dead? Because of that concussion?"

"No, thank God." I'd reached the pub. Inside, all the tables were full, and there weren't even any free bar stools. I hovered near the doorway, watching for the Hawk, while I spoke to Rowan. "Supposedly died of a drug overdose."

"Why 'supposedly'?"

That's right. I hadn't told Rowan about being summoned to Autumn, either. He'd only been gone a little while, but he'd missed an awful lot. I was about to launch into an explanation when a tall figure entered from the car park entry, looking around with the air of a man expecting to be disappointed. "I'll tell you later. I'm meeting someone, and he's just arrived."

"You just broke up with Adam the A-hole, and already you're seeing other men? Nice work."

"Rowan! It's not like that. I'll talk to you later." I hung up and slipped the phone into my pocket.

The Hawk caught sight of me as I made my way across the room toward him, and there was a slight lightening in his grim expression. He'd probably been afraid I was going to leave him hanging again.

As he neared the bar, two stools opened up as if by magic, their occupants moving away practically under his feet. It probably *was* magic, some kind of Aversion. I wouldn't put it past him. He didn't seem like the type to wait around for a seat when he wanted one.

I slid onto the stool next to him. "Sorry about last night," I began, hastening to get out my apologies. "I had a disaster and I clean forgot abou—"

He cut me off. "I don't want to hear your excuses. Your personal life is your own, but the task must come first. Don't stand me up again."

My cheeks flushed red, and I swallowed a furious retort. Inside, a war raged between mollifying the knight at all costs for the sake of achieving my ultimate goal and telling him where to get off. It would have surprised none of my friends that the latter impulse won.

"I did, in fact, have a crisis in my 'personal life', as you call it, last night. You needn't sound so contemptuous—it's not actually a character flaw to have a life. But that's not why I forgot to keep our appointment. It was more the fact that someone tried to kill me that made me just a teensy bit forgetful." I gave him a sweet, poisonous smile. "I'm sure even you might have a problem with having your house blown sky high right in front of you."

His tawny eyes stared into me with an intentness that was chilling, as if he was searching my soul for the truth. I held his gaze defiantly. Being a knight didn't give him the right to speak to me like that, no matter how gorgeous he was. He was probably used to women falling at his feet, ready to do his bidding. Well, not this little black duck.

"I can see I've offended you," he said at last. "Perhaps I was too quick to leap to conclusions."

Ya think? It wasn't exactly an apology, but it was probably the best I was going to get and, frankly, more than

I'd expected from someone like him. He gestured to Cathy, who'd been hovering nearby, and she scurried over to take his order. There was no sign of Randall.

"Can I buy you a drink to earn back your favour?" he asked.

Hmmm. That assumed he'd ever *had* my favour in the first place. Wanting to jump his bones didn't count—that was just biology. "Sure. I'll have a beer."

"Two beers, please," he said to Cathy, and she smiled and nodded and hurried away to do his bidding. Probably more the reaction he was used to. "Tell me more about this explosion. What makes you think it was more than an accident?"

"The firemen on the scene found it suspicious," I said. I explained what Jim the fireman had said about the usual pattern of fires, and how it was sheer chance that I'd been outside when the place exploded, but I kept the part about the ravens to myself. That pointed very clearly at someone from the Realms, and I didn't feel comfortable sharing that with anyone but my friends. I knew that *they* weren't trying to kill me, but everyone else was still a suspect.

"And this happened directly after your lover left?" he asked. "Perhaps he is the one trying to kill you. Some men are too possessive to take no for an answer." His eyes had tiny gold flecks in them that were positively mesmerising, especially since he stared at me with such focus. It was as if we were the only two people in the crowded room.

I had to force myself to look away, unnerved by such attention. "First, he's an ex-lover, and second, the guy can barely boil an egg. I think bomb construction might be a little beyond him."

"Who else would have a motive to kill you?"

I shrugged. "Nobody. I've done nothing, offended no one. I do my job, I keep my nose clean—it doesn't make any sense."

"Perhaps you have a crazed fan. Like that one who made such a ruckus on Monday night."

Cathy returned with the drinks, then, and he took a long gulp of beer. Knighting must be thirsty work.

He set his glass down and turned to the reason for this meeting, unaware that half his moustache was covered in beer foam. "So how did you go with the changelings?"

I took a sip of my own beer, first, trying to hide an unruly smile. "Since you're asking, I guess that means you didn't turn up anything useful with the fae?"

"No." He frowned as my lip twitched. "Is something funny?"

"I'm sorry, it's just that you have foam—" I gestured at his mouth, and he wiped at the wrong side. "Here, let me."

I leaned forward and wiped the wayward bubbles from his top lip, where they'd caught in his moustache. The hairs were surprisingly soft under my fingertips. The action upset my balance, leaving me dangerously close to falling into his lap. Suddenly, he was very close—way too close—and the sharp pine scent of his aftershave filled my nostrils. Or maybe it was his natural scent—some people's magic had a scent, if they were powerful enough. Eldric smelled of roasting nuts over an open fire. Willow trailed a faint hint of rose petals wherever she went.

Hurriedly, I sat back. "Sorry." I wasn't quite sure what I was apologising for—touching him? Invading his personal space? Maybe he was too knightly to have personal space, either, since he didn't seem to approve of personal lives. Yes, that was good. Hang onto that righteous outrage. It was better than feeling all giddy because I'd touched him. Fae men were dangerous to mortal women. Their beauty could be overwhelming if you weren't careful.

He took another, more cautious, sip of his beer, then ostentatiously wiped his mouth with a paper napkin from the dispenser on the bar.

I got the message and clasped my hands firmly together in my lap. No more touching. Suited me fine. I wasn't in the market for romance, after all. This was how it always started, feeling drawn to some guy, staring into his eyes. Watching his lips as he talked. Touching.

And then everything went to shit. When would I learn not to fall for the gorgeous outer shells of empty men? All I needed from this man was a good word from him to Lord Eldric. Nothing more.

"The changelings?" he prompted.

"Right. Ah … I spoke to everyone, but none of them knew anything about it."

"Of course they would say that," he said impatiently, "but did any of them seem nervous, as if they might be hiding something? Did you see any signs of new wealth in their homes—new belongings, different clothes?"

Different clothes? Damn it. I knew I must have been doing it wrong. It would have been nice if he'd mentioned this before I started. My expression must have given me away, because his changed to one of disgust.

"You didn't, did you? You just asked them straight out and put them on their guard."

"I thought that was what you wanted me to do. You said go out and question the changelings, so I did."

He sighed and pinched the bridge of his nose between his fingers. "Can you really be that stupid?"

"Listen, I'm a straightforward person. If you wanted me to snoop around and spy on people, you should have said so."

He shot me a glare. "I expected you to be a little subtle about it. Even a child could have figured that out."

I didn't do subtle. Shit. This wasn't going at all well. If I wasn't careful, I'd be off the case, and then I could kiss goodbye to any hope of being invited back to Autumn.

"There is another possible changeling," I said. "That guy you mentioned earlier, the one that went crazy at the gig the other night."

"Lord Eldric assured me that you knew all the local changelings. Is he or isn't he?"

Quickly, I explained my theory that he might be a changeling because he seemed to be able to see Rowan's true form, then added: "But he's dead now. Supposedly died of an overdose."

"Why supposedly? Not only are you not sure whether he's a changeling, but you can't even decide if he's dead?"

"No, he's dead, all right," I said, resisting the urge to push him off his bar stool. Jerk. At least anger was better than lust. "Shim finished him off in a matter of weeks."

"He was taking shimmer?"

"Is that its name?" I'd only heard it called shim up until now.

"Yes. Because it sparkles like glitter. This isn't the first time I've heard it mentioned, but only here in Sydney, for some reason." He eyed me speculatively, then sighed, his stern gaze softening. Those eyes really were amazing. "I have already been guilty of misjudging you once this evening. Before I leap to any more conclusions, tell me why you don't believe he died of drug use."

"Don't you think it's a bit convenient? Right when we're questioning changelings about the drake skin, he dies just before we can question him? Added to the fact that someone tried to kill me, too, it makes me wonder who doesn't want us investigating this."

He took another drink, then contemplated his half-empty glass for a moment, allowing me to admire his strong profile. Not that I wanted to admire it, of course. But it was a good thing his personality was so unappealing, or I would have been in real trouble.

"That may be the first sensible thing you've said tonight." Yep. With a personality like that, my heart was in no danger. "But it does us little good if he's already dead."

"We could search his house and see if anything odd turns up."

He drained his glass and slammed it down on the bar. "Good plan. Let's go."

"What, now? But he lives—lived—with other people. What if they're there? And I don't actually know the address. How about I find that out and we do it on Monday, when everyone is at his funeral." I cringed a little inside as I suggested it, but consoled myself that we weren't actually robbing him or doing any damage. Just having a look.

Again, I got that speculative look. "That's not a bad idea. Monday, then. Don't be late."

We pulled up in the street outside Dominion Tyres, and Willow cut the engine. "Tell me again why we have to break into this place? To find some guy's address?"

"Yes." I was only half paying attention, busy scanning the building for any sign of security cameras. There was a light over the door to the reception area—one of those blue things that starts flashing when the alarm goes off—but a lot of those were for show only, and not connected to an actual alarm system. Fingers crossed. "He works here, so I figure it'll be in his employment file."

"Why didn't you just ask him?"

I turned to look at her, eyebrows raised. "Because then he would think I was some kind of creepy stalker. Would you give your home address to some random woman off the street who'd just been asking odd questions about your dead friend?"

Willow tossed her copper-coloured tresses out of her face. "Honey, if I was a guy and some hot chick asked me for my address, I'd be offering her a gilt-edged invitation."

"And maybe a map," Sage added from the back seat.

"You guys are like twelve-year-olds," I complained. "I'm serious."

"So am I," Willow said. "You don't know much about the way men think."

I was about to protest that I knew plenty, but then I considered Adam and my dismal track record with boyfriends. "Well, I didn't know then that I was going to need the address."

I got out of the car. It was nearly midnight, and there were a couple of other cars parked on the street, but no people in sight. The quiet hum of traffic from the main street one block over was the only sound.

"Self-belief, girl," Sage said as she joined me on the footpath. "That's what it's all about. Any man would be happy to have you drop in for a 'home visit'." She made quotation marks in the air with her fingers, and I cringed. "Especially now you're wearing those clothes that someone with incredibly good taste bought for you."

"You're an idiot. And I didn't want to start a relationship with the guy, anyway."

"So now we have to break in to this place instead, when we should be at home, relaxing with a nice bottle of Chardonnay," Willow said, surveying the building with a sigh. "How is that any better? Really, Al, you need to think about your life choices."

"Princess," I said.

"Loser," she replied, without rancour.

"How are we going to get in?" Sage asked. "Those are steel shutters." Big, metal roller doors covered the three bays of the workshop area. "Can you pick the locks?"

I snorted. "I don't know about you, but my education in the Realms didn't include a course in lockpicking." And I'd tried to stay out of trouble—and mostly succeeded—since arriving in the mortal world. Sage and Willow, of course, had grown up in what had amounted to a palace, but even though their education there had doubtless been far more extensive than what my mother had taught me in our cottage in the woods, it was a fair bet that breaking and entering hadn't been on the curriculum.

"Shame," Sage said, a mischievous gleam in her eye.

"I don't think what we're after will be in the workshop anyway." I nodded at the glass frontage of the reception area. "More likely to be in there, where the computers and the filing cabinets are, than hanging with the tools."

Willow flexed her hands, cracking the knuckles. The giant amethyst ring that was her iron ward flashed as it caught the light from the street lamps. "That, we can deal with."

She strode across the empty concrete apron toward the door, Sage and I right behind her, and placed her hand flat against the glass just above the door handle.

For a moment, nothing happened as she pushed her magic past the resistance of the iron ward, then a green glow began to form around her hand. She looked as though she were just standing there, leaning slightly into the glass, perhaps thinking about something else. Uneasily, I glanced over my shoulder at the street. I felt like a sitting duck out in the open like this. Then the glass gave way to the sound of grains of sand pattering against the concrete, and a hand-shaped hole appeared in the door. Willow flashed us a grin before reaching through and unlocking the door from the inside.

"You make that look so easy," Sage said in a wistful tone. I gave her a sympathetic glance; watching magic performed always gave me the same mix of jealousy and longing for the old days that she evidently felt.

"Glass *is* easy," Willow said. "It *wants* to be sand again." She pushed the door open and waved a hand. "After you."

I slipped through the opening, glad of my black jeans and dark hoodie. An invisibility spell would have been even better, but we had to make do with what we had. The other two followed me inside.

"Uh-oh," Sage said as she entered. "What is that light?"

A red light was flashing on a panel on the wall behind the reception desk. "Probably nothing," I said, trying to convince myself as much as her.

Sage shut the door. In the darkness, we shouldn't be visible from the street—not unless someone was really looking. One computer sat on the reception desk, and two more were visible through a door behind the desk that opened into a small office. There was also a large filing cabinet in there, so I headed straight for it.

"Try the computers," I called over my shoulder to Sage, as I yanked the top drawer open.

"Me? I know nothing about computers."

"You know more than I do. You've got all those apps on your phone—work it out."

"But I—fine." I heard the swift tap of her fingers on a keyboard.

"Ladies," Willow cut in, "that red light is starting to flash faster."

"It's no good," Sage said. "I can't get in. It's password-protec—"

A shrill wailing burst out somewhere above our heads and I nearly jumped out of my skin. Dominion Tyres had a real alarm system after all, damn it. The blue light outside over the door was flashing faster than my panicked pulse rate, lighting up the whole damned interior. I slammed a drawer shut and pulled out the next one, speed-reading the tabs at the top of each file. They all seemed to be company names—suppliers, probably.

Sage stuck her head in, the blue flashing light silhouetting her form. "Let's go, before somebody comes to investigate."

My heart was pounding as I yanked open the last drawer, a prayer on my lips. If I couldn't find this address, the Hawk would look at me again as though I was something nasty he'd stepped in, and there would go my big chance to impress Lord Eldric. "Just give me one more minute. No one ever pays attention to alarms anyway."

A big, fat file at the front of the drawer had no name tag. I pulled it half out so I could read what was on the front page, then flipped through pages with trembling fingers. White light washed over me, then swung up the wall.

"Shit. There's someone here," Sage hissed.

I risked a glance over my shoulder, which almost blinded me. The white lights were the headlights of a car that had pulled up right in front of the doorway, so that the bright lights illuminated the inside of the office, competing with the blue flashes. It was starting to feel like a disco in here. Sage and Willow crouched behind the reception desk as I raced through the fat sheaf of pages.

Outside, a car door slammed, followed by the sound of heavy footsteps on concrete. The fat file held what I'd been looking for: twenty or more bundles of paper, clipped together at the top, each detailing the employment history of a different employee. I doubted they had twenty employees, so the records must cover past as well as present employees.

I found a Matthew and was in the act of ripping it out of the file when I saw the date of birth and realised the man was much too old to be the person I was looking for. Swearing under my breath, I searched faster, even as a shadow loomed on the wall above me. The man outside had stopped at the door, his shadow cast before him by the headlights behind him. Since I was crouched down behind the desk, he couldn't see me yet, but that wouldn't last long.

"What the hell?" he said, as I got to the second-last group of pages and found a Matthew Wrightson, born in the same year I was. Bingo! I committed his address to memory, then shoved the whole file back into the drawer, trying to close it as quietly as possible. "Base, I've got a hole bigger than my fist in the front door of Dominion Tyres."

A crackling sound was followed by a tinny voice. "Any other damage?"

He must be wearing one of those shoulder mics the police had. Just our luck that Dominion Tyres had a full-service alarm system with monitoring, and not just a fake set-up to deter thieves.

"Doesn't look like it from here. And you know what?" His tone was surprised, as if he'd just realised something. "It's the damnedest thing. There's no broken glass on the ground."

Joy. A full-service alarm system with monitoring *and* a perceptive bloody security guard. This was getting better and better. At least there was only the one guy.

"Any sign of the vandals?"

"Not that I can see from here. Want me to go in?"

"Negative. Wayne's not far away, I'll send him over for back up. Don't go inside until he gets there, understand?"

"Got it."

Holy crapfest. And Wayne would probably turn up with a machine gun and a police escort, the way this night was going. I crawled across the carpet to where the other two crouched, hidden from the security guard's sight by the bulk of the reception desk between us. For now, anyway. As soon as he—and Wayne and the police and the goddamn sniffer dogs and probably a marching band— came around the desk, we would be exposed. There was nowhere else to go except back into the little office I'd just come from, and that wasn't big enough to hide us all, especially once he turned on the lights.

Sage gave me a fierce grin. "Isn't this fun?" she whispered.

The sad part was that she wasn't being ironic. "You are insane. You know that, right?" I whispered back. No part of this was fun. My stress levels were through the roof; my heart pounding so hard, I was surprised the guard couldn't hear it from outside.

"Relax," Willow said. She wasn't grinning, but she didn't look worried. "I've got this."

"Be careful," I said. "He's probably got—"

But before I could say "a gun", she was on her feet and sauntering around the reception desk. Willow was a strong fae. Even here, in the mortal world, she had power to burn, though there would be consequences for using it.

I heard a muttered "Shit," from outside, then the guard barked, "Who's there? Stand still and put your hands where I can see them."

"Hey, there," she crooned, a musical lilt in her voice. This was why she was so mesmerising on stage, though she toned it down a bit for the band. Her voice was an instrument—and a weapon. "I'm Willow. What's your name?"

Something in her voice tugged at me even though I knew what to expect. The scent of roses swirled around her as she strode into the light from the car's headlights. Only the glass door separated them—the guard was right on the other side.

"Simon?" the man said, with a rising inflection, as if he wasn't quite sure anymore. He stared as she reached out and opened the door, watching incuriously as she stepped out into the glare of the headlights.

She put her hands on him and turned him around. He moved as if he were sleepwalking, unresisting but ponderous, and she guided him back to the driver's side of the car. "I'm sorry about that pain in your stomach, Simon," she said. Her magic rose around them; suddenly all I could smell was roses, heavy and sweet.

He hunched over, one hand going to his stomach. The other hand leaned against the roof of the car. She reached past him and opened his door.

"You should probably go home and rest." The sweet power of her voice urged him into the car, and he sagged into the seat unresistingly. I felt a powerful urge to join him. *Home* and *rest* sounded so good. "It's not that serious, but you'll feel better once you're moving again. Away from here."

I rose from my crouch behind the reception desk, fascinated. His eyes never left her face as he nodded and started the car. I was prepared to bet I could have walked out there in front of him and he wouldn't even have noticed.

"Take care of yourself, Simon," she said.

It seemed to me I could hear a melody underneath her words. I took a step forward, wanting to get in the car and drive away, too. Sage caught at my wrist and I stopped. Together, we stood, watching the guard back out onto the street and drive away.

Willow turned back to us once he was gone. The scent

of roses was fading now, and I blinked, half-dazed. "Wake up, ladies! Let's get out of here."

Sage moved solicitously to her side. "Are you all right?"

"Of course." Her tone was as bracing as ever, but she looked exhausted, and pale even for a redhead with milk-white skin. That had been a pretty powerful Suggestion she'd placed on the guard, and the shadows under her eyes showed how much it had taken out of her.

"Want me to drive?" Sage asked.

"I'll drive," I said.

"No!" they said in unison.

"How come you never let me drive? I'm a good driver."

Sage hustled Willow out to the street where our car was parked. By the time we got there, Willow was openly leaning on her.

"You drive like you're in a grand prix. We just want to get there without the drama," Sage said, as she opened the front passenger door for Willow.

"And without having to Charm any police officers into not giving you a ticket," Willow added. She sat back in the seat and closed her eyes. "I don't think I could manage it at the moment."

"Fine." I got into the back seat. I didn't know what they were talking about. Just because I took the corners a little faster than Sage did. She didn't love cars the way I did. One day, I'd be able to afford one of my own, instead of having to borrow other people's. His car was probably the thing I'd miss most about Adam, if I was honest.

"Sage, stop fussing," Willow said, pushing Sage away

when she tried to do up Willow's seat belt for her. "For heaven's sake, start the car and let's go before Simon's back-up arrives."

"And the marching band," I muttered.

"What?" Sage asked. When I didn't reply, she rolled her eyes at me in the rear-view mirror. "And you reckon *I'm* crazy."

12

On Monday morning, Sage was alone at the breakfast table when I came out.

"Where's Willow?"

"Still sleeping." Sage lifted the teapot with a questioning tilt of her head.

"No, thanks." I barely restrained a shudder as I turned to the coffee on the sideboard instead.

"She'll probably sleep most of the day," Sage added. "I wish she wouldn't use her magic outside the Realms, but …"

"But we really needed it last night."

"Yeah. Now she'll have to stay in the sith for a couple of days to build her strength again."

That was the trouble with being a powerful fae in today's world—there was so much iron everywhere: in the cars, the buildings, the machines we used—even the tiny ones we carried around in our pockets. And iron was toxic to magic. Any fae who wanted to be able to use their magic—which was basically all of them—had to wear iron wards at all times while in the human world. The more magic you had, the more uncomfortable the human world made you, and the stronger your iron ward had to be—which meant accessing your magic for anything more than minor spells became horribly taxing. Most powerful fae chose for that reason to spend most, if not all, of their time in the Realms. People like Willow and Jamison were too strong in their magic to be able to stand living in the human world full time, even with the help of an iron ward, which was why they both had a little slice of the Realms to retreat to.

Willow's home—and Jamison's little cottage apothecary—were in siths, little bubbles of the stuff of the Realms, but broken off from them: a complete, personal little piece of fairyland. Jamison's was anchored to the door in the pharmacy; Willow's was currently anchored to the grotty little house in the back streets of Parramatta—but either of them could be moved around at will. It was like having a home in a suitcase that you could pack up and take with you. It was the only way Willow could have lived so long outside the Realms.

"I hope it was worth it," Sage said. "You got the address, but what do you think you'll find there?"

I slathered butter on a slice of toast, trying to decide between avocado or cream cheese on top. In the end, I piled it all on. "Judging by the way things have been going lately, probably nothing. I'll have to go to the library this morning so I can Google his address. Hopefully find out when the funeral's on, too." That was another reason to miss Adam—usually, I'd just ask him to Google things for me.

Sage's phone was lying on the table beside her. She tossed it to me. "Google on that."

"But—" We were inside a sith. Belatedly, I wondered why her phone was on the table. Phones didn't work in the Realms, so it stood to reason that they wouldn't work here either. "How do you even have reception here?"

"We're in the twenty-first century here, baby." Sage grinned. "Rowan rigged up a wire. Don't ask me how it works, because I don't even understand half the things that come out of his mouth. There's a little magic, a little technology, and somehow, hey, presto! We have mobile reception. Television, too. Willow would go crazy otherwise, having to spend so much time in the sith. She likes her modern gadgets."

"Cool." I typed in the address. It wasn't far away. Next, I typed in the dead man's name: Peter de Gruner. Nothing came up, so I got onto *The Sydney Morning Herald*'s website and searched the obituaries and funeral notices. That went better. "Funeral's at ten o'clock this morning." I checked my watch. It was almost nine thirty. "Shit. I'd better get going. I'll text the Hawk and get him to meet me there."

I shoved my chair back and got up, holding the piece of toast between my teeth while I shrugged into my new leather jacket. Then I tossed the phone back to Sage.

She caught it one-handed. "The Hawk has a phone? How very modern of him."

A glob of cream cheese dropped onto the sleeve of my jacket. I scooped it up and sucked it off my finger. "I know, right? I was surprised, too—who would think a knight would be so up to date?" Of course, he hadn't thought to give me his number until I'd asked last time I'd seen him, so maybe he wasn't quite as with-it, technology-wise, as all that.

Sage sighed, watching me scrubbing at the smear left on my sleeve. "I can see why your clothes got grungy so fast. Do you have to throw your breakfast around before you eat it?"

"Tastes better that way." I made a show of licking my finger again, making her flinch. Having been brought up in the upper echelons of fae society, Sage's ideas on etiquette were a little out of touch. Overplaying my slovenly ways to get a rise out of her made breakfast taste all the sweeter. I shoved half the toast into my mouth. "Gotta run. See you later."

"Have fun," she said. "Try not to get arrested."

On the way to the station, I texted the address to the Hawk. *Heading there now*, I added. *Meet me there?*

Yes, he replied.

A man of few words. Why was I not surprised? I bet *he'd* be no fun at sleepovers.

No, wait. Firmly, I banished from my mind any images involving me having a sleepover with the handsome knight. Looks weren't everything, as I had learned to my cost, and he seemed sadly lacking in most other departments—humour, for instance, or even basic tolerance for people he considered beneath him. Though he *had* stepped in when that jerk Dansen Arbre was blowing smoke dragons at me … Not that it mattered. He was nothing more to me than a means to an end. I was done with falling for men because of their looks. Adam had only been the last in a long line of poor such decisions.

The address was in a rundown neighbourhood not much different from the one where the entrance to Willow's sith was hidden. It had the same small, dark brick houses, the overgrown front yards, often with a rusting car body resting on its axles or a pile of unidentifiable junk thrown in. Blinds sagged in windows, paint peeled off gutters and fascias, and the letterboxes leaned drunkenly. I felt completely at home.

A familiar figure leaned against a telegraph pole a few houses beyond the one we were interested in. He straightened as I approached, the sunlight flashing in his dark hair, revealing those russet highlights. A woman walking her dog on the other side of the street stared at him so intently that she tripped on an uneven section of footpath and nearly flattened her poor dog. The knight paid her no attention. He was probably used to such scenes—he'd draw attention wherever he went with his height, his physique, and his impossible good looks.

I felt almost cross as I drew level with him and met his ridiculously beautiful eyes. No one had the right to be that good-looking. He was probably rich, too, just to add insult to injury. You didn't get to be a knight unless you were from one of the powerful Houses of the Realms. Had anything ever gone wrong for him in his charmed life? I bet no one had ever thrown him out of his home into an unfamiliar world, cut off from friends and family, left to fend for himself. Everything on a silver platter.

"Yes?" Even his voice was attractive, deep and resonant. Damn him.

"Yes, what?"

"You looked as if you wanted to say something."

"Nope." Ranting at him about the unfairness of life might relieve my feelings, but it wouldn't do me any favours. "Did you check if anyone was home?"

"The house is empty," he said, which wasn't exactly an answer, but I was prepared to trust him on that. Some fae had a very finely tuned sixth sense which warned them of danger. For the first time, I wondered what kind of fae he was. With hair like that, he could be from Night or Winter, but dark-haired people could be found in most Courts, and that still left his actual type unknown. The only thing I was certain of was that he wasn't a kobold or any kind of goblin, because those dudes were short.

I turned my head away, watching him from the corner of my eye, and was rewarded with a glimpse of enormous, shadowy wings rising behind his shoulders. That didn't narrow it down much. The people of Air were all winged, but so were many other kinds of fae. Jaxen had wings, and he wasn't Air.

"Shall we?" I asked.

"After you," he said, very formally, with a gracious wave of his hand.

I led the way to the property in question. Most of the lawn was dead, and it looked more like straw than grass. Only the weeds in the garden beds flourished, choking out everything except a couple of wizened old azaleas that still struggled toward the light. I strode down the cracked and broken driveway with a confident air, trying to look like I had a reason to be there, and went straight around to the back of the house. I figured the sooner we got out of sight from the street, the better.

There wasn't a blade of grass or a speck of green in the back yard. It was tiny, and every inch of it was covered in concrete, as cracked and crazed with age as the driveway had been. In the centre of this desolation reared a rotary clothesline, an ugly grey monument to humans' love affair with steel. I'd adapted pretty well to the human world— my world, now—with its concrete and glass and steel, but every now and then, a pang of homesickness for the red and gold trees of Autumn pierced me. A place like this had no soul. How could anyone stand to live here?

I turned and found the Hawk with his hand on the back doorknob, head bowed, apparently in thought.

"How are we going to get—"

He turned the knob and pushed the door open.

"Inside. Never mind." I mounted the back steps—more concrete—and followed him in, shutting the door quietly behind us. At least there were no hand-sized holes in this door to give away our presence.

He moved swiftly through the rooms, perhaps getting an idea of the layout, or maybe he hadn't been as sure as he'd made out that there was no one home. There were only two bedrooms, a bathroom with a shower but no bath, a lounge room, and a kitchen with a small, round table crammed in one corner. Dirty dishes were piled in the sink, and a glance into the lounge room showed piles of empty takeaway containers. Housework was probably the last thing on Matt's mind right now, the poor guy.

"Well, it shouldn't take too long to search," I said. That was good, since I didn't know how long Matt would be away at the funeral. I felt guilty even for being here, as if I was intruding on his grief. "What exactly are we looking for?"

"Money. Gold. Expensive electronics. Anything that might show a recent windfall. These men don't appear to enjoy an affluent lifestyle, judging by the house they live in."

True. A pile of cash in a place like this would pretty much prove something suspicious was going on. I headed into one of the bedrooms, and he took the other. I didn't want to admit I wouldn't know an "expensive electronic" if it bit me on the arse. Sure, I knew iPhones were pricier than Androids, but I didn't think possession of an iPhone proved anything. Plenty of people had those.

Straight away, I realised this was the bedroom of the dead guy, which gave me a queasy feeling. There was a photo of him on top of a chest of drawers—probably a selfie, judging from the odd angle—with his arm around a laughing woman. They were at the beach, and they looked young and tanned and happy. Looking at it made me sad, knowing that he was gone. How had he gone from carefree to corpse so quickly?

I pulled open the first drawer and found underpants and socks. Really? I had to look through some poor dead guy's undies?

Somehow, this was not how I'd envisioned my life turning out.

No, I'd thought I could stay in Autumn forever. My mother was different—she would share her power with me. I would be the one changeling in a hundred who actually became fae and got to call the Realms home forever.

Yeah, not so much. But if this was how I got back there … I steeled my resolve and carefully looked through the drawer, then the one beneath it, and the one after that, too. I'd said I would do anything to go home, and I'd meant it. But there was nothing here to suggest Peter de Gruner had profited from the proceeds of crime. Still, there wasn't any evidence of a drug habit, either, and I knew he'd had one of those. The fact that everything looked normal on the surface didn't prove anything.

I finished checking the last drawer, even carefully pulling it out to make sure there was nothing in the cavity at the bottom, but found nothing. Where would someone hide their drugs in a room like this?

A freestanding wardrobe, just two slim doors wide, stood in one corner. A guitar case leaned in another, and an assortment of boxes lined the wall between them, piled carelessly underneath the room's only window. The blind was drawn, which was good, since it meant no one could see me going through some poor dead guy's stuff. Shoes and socks were discarded on the floor, and a pair of jeans lay flung carelessly over the bed, as if their owner had just got changed and might wander back in at any moment.

No, don't think about that. For better or worse, Peter de

Gruner was dead, and my sadness wouldn't bring him back. For now, I had to focus on what I was doing. I couldn't save him, but I might be able to save myself.

I opened the guitar case only to find there was no guitar inside. Maybe he'd sold it to get money for drugs. There were a couple of small pockets inside, meant for holding spare strings. Just right for a little packet of something shimmery—but they were both empty. I looked under the bed, next, and found nothing but a stray sock, an empty beer can, and a whole lot of dust bunnies. Under the mattress yielded nothing. Inside the pillow cases, likewise. Looked like I would have to go through everything hanging in the wardrobe.

The occasional soft sound came from the room next door—things being shifted, drawers closed. No cries of "Eureka!"

I glanced nervously at my watch. We still had the shared areas of the house to search, but it seemed most likely that if there were anything here, it would be in the dead man's bedroom, hidden among his personal things.

Quickly and efficiently, I plunged my hands into the pockets of every pair of pants hanging in the wardrobe and checked the pockets of every jacket and hoodie. I picked up every shoe and shook it to see what fell out. I even stood on the bed so I could check the top of the wardrobe.

The Hawk came in while I was doing that. He raised an eyebrow, but said nothing.

"No luck?" I asked.

"No. Nothing here?"

"Nope." I hopped down off the bed and smoothed the sheets where I'd been standing. Not that it made a lot of difference, since the bed hadn't been made anyway. When I turned around, he was almost on top of me, and I stepped back in surprise, bumping the chest of drawers with my hip. The photo of Peter and the laughing girl took a nosedive. The sound of the photo frame hitting the wood was very loud.

"Shhh!" He was facing the door, alert as a sniffer dog that's caught the scent.

I snatched the photo frame up. "What's wrong?"

"Someone's out there."

"He's home already?" Shit. Must have been a short funeral. The glass was loose in the frame; it made a slight grinding noise as my hand tightened on it, and he shot me a warning look.

"Not human. Something fae." And then he really did sniff the air.

I glanced down at the smiling faces in the photo again, feeling the glass shift under my thumb. Rocking like a seesaw, balanced on something behind it.

Something in my peripheral vision caught my attention: curls of green—smoke? mist?—crawling around the door of the bedroom like fingers of a spectral hand. Like a striking snake, the Hawk leapt forward and slammed the bedroom door shut. I dropped the photo on the floor in surprise. It bounced on the carpet and the back of the frame popped open, revealing a tiny scrap of fabric.

The Hawk caught at my arm as my fingers closed around it. "What are you doing?"

"What is that stuff?" The mist was seeping under the door, now, creeping across the floor. He dragged me across the room, toward the window, out of its path. His urgency infected me with fear. If *he* was afraid, it must be pretty bad. You didn't get to be a knight if you jumped at every shadow.

I turned to the window, heart pounding. We could get out this way. I scrabbled at the bottom of the blind, trying to pull it out of the way, but his voice stopped me.

"Don't. They'll be out there."

"Who will? What's going on?" I eyed the green mist, close to panic. It had formed a column and writhed up from the floor, like a swaying cobra about to strike.

I was so focused on the threat that I hadn't even noticed he had a sword in his hand until he slashed it through the air, sketching out a rough rectangle with the tip of the blade. Where the hell had he been hiding a sword?

The lines of the rectangle glowed briefly, then light burst from inside it, dazzling in the dim room. I barely had time to realise I could see a sunlit courtyard through what was obviously a fae gate before he grabbed my hand and dragged me through.

13

He slashed the sword through the gateway the minute we were through, and it winked out of existence. I stumbled as I landed: the courtyard looked as though it were paved with bricks, but the surface felt oddly spongy beneath my feet.

"What the hell was that? Was it trying to kill us?"

He said nothing, merely sheathed the sword in a scabbard that I could swear hadn't been hanging by his side a moment before. As soon as it was fully sheathed, I found myself unable to look at it anymore. An Aversion, then. That was one way to hide a sword, for sure.

"It was, wasn't it? That's twice in one week!" Aware that I was becoming shrill, I tried to rein myself in, but I still sounded accusing when I added: "No one ever tried to kill me before I met you."

His face, never all that expressive at the best of times, was a grim mask. "While I'm sure there's a correlation, I don't think I am the causative factor here."

I shrugged, massaging my hand. He'd squeezed it so tightly when he dragged me here, he'd ground the bones of my hand together.

He noticed what I was doing. "Did I hurt you?" I nodded, and a momentary expression of guilt flitted across his face. "I apologise if I was rough. I thought you would prefer me not to lose my grip halfway through the gate."

"Of course."

He took my hand, much more gently this time, and enclosed it between his two large ones. The warm orange glow of his magic surrounded our joined hands, and any lingering pain melted away.

"Better?" He stroked my skin, sending a little shiver through me.

I nodded. "Are you some kind of Jumper?" He had wings like Jaxen, but I'd never heard of a Jumper creating a gateway with a sword before.

"No." His thumb continued to stroke apologetic circles across the back of my hand. "The power to open gates is Ecfirrith's."

"Ecfirrith?" I looked up, confused.

He was standing close, much too close, and there was a wild light in his eyes I'd never seen before. "My sword. The name means Ghostmaker."

"Ah." I was having trouble stringing words together. The gentle stroking movement of his thumb was so distracting. "What was that green mist? It seemed so … menacing."

Mention of the green mist seemed to energise him. "I'm

sorry, I'm not doing a very good job of welcoming you to my home, am I?"

His home? I looked around, finally taking in our surroundings. The courtyard was bordered by the three wings of a house, with many doors and windows opening onto it. I could see a warm, sun-soaked kitchen through the nearest, with wooden benchtops and an open fireplace. Behind us, on the fourth side, a tiny bit of garden disappeared into forest, but through the tree trunks, I caught the occasional glimpse of sky, so the forest obviously didn't extend very far.

Still holding my hand, he led me to the door into the kitchen. When the door opened soundlessly, my heart flipped in my chest.

"Where are we?" I asked, though I was sure I already knew. Doors didn't open by themselves like that in the mortal world—not unless you were in a shopping centre or an office building, which this manifestly wasn't.

"We are on Oldriss." He let go my hand once we were inside, and I crossed the flagstones to look out the windows on the other side of the house.

I drew back sharply once I reached the glass. There was nothing to see out there but a very short stretch of grass and a world full of sky. It was like being on top of a very high mountain, except there was no valley below, no vista spread out before us, only blue sky everywhere I looked. Oh, wait, no, not everywhere—I found the clouds. They were below us.

I must have swayed, because he appeared at my elbow

and guided me to a chair. Not being able to see the ground was disorienting. My eyes made my brain doubt the evidence of solid floor and walls about me. I felt unbalanced, as if I might fall at any moment.

I'd thought we must be in the Realms, but not until this moment had I realised we were in the Realm of Air. Few people got to see it, unless as a shadow passing between them and the sun. Usually, the fabled floating islands of Air could only be accessed by those with wings. Thinking of all that empty sky between me and solid ground made me feel almost ill.

He pressed a glass of water into my hand as I stared queasily up at him. "You're from Air?"

"Yes." He crouched beside my chair, watching me solicitously. This was a side of him I hadn't seen before—he must take his duties as a host seriously. Fae generally did. It was largely due to the laws governing hospitality that the fae hadn't all managed to kill each other long ago.

"Is Oldriss a very big island?" It certainly didn't extend far past the kitchen on that side. I got a mental image of a house perched in mid-air, with clods of earth crumbling away at the edges, and shuddered again. I really wanted to ask him what was keeping it up, and if it had ever fallen down, though I knew the answer already.

But somehow, knowing intellectually that the islands of Air floated by magic, rising and falling at the whim of the Air fae who called them home, wasn't anywhere near as good an explanation now as it had seemed when I had my feet firmly planted on the ground. What if the magic failed?

Had any of the islands ever crashed? Maybe these questions didn't seem so pressing if you had wings yourself, but they felt pretty bloody crucial to me right now.

"One of the smallest," he said. Oh, great. A few more pieces of earth crumbled away from my mental image of the floating house. "I'm the only one who lives here."

Right. A private island. Somehow, that didn't seem as glamorous when we were discussing a floating island as, say, an island in the Caribbean. And it was tiny. I wouldn't be able to venture outside again for fear of accidentally falling off the edge.

I took a big gulp of water, then set the glass down on the table next to my chair. My other hand was still clenched so tight it was cramping, and as I eased it open, I remembered what I had found hidden behind the photo in its frame.

I opened my hand and held it out to him. "Look at this."

He caught his breath and plucked it from my hand. It was a tiny scrap of something that looked like fabric, but I knew it wasn't, shimmering like mother-of-pearl in the light from the windows. In the centre of it sat a tiny emerald jewel, a perfect half sphere. It had left a matching round indent in the skin of my palm.

His tawny eyes were full of storms. There was something strange about him—he seemed tense, almost feverish with some inner excitement. "You found this in the dead man's room?"

"Yes. It was hidden inside that photo frame I knocked down. I never would have found it otherwise."

He shut his eyes and let out a shuddering breath. "I

would say the Lady smiled on us, but this has become much more than a matter of some stolen skins." He ground the corner of the fragment between his thumb and forefingers. It flaked and crumbled into a fine powder that clung like glitter to his skin. "I think we have found the source of this strange new drug."

Holy shit. I stared at the sparkling particles. This was shimmer? "How does something that's rare even in the Realms become a drug for sale on the streets of Sydney?"

"If this man was a changeling—"

"But I'm not sure he was, now. I mean, I was prepared to believe there was one changeling that I hadn't known about, but he's not the only user. They can't all be changelings, can they?"

The Hawk rose from his crouch like a spring uncoiling and began to pace across the flagstones, as if he couldn't keep still a moment longer. "*Someone* is bringing the skin from the Realms."

"And you'd like to believe that someone was a changeling, would you? Somehow, that's easier than imagining a fae stealing from their own?" Anger flared inside me. Typical fae—thought the sun shone out of his own people's arses, but changelings! Yes, kicking them out's not enough. Let's blame the evils of the world on them, too. "You do realise that there are thousands and thousands of fae, compared to maybe a few hundred changelings? Statistically, it's far more likely to be a fae, never mind the fact that they'd have far more opportunity. Changelings can't get such easy access into the Realms as fae can."

"*You* can."

My hand crept to the gate glyph around my neck.

He had stopped pacing, and was standing with his back to me, gazing out the window. "Your Spring friend could probably persuade her hearth sister to take her anywhere in the Realms she wanted to go."

"Are you accusing *Sage*?" I sprang from the chair, outraged. "Or me?"

He waved an impatient hand. "I'm not accusing either of you. Merely pointing out that many outcasts have ways around their apparent exile." He slammed a fist against the wall, rattling the plates on the shelf above the sink. "Everyone is a suspect."

I had jumped nearly as much as the plates, so I folded my arms across my chest, trying to look unconcerned by his temper. "I didn't think you cared about the thefts. I got the impression you had better things to do than chase around after the queen's missing clothes."

He sighed and leaned his forehead for a moment against the window frame. It was a peculiarly vulnerable pose, and made my anger melt away. Something was obviously eating at him. He seemed a different person to the buttoned-up knight I knew.

"And so I do. Only now it's clear to me that this task is not so far removed from my own interests after all." Then he whirled, reaching down two small glasses from a shelf, digging out a bottle from a cupboard. "I need a drink. Want one?"

Clearly, he meant something stronger than water. The

liquid he poured into the first glass was a deep honey-gold—almost the colour of his eyes, in fact. "Sure. Why not?" It had been the kind of day where drinking before noon was totally justified.

The Hawk downed his glass in one gulp, then poured himself another, staring moodily into the golden depths of his glass. "I've seen that green mist before." He could have been talking to the wine. He swirled it in his glass, watching the light play on the liquid gold.

"Really? Where?"

"Deep in the forests of Autumn, actually." His tawny eyes met mine, haunted by memories. "When the king's enemies came for him."

Ah. Now I could see what had him so stirred up. Yet my sympathy for his painful memories was quickly drowned in a rush of outrage for what he was implying.

"Are you suggesting that *Autumn* had something to do with that?" Eldric might be an elitist arsehole where changelings were concerned, but that was no reason to think he was a traitor to his monarch. "That was a plot by Illusion."

"You were there, were you? You know all about it?"

The curl of his lip made me feel small. I straightened my shoulders. "Of course not. But everyone knows it's true. Illusion was even struck down by the Curse of the Brenfells." Most people considered that as proof enough, if Randall was to be believed.

His glass clinked as he put it down on the table and held out his hand imperiously, a man with a point to prove. "Come with me."

I let him pull me outside, across the sunny courtyard and onto the grass. It looked so green and soft that I wanted to take off my shoes and sink my toes into it. Like everything in the Realms, it made the earthside equivalent look like a second-rate copy. The trees here were straight-trunked and beautiful, the birds more brightly feathered, the sky clearer. The grass really was greener on the other side.

The sun beat down on our heads as we stood there in the little clearing before the trees began.

"Oldriss," he said. "Open."

The earth beneath my feet shivered—there was no other word to describe the strange ripple that ran through it— and a crack appeared in the green grass. The crack widened and deepened until it was a chasm, dark earth yawning open, so incongruous in the pretty, sunny meadow. I tried to step back, but his hand tightened around mine.

"Don't be afraid. Oldriss won't hurt you."

He spoke about the island as if it were a living thing. I glanced at him sidelong. "Are you doing this?"

"No." An earthen staircase appeared, leading down into a narrow pit. He tugged on my hand, and I followed him down gingerly. "Oldriss is. The islands of Air aren't truly made of earth, though they look as though they are. They are living creatures." He trailed a hand over the side of the pit, almost like a caress. "Oldriss and I have known each other a long time."

The pit wasn't deep, and it was still open to the sky and the light, but that was little consolation as I stepped off the bottom stair onto the floor. The walls were steep and narrow, and it felt uncomfortably like standing at the bottom of your own grave. I clung to his hand a little tighter, suddenly glad of the contact.

"Look at this," he said, directing my attention away from the square of blue above us. On the floor of the pit was a strange indentation. After a moment, I realised it was in the shape of a body lying curled on its side. Sure, that wasn't creepy at all. "I lay here for seven years while Oldriss cradled and protected me, keeping me from harm."

I glanced uncertainly from the outline on the floor to his shadowed face. "You lay here, in the pit?"

"No. Under the earth. Hidden from prying eyes."

"I don't understand." Had he been buried alive?

He led me back up the stairs and my breath whooshed out in a great rush of relief to be back on the grass with the sky above and the breeze ruffling my hair. Soundlessly, the pit closed up again, and he sank down on the grass where it had been. After a moment, to be sure he wasn't going to be sucked under the ground, I sat next to him.

"One day, nearly twenty years ago, at the height of summer ..." He considered me for a moment, then sighed. "You were probably only a child of three or four at the time. King Rothbold was journeying to Summer, to the home of his wife's brother, Lord Kellith. With him was his dearest friend, Perony, Lord of Illusion, and several of their men, as well as a group of the king's other favourites, his guards, and two of his knights, the Bear and the Hawk."

"That was you?"

"Yes. That was me. It was a large, convivial party. We could have created a gate, of course, and been there instantly, but the king was tired of being cooped up in the palace, I think, and decided to travel overland as a little holiday from responsibility." He smiled, as if at a fond memory. "There was certainly a lot of fine wine consumed, and a lot of laughter around the campfires at night. Not that it was a holiday for the Bear and me. We took our duty to the king seriously, even though it seemed he could hardly be safer even in his own castle than he was with this handpicked group of loyal men."

Oh, dear. I had a bad feeling that I already knew how this story ended.

"We spent our last night on the road in the forests of Autumn. We could have pushed on to Lord Eldric's halls, but the king insisted on the campfire as usual. We found a place on the banks of a stream late in the afternoon. Once the camp was set up, I went to bathe in the water. It had been a hot day, and we'd been riding for days. I didn't want to arrive in Summer the next day stinking of horse and sweat." He plucked a flower from the grass and began to fiddle with it, twirling it between his fingers. "I'd just finished dressing again when I heard shouts from the camp, and then the clash of swords. I grabbed Ecfirrith and ran."

He swallowed hard, lost in the memory. Even after all these years, it was obvious it still pained him.

"I saw the Lord of Illusion cut down. Enemies swarmed the camp, but they wore no uniform, no insignia. They could have been anyone. The king was surrounded by a knot of guards, fighting to protect him, but a strange green mist writhed around their feet, though the sun had not yet set and the day was too warm for fog." He began to pull the petals from the flower, one by one, very delicately. "Even as I ran into the clearing where they fought, the mist rose up and enveloped them—and they all fell to the ground, senseless."

"What about the other men? The ones attacking them?"

He shrugged. "The mist had no effect on them. I cut down a couple, trying to fight my way to the king's side, but the mist came for me, too. I held my breath as long as I could, but it was hopeless. Seeing it was useless, I resolved to go for help, but as I began to open a gate with Ecfirrith, I breathed in a whiff of the mist. My head spun, and I could barely keep my feet." The flower was nothing now but a stalk, its petals scattered on the grass beneath his restless hands. "In my confusion, I made a mistake. I had meant to open a gate back to the palace. Instead, I fell through onto this spot and blacked out."

He stopped. I wanted to reach out and comfort him, heal the ancient pain in those tawny eyes. He'd carried this guilt for twenty years. When he didn't go on, I prompted him. "And what happened when you woke up?"

"When I woke up, I thought I'd been buried alive. Seeing I was unconscious and defenceless, Oldriss had taken me into itself."

I shuddered. "How did you not suffocate?"

"Oldriss knew I needed air. It provided ventilation. The magic of the green mist that put me to sleep kept me nourished and alive." He met my eyes, his fingers at last still. "Which was just as well, since I slept there, under the earth, for seven years."

Seven years was a hell of a long time. It still seemed incredible, but the sombre look on his face assured me he was telling the truth. I'd seen some strange things in the Realms, and I knew perfectly well that there was more I hadn't seen that was stranger still. The Hawk had no reason to lie to me.

He laughed, though it wasn't a happy sound. "It sounds unbelievable, doesn't it? The ravings of a madman. That was what they thought me when I turned up at Whitehaven, shouting that the king had been attacked. It took them a long time to convince me that he'd been gone seven years. The queen had been pregnant when I left. Not until I saw her daughter, now a seven-year-old child, would I believe what they were telling me."

"That must have been awful." I laid a tentative hand on his knee, and he covered it with his own, though his face was still a grim mask as the memories racked him. This new, more vulnerable Hawk was even more attractive than before, dangerously so, but what could I do? I'd have to be made of stone to ignore such pain.

"They sedated me."

I snorted. "You'd been asleep for seven whole years, and the first thing they did was put you back to sleep?" Indignation on his behalf swelled inside me. What sort of treatment was that for a loyal knight?

"When I woke the second time, under the care of Whitehaven's healers, I resolved to take things more slowly, to gather information before I spoke again, so that I could understand this new reality. Though my natural impulse was to turn the world upside down in order to find the king, it occurred to me as I lay there that I had no idea who was responsible. It could be anyone, and I did the king no favours by letting myself be taken out of play." He patted the grass. "It also occurred to me how odd it was for Oldriss to have hidden me like that. I was forced to conclude that someone had come looking for me and Oldriss had been suspicious of their motives."

"Can you communicate with Oldriss?"

"Not well enough, I'm afraid. The communication is one-sided—Oldriss cannot speak to tell me what it has seen. I discovered that everyone believed the king dead, and the queen ruled as regent for her daughter, assisted by her brother, Kellith. Illusion had fallen, scant weeks after the king's disappearance, destroyed by Summer as punishment for their supposed treachery." He shook his head. "If Lord Perony was responsible for the attack, he did a damn bad job of the planning. He was one of the first to die."

"Maybe he faked his death?" He was the Lord of Illusion, after all.

"You can't fake a sword through the guts. And what would be the point, anyway? He was the king's closest friend, but he wasn't in the line of succession. He had nothing to gain from the king's death, and even less from faking his own."

"But …" I was having trouble making sense of all this new information. I rubbed at the back of my neck, which was hot. We'd been sitting in the full sun for a while. "The Curse of the Brenfells fell on Illusion."

He made a sound of disgust. "No, Summer fell on Illusion, without proof or warning. Apparently, the bodies of Perony and his men were removed from the scene. Someone went to a lot of trouble to make Illusion look guilty, and they paid the price."

"Did you ever tell anyone that you saw Lord Perony die?"

"Who would I tell? The queen? She was determined to hate Illusion for costing her her husband. My fellow knights? They thought I had abandoned the king in his hour of need. Said I should have died along with the Bear, to protect him." He shrugged. "I was finding nothing but suspicion everywhere I turned, and Illusion was already long gone, anyway. What was the point? I've been searching for the king on my own, but I've never found a trace of him, or seen any sign of the green mist again. Until now."

His tawny eyes burned with excitement. Why was he telling me all this, when he'd never told anyone else? He'd barely strung enough words together to be civil before this, and now he was spilling all his secrets. Must be the excitement of finding his first clue after all those years of searching.

"But do you think the king can really still be alive? After all this time?" I didn't want to burst his bubble—I liked this less aloof version of the knight—but I hated to think of his enthusiasm turning to despair when he failed to find any trace of his beloved monarch. "I know they sleep for a hundred years in fairy tales, but twenty years seems excessive."

"That green mist put me to sleep for seven years, and I only caught a tiny whiff of it. The king was surrounded by it, breathing it in fully. How much longer must he have slept? I'm convinced he's out there somewhere, Allegra."

That was the first time he'd said my name, and it sent a jolt of pleasure through me to hear it in his deep voice. Almost like a caress. There was a light in his gold-flecked eyes that made me feel I could fall into them and lose myself.

"His enemies orchestrated the whole thing so they could take him alive. If they'd wanted him dead, why bother with all that? It stands to reason, therefore, that he *is* still alive— and, finally, I have a lead. The green mist is now connected to the drug. If I find the people responsible for the thefts, for marketing shimmer to the humans, I will find the people who stole my king."

"Okay." I covered the back of my neck with my hands, leaning forward to rest my elbows on my knees. I could feel the warning prickle of heat on my neck which promised a sunburn in the making. "But how will that help if you have to flee every time the green mist makes an appearance, so you don't lose another seven years?"

The sparkle in his eyes faded somewhat. "I don't know. I'll think of something. What *are* you doing? You don't look comfortable."

It was beautiful outside, but maybe it was time to go back in. Or even move into the shade—the trees were very close. "I think I'm burning." He was so tanned he'd probably never had to worry about sunburn in his life. "It's hot out here."

There was a creak of wood and a rustling of leaves, and cool shade fell over us. I looked up to find a tree spreading its branches over our heads, which before had been stretching up towards the sky.

He grinned, his teeth very white against the dark of his beard. "Oldriss likes you."

"Ah … thank you, Oldriss." I'd never talked to an island before, and felt pretty stupid, but it seemed only polite.

"I should take you home—or wherever you're staying now. The day is wasting." He stood up and offered me his hand. I let him pull me up for the pleasure of having him touch me again. He was so ridiculously handsome, it honestly made me a little giddy to be near him. More, his passion had brought him alive, so that he seemed a different person. A much more likeable one.

Danger signals were going off all over my brain. My next boyfriend was supposed to be the most ordinary-looking man I could find. I couldn't trust my own stupid feelings—they'd got me into too much trouble in the past.

"You have been an immense help," he added, "but I can't in good conscience have you involved any further in this. These are dangerous people, and I would never forgive myself if something happened to you."

Oh, hang on. He wasn't getting rid of me that easily. Imagine if I actually found the king—Eldric would have to let me back into the Realms then. I'd practically be a celebrity. I wasn't going to let him dump me back in the mortal world and go questing on his own.

"It seems to me you still need my assistance."

His dark brows drew together in a frown. "How so? You helped me with the changelings, but I'm done with them now."

"So? Are you an expert on the mortal world, too, all of a sudden?"

He straightened, some of his usual haughtiness returning. "I daresay I know as much as any changeling."

"Says the guy who didn't even think to give me his phone number until I asked for it. Do you know how to use the internet?" Not that I was any great expert, but I was willing to bet I was better than he was. "Have you lived there for four years? Do you know how to talk to people without sounding like there's a stick up your butt? Would you even know the first place to start looking for a drug ring?"

I could feel the sun on my neck again as the branches withdrew their shade. Maybe Oldriss reflected its master's moods. The Hawk had put some distance between us, and was watching me with a hard stare, his lips pressed together in a thin line. "Are you quite done?"

Belatedly, I remembered that he was a powerful fae, and I was supposed to be winning his favour, not pissing him off. Sometimes I let my tongue run away with me. Still, I wasn't going to let him shunt me aside when something as big as finding the king was at stake. I was no royalist—after all, it was Rothbold who had decreed that changelings must leave the Realms by their eighteenth birthday, so he was hardly one of my favourite people—but I knew there'd be rewards handed out like how-to-vote cards on election day for a feat like that, and I planned to be in line for one of those rewards.

But what did I really have to recommend me? I had no great powers, and very little skill, really, unless you counted playing musical instruments, and I had the feeling that the Hawk wouldn't have a pressing need for a guitarist in order to save the king.

"Lord Eldric commanded us to work together," I said, falling back on a plea to authority. He was a knight; he should respect the wishes of a peer of the Realms. "He told us to find his lady's cloak, and the queen's dress, and I'm not stopping until I do. You should just hope that I let you tag along, because you need me."

A smile tugged at the corner of his mouth, spoiling the frosty look he was trying to blast me with. So Mr Tall, Dark, and Self-Important had a sense of humour after all. "I need you, do I? Please, enlighten me."

My brain had been spinning for the last few minutes, desperately trying to come up with something truly convincing. At last, I hit on it. "I know someone who can help us fight the green mist."

So, that was true. I did know someone who might be able to help—for certain definitions of "know". "Know of" might be a better way of putting it. I'd never actually met Yriell, though I knew roughly where she lived, and I'd heard Willow talk about her. Mainly to say that she was a little on the scary side, and best avoided.

But hey, if I had a choice between a possibly crazy old fae and the creepy green mist, I was picking the crazy lady every time.

The Hawk created another gate with his sword. He took my hand and we stepped through into a quiet, leafy suburban street.

"Where are we?" We were back in the mortal world, but I didn't recognise the neighbourhood. It looked a lot more upmarket than the one where Willow's sith was anchored, or even where I'd lived in Rowan's garage. A bellbird was calling somewhere off to the right. There were no houses on that side of the street; it all looked like wild bushland. I felt a pang of homesickness for the forests of Autumn, though they looked quite different from the dusty green gums that made up most of the trees here. But the breeze rustling through the leaves was the same, and the sound of bird calls.

"I live here," he said. "Sometimes, anyway."

"What? In the bush?"

"No." He jerked his head behind me. "There."

I turned around and found a large house perched on a shelf of rock above the street, with steep stairs cut into the rock winding up to the entry. He probably had a great view from up there. "What are we doing here?"

He threw me an impatient look, as if it should be obvious. "Ecfirrith can only open a gate to somewhere I've been. I assume we will need transport."

At street level was a single garage, and he hauled on the roller door to reveal a low-slung black sports car. My little car-loving heart nearly skipped a beat.

"A Maserati?" It was a GranTurismo. "4.7 litre V8 engine. Can I drive?"

"I don't know. Can you?"

"Of course." I was affronted that he'd even asked. I bet I'd spent a lot more time in the mortal world than he had.

"There's no 'of course' about it. What are you, seventeen?"

"I'm twenty-two. So can I?"

"No."

He got into the driver's seat and I shrugged. Oh, well. It had been worth a try. I climbed in beside him, breathing in that delicious leather-and-money new car smell. It was still heaven to get to sit in such a car. Then he took off with a throaty growl from the engine, and I sighed with pleasure. This thing was sex on wheels. Willow's car was expensive, but it had been chosen because it fit the band's gear, not for its performance. I settled back into the leather seat and resolved to enjoy the ride.

"So, where are we going?" he asked.

"Over on the east side. The Royal National Park."

He quirked an eyebrow at me. "Your friend lives in the national park?"

"She likes forests." Rather more than she liked people, if Willow was to be believed, but hopefully she'd make an exception for a visit from a Knight of the Realms.

We were soon roaring down the Pacific Highway, weaving in and out of the traffic, and I had to revise my estimate of how much time the Hawk had spent in the human world. He took shortcuts that I hadn't known, and never once consulted the GPS. He drove fast but confidently, as if he'd been doing it all his life. Most fae had an automatic aversion to the "metal machines" as they were often called, and rarely drove unless they had to. The Hawk must have a pretty spectacular iron ward. He seemed to enjoy driving as much as I did.

"Have you got an Aversion on this car?" I asked eventually.

"Why?"

"You just drove past a police car doing"—I leaned closer to him so I could see the speedo—"at least thirty over the speed limit, and nothing happened. Either that cop's asleep on the job, or you're cheating."

"It's not cheating, it's using all available resources. Does my driving bother you?"

"It's a little slow for my taste, but I can put up with it." I gave him a cheeky grin.

He tried to keep a straight face, but a smile cracked through his façade. "I'm glad you're not going to have the vapours on me." There was a note of approval in his voice, and I couldn't help feeling pleased that I'd managed to impress him. "We're in a hurry."

"Are we? The king's been missing for twenty years. A little bit longer isn't going to kill him."

Oops. That was the wrong thing to say. The smile was replaced by his usual aloof expression and the mood of camaraderie evaporated.

"Neither of us know the king's situation. He may be suffering, in which case I'm sure he'd prefer not to endure it for 'a little bit longer'. You speak as if he's some remote character in a story, not a living, breathing man."

"I'm sorry, I didn't mean—"

"Forget it."

I closed my mouth and looked out the window for the rest of the journey.

Twenty minutes later, we turned off the highway into the entry to the national park, and the car rolled to a stop at the ticket booth.

"Twelve dollars, thanks, mate," said the bored-looking ranger on duty in the booth. "Gate shuts at eight thirty tonight."

The Hawk pulled a scrap of paper out of a compartment in the console and handed it to him. The ranger gave him an entry ticket and the Hawk drove through.

"You Charmed him," I said. "Why didn't you just pay the twelve dollars?"

"Why do you care?"

"Now his till won't balance at the end of the day. You pay for drinks at the pub. How is this different?" Apart from the fact that Randall would whoop his ass, knight or not, if he tried to pull a stunt like that at The Drunken Irishman.

"Randall's fae," he said, as if that explained everything.

"That's elitist bullshit. Humans are not some kind of subspecies." He was no better than me, despite his pretty face and his magic sword. "They deserve to be paid for their efforts the same as fae do. Just because you *can* rip them off doesn't mean you should."

"Perhaps we could save the Marxist lectures for some other time," he said. "Where are we going?"

I directed him to the car park at Audley Weir. Sunlight danced on the water as we got out of the car, but my mood was far from sunny. Just when I'd started to think that maybe he was different, he turned out to be just as much of a jerk as the Lords and the other high-born fae. Why did I even want to help him find his stupid king? Rothbold was probably the biggest jerk of them all.

That's right, because I wanted to go home. I set off on one of the bushwalking tracks, walking fast, as if I could leave my problems behind if I outpaced him. That was never going to work, of course—with his longer legs, he soon caught up. Instead, I took a childish consolation in pushing overhanging branches aside, then letting them thwack back into his chest as he followed me down the trail.

After about fifteen minutes of this, he broke the silence.

"If I shower that man in gold on the way out, will you stop attacking me with bushes?"

"Fairy gold or real gold?"

"Real gold. I'll make him rich beyond the dreams of avarice."

He was trying to charm me, but I refused to play the game. "You don't have that much real gold, which means you're just going to steal it from someone else. So, no."

Silence fell again. I needed to concentrate, anyway. Willow had said there was a charred stump off to the side of the track that had been struck by lightning long ago, and that Yriell's house wasn't far past it. You just had to force yourself to go there.

I was starting to worry that I'd missed the blackened stump, when it loomed on my left, crouching like a wizened old man above the bracken. I plunged off the path and headed for it.

"Allegra." Again, I felt a thrill of delight at my name in his deep voice and had to remind myself that he was a stuck-up fae. "Who in the name of the Lady are we going to see out here in the middle of the bush?"

"Yriell." As soon as I passed the stump, I felt it—a powerful Aversion. Even though I'd been expecting it, my steps slowed, and it was an effort to keep walking against its suggestion that I should turn back, that there was nothing for me this way but danger and pain. "She knows Earthcraft. Willow said she had a potion for everything under the sun."

Most fae—and a few changelings, too—knew a little Earthcraft, but these days, it was limited to the kind of herb lore that I'd learned, and some basic potions. Earthcraft was a dying branch of magic, even though it was the first thing a lot of humans thought of when they thought of magic. Witches and their potions were a standard part of the average person's image of magic.

Behind me, his footsteps slowed, too. "Is that her Aversion I feel? She's strong." He caught up to me and looked down into my face. "Wait. You said, 'Willow said'. Haven't you met this Earthcrafter? You told me you knew someone."

"I do. Kind of."

I started walking again, aiming my steps for where I felt the most resistance, a barely visible track that curled around the base of a large red gum tree then disappeared into a straggly thicket. We both stopped in front of the thicket. It was made up of spindly plants whose branches crisscrossed to form a seemingly impassable barrier. There were thorns among the grey-green leaves, too. I rubbed at my bare arms. Who wanted to be stabbed by those suckers? It would be so much easier to turn back.

"Maybe this isn't such a good idea after all."

He gave me a sharp glance. "That's the Aversion talking. Come on."

He took my hand and led me into the thicket. I dragged on his hand, dreading the attack of those wicked thorns. If I could have freed myself, I would have headed straight for the car park, but he refused to let me go, pulling me along in his wake. My shoulders were hunched, expecting any moment to feel the bite of a thorn, but nothing worse than a few twigs battered at my unprotected skin.

Suddenly, we were through, and the terrible dread lifted. I felt like the champagne cork popping out the top of the bottle with the sudden release of pressure. When I glanced back, I couldn't even see any thorns. Was it all a Glamour to deter visitors?

Ahead of us lay a cottage that would have looked completely at home in some beachside town—a snug little weekender with a wide front porch. The house was painted a dull green so that it blended in with the trees surrounding it, but even so, it looked rather odd stuck on its own out in the middle of the bush. A small curl of smoke rose from the brick chimney at one end of the house.

Now that we were past the Aversion, it was no trouble to walk up the path to the front porch. As we climbed the steps, it did occur to me that someone who went to such trouble to avoid visitors might not be too happy to see us. I'd just have to hope that my charm and good looks got us in to see the Earthcrafter.

Or maybe my charm and *his* good looks. I cast a sideways glance at my companion. His looks had probably opened a thousand doors for him before. Why not this one?

I raised my hand to knock, but the door opened before

my knuckles landed on the rough wood. A small woman stood there. And by small, I mean I could see straight over the top of her head into the cottage's interior, and I was no giant. Dark strands in her hair hinted that it had once been as black as a raven's wing, but it was now mostly grey, and fell in long waves around her shoulders. It was also full of bits of twig and grass, as if she'd been rolling around on the ground just before she'd opened the door, but she seemed unaware of it.

Her eyes were a deep, warm brown, like rich soil after rain, and they glared at me from under thick, greying eyebrows. Her gaze slid from me to the Hawk, then back to me, apparently unimpressed with the gorgeous fae knight on her doorstep.

"How the bloody hell did you bastards find me?" she demanded.

"I—" That was *not* what I'd expected to come out of her mouth.

"Well? Cat got your tongue?" Impatiently, she glanced again at the Hawk. "What about the pretty boy? Is he mute?"

"Not at all, my lady," he began smoothly, but she waved him to silence.

"Doesn't matter, anyway," she said. "I'm not interested."

Then she slammed the door in our faces.

I flinched in surprise. Now I knew how the Jehovah's Witnesses felt. The look of outrage on the Hawk's face made me giggle, then snort, and finally break out in full-on laughter.

"Why are you laughing?" he asked. "May I remind you that this is not a game?"

"I know, I know, I'm sorry," I said, forcing my face into more serious lines. Then I raised my voice. "Lady Yriell, please, may we have a moment of your time? My friend, Willow Andrakis, sings your praises, and we have great need of your talents." I was sure she was still standing right on the other side of the door and could hear me perfectly well.

For a long moment, nothing happened, and I was wondering what other tactic I could try when she spoke.

"You're full of shit, girl, and so is that Willow. Came here wanting gardening advice when everything in her sith was dying." The door flew open again. "Can you believe that? Gardening advice! Do I look like a bloody garden centre?"

She stood there, hands on her hips like some tiny, aggrieved gnome, and my lip twitched again. I couldn't understand why Willow had said she was scary—she looked adorable. I bet she'd be great fun at parties.

"Shocking," I agreed. It seemed like a different approach might work better. "Willow can be such a princess."

She eyed me for a moment, as if weighing up her options. "I like your moxie, but I don't have time for you."

Then she slammed the door again.

After a moment of stunned silence, the Hawk tried again. "My lady, we need your help in the search for King Rothbold."

"That idiot."

"We've found something that will lead us to him."

Dead silence, and then the door opened once more.

"Lady's tits," she muttered. Out of the corner of my eye, I caught the Hawk's flinch at the blasphemy. Grudgingly, she held the door wider. "In that case, you'd better come in."

I stepped inside and found myself in a large room that reminded me very much of Jamison's apothecary, though clearly, this was no sith. I could see the dusty greens of the Australian bush outside the large window at the back of the room. Shelves along the walls groaned under the weight of glass jars and bottles full of odd ingredients, and a worn bench under the window showed the scars of many cuts and even burns, presumably from years of mixing potions there.

Unlike Jamison's apothecary, however, a modern kitchen took up another wall. She even had a fridge and microwave. How on earth did she get electricity all the way out here? And how did she manage to coexist with so much metal without escaping into a sith? If what Willow had said was true, she was very powerful—much too powerful to deal with the iron-drenched modern world. Yet she seemed to have made a home for herself here. Her iron ward must be something special indeed.

We'd obviously caught her in the middle of something. A great many bits of greenery were spread out on a circular table in the kitchen end of the room, as well as some oddly shaped roots and other dried up, wizened things that might have started life as mushrooms, but were a little hard to identify now that she'd chopped them. The herbs, I knew, but there were also leaves from Australian natives, some dried, some fresh, and bark from trees I didn't recognise.

She went back to chopping something that looked like ginger root into tiny pieces, leaving us standing awkwardly in the middle of the room. The blade of the knife tapped away against the chopping board, like a tiny woodpecker. Tap tap tap.

"Get me that green bottle behind you," she said, without looking up.

There was nothing behind me but the window, so she must have meant the Hawk. On the shelves behind him were several green bottles, scattered amongst the clear ones, and some brown ones that looked suspiciously as though they'd started life as beer bottles.

He reached out for one that contained an unidentified dark fluid.

"Not that one," she said impatiently. "On the shelf beneath that."

He handed her something that looked horribly like a bottle full of eyeballs. I shuddered and gazed out the window instead. Maybe she wasn't quite as adorable as I'd thought.

"Well, then?" she said briskly. "I didn't ask for company, and I'm not getting any younger here. What do you want?"

"Lady Yriell," the Hawk said. "I'm a Knight of the Realms—"

"I'm not blind," she interrupted. "I can see that sword you're concealing."

She could? Even when I looked sideways at him, I

couldn't see it, though I caught the outline of great wings rising up behind his shoulders.

"You're the Hawk, I suppose, being a fly-boy. Not that I care. You could be the king himself and I'd rather see the back of your head disappearing down my front path again. Get to the point."

She wanted to cut to the chase? I could do that. "We need help fighting a toxic green mist," I said hurriedly, before the Hawk could launch into any long-winded explanations.

The tapping of the knife paused, and she looked up. "Toxic green mist? Are you drunk, girl?"

"I wish. I could do with a beer after the day I've had."

"It's not even mid-afternoon," she scoffed.

"My point exactly."

That startled a laugh out of her, though it sounded creaky from lack of use, and she put the knife down. "All right, you've got my attention now. Make it quick and make it good. Tell me about this green mist."

So I launched into the story of going to Peter de Gruner's house, the attack of the green mist, and then described how the Hawk had come up against it before, when the king had been attacked, and its effects on him. In a couple of minutes, I had the problem laid out for her: if we were to continue the search for the source of the drug and find the thief who'd stolen the rainbow drake skin, we needed a way to counteract the mist.

"I thought, since you're so good with herbs and things, that you might know of some potion or counterspell." I waved a hand, encompassing all the weird and wonderful tools of her trade that lined the shelves of the room.

"Herbs and things," she repeated, in a tone of disgust. "That's all anyone thinks Earthcraft is anymore." She picked up the knife and began to cut again, wielding it as if the ginger root had personally offended her. "I remember when Earth was one of the most respected of all the Realms. And feared." She waved the knife at me pointedly. "If you can't be liked, be feared, girl. That's always been my motto. Worked like a charm for centuries, and why screw with a winning idea, I ask you? Those fools Untaro sired were never true Earth. Their mother's blood was full of salt water."

Who the hell was Untaro? And why was she ranting about him now? I raised an eyebrow at the Hawk.

"Untaro was the Lord of Flowers, before it joined with Spring," he said, for my benefit.

"Lord of Flowers, my arse," Yriell snarled. "He was the Lord of Earth, when it was still called Earth, before those lily-livered daughters of his decided to turn their backs on the forest and rename the Realm Flowers. Flowers! How can you respect a Realm that denies the existence of its very source of power?"

This must be ancient history, indeed. How old was the tiny woman in front of me?

"All they cared about was how pretty things were. They wanted roses, and perfume, and white doves cooing in the garden. That's not Earth." Every point was punctuated by an emphatic wave of the knife. "Those of us who were true

Earthcrafters weren't welcome any more at Court—not that we wanted to go there. Stupid, superficial place. In the end, the trees and the beasts and everything uncomfortable—everything that made up the real Earth—was banished to the Wilds."

"Is that why you moved to the human world?" I asked.

She shrugged. "After a while, the Wilds got lonely, even for an antisocial old bitch like me. Anyway, that hole's been dug a long time. This green mist of yours … I can't say I've ever seen it before."

I sighed. If Yriell couldn't help us, who could?

"Keep your fur on, girl. I might still be able to knock something up for you. In the old forests of Earth, we had a little proto-dragon. Not much bigger than a rainbow drake. We called 'em smokers, because they couldn't breathe fire. All they had was this smoky breath, but there was a poison in it that would stun their prey long enough to make an easy dinner. You've never seen a rabbit go down as hard as when he caught a face-full of a smoker's breath." She smiled at the memory.

"I've never seen such dragons," the Hawk said.

"You calling me a liar, fly-boy?" He began to protest, and she waved him to silence. "Just yanking your chain. No one's seen a smoker in centuries. I don't think they survived the sanitisation of 'Flowers'. Poor little bastards."

"And you had something that would protect you from this breath?" the Hawk asked. I was fascinated by the old fae's stories, but he was keeping his mind on the job.

"There used to be a potion that we drank if we knew we

were going into smoker territory. Oak and ash, I haven't thought of that for centuries." She turned to a shelf that had a row of books among the jars and bottles, and took down one with a brown leather cover. "I wonder if I've still got it here? It was bloody good, I can tell you. Those smokers may have been small, but if you breathed in their stink, you'd be out for the count, and liable to wake up and find the little bastard had been chewing on you while you slept." She flipped through the pages as she spoke, sending little puffs of dust into the air. "I knew a lad once who walked into a nest of them. Got lost and hadn't been expecting to go anywhere near them, so he hadn't taken the potion. He never woke up at all."

An image of a swarm of tiny dragons chewing on an unconscious man popped into my head. Erk.

"Here it is. Oh, I'd forgotten about the ragweed." She grinned. "Tastes like cats' piss. Are you sure you want this? I don't even know if it will work against whatever this green mist is."

"We're sure," the Hawk said. "How long will it take to make?"

"Come back in a couple of days. Should be ready by then."

"Thank you," I said. "You've been very helpful."

She shuddered. "For Lady's sake, don't tell anyone that. I'll have a line of damn fools at my door wanting me to do shit for them."

16

Late that night, I was lying in bed in my new room, not too hot and not too cold, wearing my comfortable new pyjamas. A nightingale was singing sweetly in the garden outside my window, and moonlight lay on the floor in silver squares. The conditions were damn near perfect for sleeping, and yet I was still wide awake, my stupid brain running a million miles an hour, busily trying to solve the puzzles the day had presented. As if they were so easily solved. The king had been missing for twenty years. Everyone but the stubborn Hawk presumed he'd died long ago. And now, it seemed the person or persons responsible were active again, stealing rainbow drake skins and selling them to humans for drugs.

That was the bit I just couldn't puzzle out. Anyone who was so well-placed in the Realms as to have a hand in the disappearance of the king should have less than zero interest in the human world. And if they were already rich as Midas in the Realms, as all the older fae were, why would they be out chasing human dollars? Humans were a sideshow, like watching pigs wrestle in the mud, or chickens peck each other. A small, idle amusement, nothing more. With all the magic of the Realms at their disposal, the high fae had turned their back on this world centuries ago, even before industrialisation had filled it with poisonous iron. Most of them had probably forgotten it even existed, caught up in their own centuries-long schemes.

My bedroom door opened a crack, spilling golden light from the hallway into the room.

"You awake?" Sage asked, in a stage whisper that could have been heard down the other end of the house.

"If I wasn't, I would be now," I said. I wasn't sleepy, but I had the morning shift at work tomorrow, so I really needed to try racking up a few z's. "What's up?"

"Nothing. Willow just got home with six different flavours of ice cream. Thought you might want some."

I groaned. "Dammit. You know ice cream is my kryptonite."

She grinned and opened the door wider. "Hurry up, then, before she eats all the honey and macadamia."

I padded down the hallway after her and out into the garden. Willow was in the pavilion at its centre. It was open to the night, except for the roof. That might have been a problem if we were really in Sydney, where the mosquitoes were just about big enough to carry you away, but here in the sith, it was beautiful. A soft breeze lifted the short strands of my hair, and as I slumped down on a pink velvet couch, the nightingale started up again.

"Which one do you want?" Willow wore a gossamer gown that hadn't been sewn anywhere in the human world. Its green matched her eyes, and it clung to her figure in a way that any red-blooded man would have found immensely distracting. She had a row of five small ice cream tubs, each with a spoon stuck into it, set up on the low table in front of her. The sixth tub, which was indeed the honey and macadamia, was half empty, and she was busy spooning the rest into her mouth.

I checked out the offerings: spearmint, vanilla, choc chip, strawberry surprise, and … what the hell? "Pecan and seaweed? What kind of abomination is that?"

She carefully licked all the ice cream off her spoon before replying. "I got these from that new Japanese takeaway. The Japanese have unusual tastes."

I shuddered and picked up the spearmint. "That one's yours."

Sage flopped down on the couch next to me. "Isn't this fun? Slumber party time! We can eat ice cream and watch soppy eighties movies."

"I don't think I could stomach a romantic movie at the moment," I said, around an explosion of icy spearmint goodness in my mouth.

"Cheer up," Willow said. "At least Adam's stopped ringing you."

"True." In fact, I hadn't thought of Adam all day. "Not that he would have got me for part of it, since I was in the Realms."

Sage frowned, her spoon halfway to her mouth. "In Autumn? Did Eldric summon you again?"

"No, in Air. On a floating island called Oldriss, with the Hawk."

"What on earth for? Is he trying to seduce you?"

"Don't be ridiculous," Willow said. "He probably wanted a nice, quiet place to interrogate her."

"What would he be interrogating me for? I haven't done anything wrong." Although I wouldn't mind if the Hawk wanted to interrogate me. I smiled as I spooned more ice cream into my mouth, imagining him patting me down. He'd have to do a *very* thorough search, to be sure I wasn't hiding anything. Maybe even a strip search, just in case. My smile widened.

"I thought he wanted you to talk to all the changelings? You can hardly interrogate yourself, so I figured he'd do it."

"He wouldn't be working with her if he didn't trust her," Sage objected.

"A man like that doesn't trust anyone," she said. "He's as paranoid as they come. He hasn't been the same since the king died."

"Actually, about the king …" My smile faded as I filled them in on all that had happened that day—what we'd found at Peter de Gruner's house, the attack of the green mist, and then the Hawk's explosive revelations about the attack on the king and our visit to Yriell. This was serious shit. "You should probably keep that to yourselves, though. I don't think the Hawk would be happy with me blabbing his secrets to everyone."

"We're not everyone," Sage said. "We're practically family."

"And I've heard something like that before, anyway,"

Willow added. "From my father." Willow always had the best information. It helped when your father was the Lord of Spring. "There were rumours when the Hawk reappeared seven years after everyone had given him up for dead. Some of the Lords thought he might have had a hand in the death of the king, but Father never bought into that. He said the Hawk had no motive."

"No one who knew him could believe he would harm the king. He's been searching for him all these years. He's all fired up now about the green mist reappearing—says that if we find who's responsible for stealing the drake skins and turning them into drugs for humans, we'll find whoever took the king."

"Surely he doesn't think the king is still alive?"

I shrugged. "He seems to. And even if the king's dead, whoever did it should be punished."

"True. Does he have any theories on who it might be?"

"If he does, he's not sharing them with me."

"But it doesn't make sense," Sage said. "I mean, I can see how he would think the green mist would be from the same person or the same organisation, but how can the disappearance of the king be connected with this drug-running?"

"I don't know. Bad people can be bad in more than one way, I guess."

"But if they're using drake skin to make this drug, how can anyone possibly afford it? That stuff is ridiculously expensive."

"If they're stealing it, they're not paying for it," Willow pointed out.

"Yeah, I know, but why waste it on selling it to junkies for thirty bucks a hit or whatever? They're not millionaires; they can't be paying that much for it. If it costs more than other drugs, they'd just use those instead. It's like tearing up hundred-dollar notes to give people change."

"And it's hard to get," I said. This had been bothering me, too. "Once they've stolen all they can, what then?"

"This guy, the one who died—what did he do for a living? Was he rich?"

I snorted. "Judging by the house he was living in, definitely not. I have no idea what his job was."

"Let me Google him." She put down the ice cream and reached for her phone. "What was his name again?"

"Peter de Gruner."

Her thumbs flew across the key pad. I eyed her strawberry ice cream, wondering if I could sneak a bit while she was preoccupied.

"Okay, found his Facebook account. Looks like he worked at a nursing home. Alder Grove."

"No money in that, unless he was the manager—but he looked too young."

"Yeah, he was twenty-one, according to this."

Damn, that was young. What a waste.

"Maybe one of his workmates might know where he was getting it from?"

"Maybe." It didn't seem likely, if his housemate didn't. "I suppose it's worth a try. The Hawk says he knows a few places where you can score. He's going to check out who's dealing what. Just in case he turns anything up that way."

"Why don't we have a look at this nursing home tomorrow?" Sage asked. "We could pretend we're visiting someone."

"Sure. We can't do much until Yriell's potion is ready, anyway."

"It'll be fun."

Willow rolled her eyes. "For certain definitions of fun, maybe. Enough of dead guys and drugs. You guys are doing this slumber party thing all wrong."

We arrived at Alder Grove mid-afternoon the next day, after I finished my shift and Sage finally managed to drag herself out of bed. A neatly manicured garden fronted the street, but the buildings were old and looked uncomfortably institutional.

A faded sign on the building closest to the street said "Office". We walked straight past that and headed for the entrance of a larger building further down the long driveway.

"This is good," Sage said as the glass doors opened on a foyer devoid of life. "No one's around."

A long hall extended off the foyer, with numbered doors on each side. Some were open, showing glimpses of small rooms with two or even three beds crammed into them. There was a pervasive smell of disinfectant that failed to completely cover the underlying stench of urine, and somewhere, a quavering old voice was calling for help, over and over again.

"Yeah, but who are we going to talk to?" I asked. Not the old people lying in their beds, staring vacantly at TVs or just at the ceiling. What would they know of drug deals? Most of them looked too drugged to even remember their own names.

A middle-aged woman in dark blue pants and tunic came out of one of the rooms and checked at the sight of us. "Can I help you?"

"No, we're fine," Sage said. "We're just going to visit someone."

"Did you check in at the office? Where are your visitors' badges?"

"Oh, we won't be long," Sage said, starting to walk away. "It's not worth getting a badge."

The woman moved to block the corridor. "Who are you visiting?"

Seeing that the woman wasn't going to be easily put off, Sage changed tack. "Actually, we were looking for our friend, Peter. He works here, and when he found out we were looking for a place for our dad, he said he'd give us a tour."

"Your dad?" She looked from one to the other of us, her expression clearly showing that she didn't believe two such different-looking women could possibly share a father.

"Yeah. Is Peter here? He said he was working today."

"Peter Lee?"

"No, Peter de Gruner."

Her expression changed, her hand creeping to her chest uncertainly. "Oh, I'm so sorry. You didn't hear? He—he died."

I'd never realised what a good actress Sage was before that. She took a step back, covering her mouth in shock. "What? But … I only saw him last week. What do you mean, he died?"

"Do you need to sit down?" Her nursing training was coming to the fore—or maybe she just didn't want to fill in the paperwork if Sage collapsed right there in the hallway. "I'm very sorry. It was a shock for all of us. He was so young."

"But what happened?" Sage asked.

"Drug overdose, apparently. So sad. He was such a favourite with the patients in the dementia unit, always so calm and helpful." She shook her head. "The funeral was yesterday. His poor father was leaning on his walking stick as if he'd fall over without it. Do you know his dad?"

Sage shook her head.

"An older man. He must have had Peter quite late. He looked devastated. Just devastated."

"Did you know Peter was on drugs?" I asked.

"No. He was a little … off, the last couple of months. Not quite himself. But I thought maybe he had romantic troubles. Not drugs. He just didn't seem the type."

"That's awful," I said.

"Poor Peter," Sage said. "I can't believe it. And now we've come all this way to see the Grove for nothing." She turned to the woman as if she'd suddenly had a great idea. "Unless you could show us around? Or one of Peter's friends?"

Good thinking. This woman was too old to be a close

friend of Peter's, but if she would hand us over to someone younger, we might be able to find out more. And Sage was so appealing with her big, dark eyes and soulful expression.

Sadly, the nurse seemed well able to resist soulful expressions. Her shoulders straightened at the suggestion, and her manner became less personal and more businesslike. "I'm sorry, I really can't help you. All tours of the premises need to be booked at the office. We can't have strangers walking around here with all our vulnerable residents."

"Of course," Sage said. "I understand. We'll just head back to the office, then. This way?" She pointed back down the hall the way we'd come.

"Yes, at the front of the dementia unit. There's a sign when you come in from the street. You can't miss it."

We thanked her and headed outside, trudging back down the long driveway.

"Should we check out this dementia place?" Sage asked. "She said Peter worked there. Maybe we'll find some friends of his."

We were approaching the entry to the unit when a side door opened and an old man tottered out into a tiny paved area where three rather sad-looking outdoor chairs huddled together in a circle. The little courtyard had a high steel fence around it, with no gate. That didn't stop the old guy from making a beeline for the fence.

"Have you come to take me home?" he asked, with such an air of hopefulness it nearly broke my heart. "Mother will be wondering where I am."

"Um ... hi," I said. "We're just visiting. Have a nice day!"

He looked about ninety-three in the shade. The poor old thing's mother had probably been dead for decades. "She always sings to me of the crystal cliffs when I can't sleep. Do you know that song?"

"Sorry," said Sage, shaking her head.

As we reached the main entry, a huge guy in a nurse's uniform came out into the courtyard. "How did you get out here, Mr Nicholson? You know you're not supposed to be outside on your own. Come back in." He took the old man's arm and propelled him back inside. The old guy looked back at us pleadingly before the nurse slammed the door behind them.

At the entry, we had problems of our own. The door was locked, so we pressed the buzzer by the door. After a long pause, a tinny voice responded. "Yes?"

Sage tried her previous trick again. "Hi, we're here to see Peter de Gruner."

"Sorry, he's not here today."

Sage raised her eyebrows at me. "Do they not know he's dead?"

I shrugged. That didn't seem likely, if what the other woman had told us was true and he was a crowd favourite in the dementia unit. "Maybe they're short-staffed and they just don't want to deal with us."

She pressed the buzzer again a couple of times, but no one responded. In the end, we gave up and headed for the car.

"Not very friendly, are they?" I muttered as she unlocked the doors. A raven flew overhead, its harsh caw sounding as though it were laughing at me. "I hope the Hawk is having more luck."

"Well, we learned one thing, at least," she said.

"What's that?"

"Getting old sucks." She shuddered. "I never want to end up in a place like that."

I nodded. Seeing all those old people lying in their beds like that, and the poor crazy guy trying to get home to a mother who only existed in his muddled brain, had been miserable.

"The trouble is, the alternative is dying young, and I don't think that's such a great option, either."

17

This time when we stopped at the ticket booth to pay for entry into the Royal National Park, the Hawk handed over a twenty-dollar note with a flourish and a sidelong glance at me.

"See, that wasn't so hard, was it?" I asked as he drove the Maserati through and headed for the car park. "I'll make a model citizen of you yet."

He got out and slammed the door behind him. "I could hardly think of anything worse than having to live in this place forever."

"Yeah, it's the pits," I said, a little snippily.

"Oh." Belatedly he appeared to remember that I *was* actually stuck here forever. "I'm sorry. That was thoughtless."

When he looked at me like that, his tawny eyes full of contrition, it was too hard to stay offended at him. I lifted one shoulder in a shrug. "It's no big deal."

"Of course. That's why you're doing all this, because

you don't care whether or not you get back into Autumn. It's no big deal."

I lifted my chin. He made me feel like some desperate loser. "Some changelings turn their backs on the Realms afterwards. They wouldn't go back if you paid them."

"But you're not one of them, are you, Allegra?" His voice was gentle and his eyes serious. "Is it really worth risking your life? Home isn't a place, you know. It's the people you love."

Easy for him to say, when he had a whole beautiful island to call home. But I was touched that he was trying to help, and he seemed so much more approachable today that, on impulse, I asked: "What's your name?"

He stopped at the entrance to the trail and turned to look at me, surprised. "My name?"

"Yeah. You must have one—your mother didn't call you the Hawk when you were born. I feel funny calling you 'the Hawk' all the time, when you use my name." And it sounded so sexy in his deep voice, too. "It's so impersonal. It'd be like you calling me Changeling Scum."

"The Hawk is my title. Is Changeling Scum yours? I could call you that if you wished." Laughter glinted in his eyes.

"Don't try to wriggle out of it. Is there some reason you don't want to tell me your name? Is it something embarrassing?" Some Realms had odd naming conventions. Spring liked to use plant names, like Willow and Sage. The old Realm of Dusk had favoured long names, the more syllables the better. "I bet it's Dick. Or Percy."

"Percival is a very respectable old name," he said mildly. "Do you think of Dick when you look at me?" He managed to keep a straight face, but there was a wicked gleam in his eyes.

Heat roared up my face from my neck to my cheeks, and I pushed past him onto the trail so I wouldn't have to look at him anymore. "I walked right into that one, didn't I?"

He laughed, and I hurried my pace. It hadn't escaped my notice that he still hadn't told me his name. Maybe he liked to remind everyone of his fancy title. Maybe he was just a raging snob and didn't think a mere changeling should be throwing his name around as though she was his friend. I forged ahead, arriving at the charred stump in record time, and plunged off the path. But soon, my feet stopped walking of their own accord, and he caught up with me. The Aversion was just so strong.

He took my hand and pulled me along with him, towards the vicious thorns that still looked so horribly real, even though I knew they weren't. "Come on. Nearly there."

We popped out the other side of the thicket, and I gasped in relief as the pressure disappeared. It felt like a literal weight had been lifted from my shoulders. The Hawk strode ahead and rapped sharply on the Earthcrafter's front door.

Nothing moved inside the house, and no one answered the door. He knocked again, but after a few minutes, it became clear that no one would. A scowl darkened his brow, and he turned the handle impatiently. To my surprise, it opened.

I guess that made sense. With such a powerful Aversion protecting the approaches to her house, why would Yriell need to lock the door? The Hawk stepped inside, and I followed him in. Something circled lazily in the microwave, so she couldn't be far away.

"Lady Yriell?" he called.

A distant laugh floated through an open door by the fridge that I hadn't noticed on our last visit. "Down here, fly-boy. And you don't need to go wasting your pretty manners on me. I haven't been called a lady in a hundred years."

Beyond the door was a set of steep wooden stairs, lit by a globe so dim that it was lucky we both had excellent night vision. Halfway down was a landing, then the stairs switched back the other way. Expecting a cellar or basement, I was brought up short by the view of a large cave that opened up before us.

I stepped onto an uneven rock floor. The space was large, but comfortably arranged, with chairs and a table. The walls were lined with even more shelves than the room above, these ones holding jars and bottles whose contents made the ones upstairs look tame by comparison. Many contained body parts—bones, ears, eyes, even organs—suspended in some kind of thick fluid. The most disturbing ones were the ones where I couldn't quite tell what kind of body the part had come from: leathery wings, or oddly jointed hands. Strange skins and scalps with hair attached that had never adorned any humanoid head. The Earthcrafter who worked down here seemed a very different proposition to the amusingly rude old fae we'd met in the sunlit cottage last time.

There was no sign of her. Two tunnels led off from the cave. The shorter one appeared to end in the outside world—hanging leaves covered much of the end of it, but bright light filtered through them. The longer one was so dark it defied even my night vision. Beyond a few paces in, the tunnel was completely black.

Naturally, it was from this tunnel that Yriell's voice came again. "Make yourself useful, fly-boy, and come carry this for me."

The Hawk headed for the black tunnel, and I trailed behind him, not quite comfortable at being left in a cave where bottled eyeballs glared down at me from the high shelves. The tunnel twisted and turned more often than a snake in a sack. The air smelled dank and earthy, and our footsteps crunched on bits of dirt and small pebbles. Around the next bend, a soft blue light glowed.

Fungi of all shapes and sizes clung to the walls and crowded the floor of the tunnel. Some even hung from the ceiling, and it was these that emitted the blue light. Others glowed purple, or sickly green. Was this whole cave a sith, and I just hadn't noticed the shiver of threshold magic when I'd entered? Some of the mushrooms looked like they were straight out of a children's book of fairy tales, their cheerful red tops spotted with white. Others would have been more at home in a science fiction novel, with their outlandish shapes and strange fringes. Some were no bigger than my little fingernail, while others were the size of elephant ears. A pungent smell filled the tunnel, part rot, part dead thing, and part God-knew-what—but it was strong. Even the Hawk's nostrils flared as we stopped amid the mushroom wonderland.

"Take a couple of these," Yriell said. I'd been so busy gawping at the fungi that I hadn't even noticed her crouched down next to a pile of wooden boxes. "Or are those muscles just for show?"

The Hawk bent down and hefted the top three boxes easily. They were filled to the brim with the weird fungi. Yriell got to her feet with an audible cracking of joints, and I hurried to take the last box for her.

"Is the potion finished?" the Hawk asked, holding his boxes as if they weighed nothing at all, though the one I had must have been at least ten kilos.

"You young things are so impatient," Yriell said, leading the way back toward the cave.

I stumbled on an uneven patch of floor as the blue mushroom light faded behind us. It was blacker than the Caverns of Night in the damn tunnel.

"Just put those on that bench," she said as we came out into the cave again. It positively blazed with light compared to the darkness of the tunnel. "Did you figure out who was supplying the humans with drake skin? Because I'd love to know. I'm nearly out."

"You use it? What for?" I let the wooden box thud down on the bench with relief. A mushroom rolled out of the top and plopped onto the work surface, but I didn't pick it up in case it was poisonous.

"It has quite a few uses in Earthcrafting. It's not just pretty jewels and expensive clothing, you know. A jewel dissolved in blood and mixed with the juices from a snapped hydrangea stem will make quite a tidy poison. Fresh skin has minor hallucinogenic properties. Dried and smoked, it can also be used as a sedative. And that's just the beginning. Once you throw magic into the mix, the sky's practically the limit. Is it any wonder the poor beasts were hunted nearly to extinction?" Yriell picked up the little mushroom and popped it into her mouth. I guess that answered the question of whether or not it was poisonous. "The males have a poisonous spur on their hind legs, too. I've heard rumours that that was involved in Illusion's magic somehow, though of course you can never get an Illusionist to spill any secrets. Bunch of tight-lipped bastards." She considered that for a moment, then sighed. "Dead bunch of bastards, now. Their secrets all died with them."

She headed up the stairs, and we followed. I was glad to be away from the dark cave and its ominous contents.

"Our investigations seem to have arrived at a dead end," the Hawk said as he closed the door to the stairs behind us. "Allegra couldn't discover anything at the dead man's place of work, and I've had no luck yet with the dealers on the streets. They all swear they know nothing. For once, I think they're telling the truth."

"Then you need to work back the other way," she said. "Who benefits from supplying the humans with this drug? Who has a motive?"

Motive. I felt as though I was living inside a detective

novel, working on a case that was rapidly going cold. I was reminded of Willow's father, saying he didn't believe the Hawk had anything to do with the king's disappearance because there was no motive. If only motives were as easy to discover as they seemed in murder mysteries.

"That doesn't narrow anything down," the Hawk said. "Making money is the oldest motive of all. It could have been anyone. There are plenty of fae with access to the Realms who could benefit from stealing skins and selling them off in pieces. It's not as if they could sell such recognisable items whole, so why not chop them up and make a fast buck from the humans? Fae are coming and going from the Realms all the time." He glanced at me. "Your friend the drummer disappeared recently, didn't he? You said he wasn't there the night your home was destroyed. Where did he go?"

I drew an angry breath. How dared he suggest Rowan could have done such a thing? "To Dubbo to look at a drum kit he was thinking of buying."

The Hawk shrugged. "But he could have gone to the Realms as well. Or even lied about going to Dubbo. You have no way of knowing where he actually was."

"I don't need to know where he was to know he's not a thief. He's a good person. He certainly wouldn't go around accusing people he didn't know of being thieves and murderers."

"I'm not accusing him," he said, with a touch of impatience. "Just pointing out that he is one of many people who had the opportunity."

"Oh, yes, I'm sure Rowan has *plenty* of opportunities to wander into Whitehaven and nick stuff out of the queen's closet. He probably does that every second weekend."

"You seem to have a lot of anger," he said, as if I was some weird specimen he was analysing for a science project.

"And *you* seem to have no idea how to judge character. You can't treat the whole world as a suspect. You have to trust someone."

"I trust myself. I've learned the hard way not to put my faith in other people. As far as I'm concerned, the whole world has been a suspect since I woke up."

The microwave pinged, drawing all our eyes.

"Ah, there's your potion done," Yriell said.

Wisps of steam and a foul smell like swamp gas rose from it as she removed it from the microwave. I hoped it tasted better than it smelled.

I ignored the Hawk, still fuming. How dare he make assumptions about Rowan's character? What motive could Rowan possibly have? He wasn't exiled, he'd just always preferred human music to fae music, so he'd chosen to make the human world his home. Some fae thought that an odd choice, but it didn't make him a criminal. He was perfectly happy with his life—playing in the band, sleeping in, going back to Autumn now and then to visit family.

What had been missing in Peter de Gruner's life that had led him to experiment with drugs? And where had he gotten the money? The poor bastard would have been better off saving his money to get a better place to live. He'd seemed like a nice enough guy, at least before the drug had taken hold, just sitting there at the bar sharing a beer with his mates. I'd even thought of suggesting him to Sage as a potential date.

I still felt like I'd seen him before, somewhere. Something about his smile had seemed familiar. Now he was in the ground, his whole life gone when it had barely started. His poor family. His father had been devastated, that nurse had said. An older man with a walking stick.

I froze as an idea exploded into my mind. *An older man with a walking stick*. Oh, my God. It couldn't be, could it? Old men with walking sticks were a dime a dozen. But that smile— No wonder it had seemed familiar.

Yriell passed the Hawk a small bottle of something brown and vile-looking, and he turned to me. Something in my expression must have alerted him. "What's wrong?"

"We have to go see Edgar right now."

"Who's Edgar?"

"Edgar Woodbine. He's a changeling. And he may be the man who can answer all our questions."

18

I rang Edgar's door bell and waited, but it seemed today I wasn't my day for having doors opened. Nobody came, and I hesitated on his neat front porch. Maybe I was wrong. Friday was his usual grocery shopping day. He could be down at the supermarket with not a care in the world.

But if what I suspected was true, he would be here. I rang the door bell again, eyeing the big pot of lavender by the front door. I knew he kept a spare key underneath it. But if everything was fine, he would think it peculiar to come home from shopping and find that I'd let myself into his house in his absence.

"Maybe he's not home," I said to the Hawk as the silence stretched.

"Someone is," he replied. "I heard movement from the back of the house."

"Could be the cat." I pressed my face against the window of the front room, trying to see inside through the gap between the curtains.

"It wasn't the cat."

He must have good hearing. He was fae, so of course he did. And Edgar's walking stick, with its distinctive handle carved into the shape of an eagle's head, was leaning against the wall by his favourite arm chair. So he wasn't out grocery shopping.

I tipped the lavender to one side and retrieved the key, unlocking the door and pushing it open. "Edgar? Are you here? It's me, Al."

"Al?" the Hawk repeated. "You have a beautiful name like Allegra and you call yourself Al? That's criminal."

Ignoring him, I stepped inside. "Edgar? Where are you? Are you all right?"

A sudden vision of Edgar sprawled on the kitchen floor hastened my steps down the long, dim hallway to the kitchen, which was at the back, its windows—trimmed with lace curtains—overlooking a little garden. Edgar was sitting at the small table in the corner, facing the window.

"Edgar?" He looked shocking, as if he'd aged overnight. His eyes, red-rimmed, saw nothing, staring blankly at the window. He was wearing rumpled pyjamas and hadn't shaved in a couple of days. His gnarled fingers were clasped loosely on the table top in front of him. "What's the matter?"

"My son is dead."

Even though I'd been more than half expecting him to say just that, I still caught my breath. I sank down in the chair to his right, my back to the faded apricot countertops and the old-fashioned sink.

"You never told me you had a son."

The Hawk stood in the doorway, watching us both but saying nothing. Edgar didn't acknowledge his presence. Hell, he didn't even look at me, just kept staring at nothing, as if the words he spoke had nothing to do with him.

"I never told anyone. His mother and I were only together a short time. She left me before he was even born. I only saw him half a dozen times in his whole life." Now he looked at me, and the grief in his eyes was terrible. "One of those was identifying his body in the morgue."

The difference in their surnames had thrown me. Peter must have taken his mother's last name. I covered Edgar's weathered, old hands with my own. They were shaking, and his face was grey with exhaustion.

"Have you eaten? Let me get you something."

He shook his head. "I'm not hungry."

"A cup of tea, then." I made as if to rise, but the Hawk stopped me with a gentle hand on my shoulder.

"I'll do it." He moved to the sink, flipped the kettle on, and started opening cupboard doors in search of cups.

"That one in the corner," I said. "And the tea's on the second shelf." This was probably the first time the knight had ever made tea for a human. He even found some biscuits and put them on a plate. Assured he had it under control, I turned my attention back to Edgar. "What happened? Tell me."

"They said he died of a drug overdose. A new drug. Very dangerous."

"Shimmer?"

"Yes."

"Do you know where he got the drug from? Who supplied him?"

He shook his head. "No. Last time I saw him was a couple of months ago. He came here, begging me for money. A loan, a gift, he didn't care. Said I owed it to him, that I'd never been there for him. That a father should do more for his son than sire him. He became … quite heated when I refused."

"Did he say what he wanted the money for?"

"He said he was behind on his rent, and that he would be kicked out of his home if he didn't pay. I offered to let him live with me until he got back on his feet, but that didn't suit him." His fingers moved restlessly under my hands, a spasm of regret. "He said he had nothing left, not a penny to his name. He was living from pay to pay. Where does someone like that find the money for drugs?"

Usually, they stole it, but I wouldn't suggest that to a grieving father. Helplessly, I looked over his bowed head at the Hawk, who quietly set the cup of tea and plate of biscuits in front of Edgar. We were no further advanced. Edgar knew nothing that could help us.

"What about his friends?" the Hawk asked. "Do they know anything?"

I'd already spoken to his housemate, but perhaps there were others. Edgar glared at the Hawk, and I pushed the biscuits towards him. "Have something to eat."

"I don't know any of them; I barely knew Peter." A tear dripped onto my hand, and I gripped his gnarled fingers tighter. "What would they tell me, anyway? My son is dead—what is the use of knowing how he obtained whatever killed him?" He looked up at the Hawk, his eyes burning. "Look at you, still young and beautiful after centuries, while I am old and broken, my life wasted in regrets. The fae stole the life I should have had, showed me the glory of the Realms then denied it to me. Ruined my life."

"Edgar—"

"It's true," he insisted. "They meddle with our lives without thought for the consequences. We poor humans can never know the kind of immortality the fae enjoy. Children are our immortality, our chance to prove that we were once here, that our lives meant something. And now he's gone. What is the point of any of it?"

There was such anguish in his voice that I leaned in and flung my arms around him. I had no answers for him. No hope to offer. All I could do was hold him while he wept.

I slept badly, tossing and turning in my luxurious bed. Every time I closed my eyes, I saw Edgar's face again, ravaged with grief for a son he'd barely known. My own mother had had the raising of me for seventeen years, but I doubted she would suffer so much when I died. If she even noticed. She'd finished with her stolen human baby and had no further interest in the changeling she'd raised as her own. She'd made that very clear when she'd shoved me back into the human world like so much discarded rubbish.

I staggered out to the kitchen as dawn's light silvered the sith and made myself a cup of coffee—it was too early even for the staff to be awake, and they were early risers. No point attempting to sleep any longer; I still had stolen goods to find if I wanted to endear myself to the Lord of Autumn. I'd pretty much given up on endearing myself to the Hawk, after last night's lead had ended in a dead end. He'd probably tell Eldric that his changeling sidekick had been no bloody use at all.

Had Edgar gotten any sleep? Probably not. The image of his face tore again at my heartstrings. I hadn't seen as much of Edgar since I'd been busy with the band, but he'd been a rock of stability for me when I'd been finding my feet among the exiles, like a kindly uncle, or even a grandfather. I didn't know how old he was, but he was the oldest changeling I'd ever met. More importantly, one of the kindest. I resolved to head over to his place to check on him later in the morning.

But my resolution came to nothing. Though I pounded on the door and called out to him, he didn't answer. Again, I peered through the windows, even going around to the back of the house to see if he was in the kitchen. He'd moved the spare key from its hidey-hole under the lavender so, unless I wanted to break in, I was stuck outside. Either he was out or not in the mood for company, and if it was the latter, I figured moving the key made it clear that he didn't want to be disturbed. So I left, feeling helpless and sad, and spent the rest of the day moping around Willow's sith playing melancholy tunes on my guitar. Fortunately, that lived with the rest of our gear at Willow's place, otherwise I would have lost it in the explosion.

My phone rang in the middle of a complicated progression of minor chords, making me jump. I checked the display and felt a stirring of relief. Well, at least the Hawk was still talking to me.

"What's up?"

The Hawk ignored my question, getting straight down to business. "What are you doing?"

"Just practising. We have another gig next week." Not that I'd be playing any of these mournful tunes at it, but at least the practice kept my fingers limber.

"Meet me at The Drunken Irishman for dinner."

"Dinner?"

"You get hungry, don't you? Do you have some objection to eating?"

"No objection. Especially if you're paying. Just a little surprised—I thought we were out of leads."

"I don't give up just because things get difficult." His voice was cool. "Do you?"

"No, of course not." I took a deep breath before I started babbling. If we were still partners, I needed to impress this guy. "I can be there in half an hour."

"Good," he said, and hung up. Not a man for idle chitchat, but whatever. It was a business meeting, not a date. I shrugged into my leather jacket and left the house.

Twenty minutes later, I arrived at The Drunken Irishman. As I entered, my phone began to vibrate in my pocket. I pulled it out, scanning the room for the Hawk.

He wasn't hard to spot, looking like a brooding romance hero, one elbow propped on the bar.

It was a number I knew well. "Edgar? Are you okay? I dropped in on you this morning, but you weren't home."

"I was out hunting."

"Hunting?" I slid onto the empty stool next to the Hawk, imagining the old man with a bow and arrow and feeling very confused.

"I think I know who your thief is."

"*What? Who?*"

"I don't want to say any more over the phone. Can you meet me?"

"Of course!" I beamed across at the Hawk and hissed, "Edgar thinks he's found the thief!" What on earth had Edgar been *doing* today? How could he have solved so quickly what we had spent days on without success? "At your place?"

"Yes. As soon as you can. Bring the knight—he needs to see this."

Before I could reply, he hung up on me.

"*Bring the knight?*" the Hawk repeated, one eyebrow arched in disdain. "Am I your dog, to be led around on a leash?"

"He knows we're working together on this investigation," I said, hurrying to make excuses for Edgar's abruptness. He wasn't normally like that. "And he's just lost his son, so cut him some slack. Manners aren't top of his priorities right now."

"I'm surprised this investigation is. He didn't look capable of even leaving the house yesterday."

That was true. But grief could do strange things to a person. "Maybe something happened. I guess we'll find out when we see him."

"I was going to buy you dinner," the Hawk said. "We should eat first."

My stomach rumbled at the mere thought of food, but there was enough background noise in the pub to cover it. "I can wait. I'm dying to know what he's found."

"My car's round the back."

Awesome—I got to ride in the Maserati again.

I sighed as I settled into the luxurious leather seat. It cradled me as if it had been moulded for my body. Maybe one day he'd let me drive it.

Edgar opened his door to our knock and stepped out onto the porch. He still looked red-eyed, but calmer than he had yesterday, though he leaned on his walking stick more than he usually did. It struck me all at once how old he was getting. He'd always been old, ever since I'd met him, but he'd worn his age lightly, one of those wiry older men who seemed as if they might go on forever. Now he looked frail, like he might topple over in a light breeze without the support of his stick.

He nodded respectfully at the Hawk. "Sir Knight, if you would be so kind as to open the Way, I have something I want to show you."

"Where would you take us, changeling?" The Hawk's tone wasn't exactly suspicious, but he was wary. This was definitely odd. How could Edgar have anything to show us in the Realms? As far as I knew, he hadn't been there for close to thirty years—longer than I had been alive. "If it's somewhere I know, we have no need to risk the Wilds. Ecfirrith can open a gate directly for us."

"I discovered something about my son," Edgar said. "I know how to find his drug dealer, but we must take a hidden Way through the Wilds."

The Hawk studied him, frowning. "You have a charm on your walking stick."

My gaze darted to the walking stick Edgar leaned on, but I could see nothing odd about it, of course.

"To help me find the Way," Edgar said.

"Who gave it to you?"

Edgar sighed. "It would be easier to show you than explain. If you would?"

He gestured at the front door behind him. The Hawk glanced at me, as if seeking confirmation, then laid his hand on the door frame. Magic flared briefly beneath his fingers, and the view of Edgar's hallway through the door rippled and pulsed, blurring into indeterminate shapes. Without hesitating, the knight strode through the door, and Edgar and I followed.

The house faded as mist billowed around our feet, and I felt the familiar shiver of threshold magic over my skin. Between one step and the next, the quiet chirping of insects began, and ghostly grasses brushed against my legs. There was a heavy, expectant feel in the air, as if a storm was about to break, and then the mist cleared and we were in the Wilds.

We stood in a clearing with seven paths leading from it,

but I barely had time to register the fact before the Hawk chose one and strode off with brisk assurance. It felt good to have a confident guide. Edgar and I followed, but Edgar couldn't move as fast as us. Courteously, the Hawk gestured for him to take the lead, so that he could set the pace.

I was last in line, and my shoulder blades itched with unease. The path was dark even for my night vision, with the trees looming above us. Their branches met overhead, forming a black tunnel down which we must pass, like the gullet of a mighty beast.

Damn, why did I have to think of beasts? My ears strained to sort the sounds of the forest around us. Were they the innocent shiftings of leaves I heard, or the rustle as something big slipped past? The feeling of being watched grew in me, just as it had last time I'd walked the Greenways.

"They'll know we're coming," I said, suddenly remembering what the Hawk had said about watchers in the Wilds, though he didn't seem concerned now. "The Greenways are being watched."

Something rustled in the gloom off to our right, and a sapling there shivered as if something moved through the undergrowth around it. I shivered, too. This place gave me the creeps. Why did I always end up here at night?

"They won't," Edgar said, voice still calm, as if he were unaffected by the gloom. His walking stick made a soft, regular thunk on the leafy ground as he placed it with each step. "I found instructions among my son's effects. The charm will help shield us until we find the hidden Way. Once we are on it, we will be untrackable."

The harsh caw of a raven punctuated his sentence. I looked up in time to see its black shape pass overhead in a gap between the branches. I wasn't sure how I felt about that now. I'd been accustomed to thinking of the ravens as my friends— and, when all was said and done, Thing One and Thing Two *had* saved my life. But knowing that they had been spying on me weirded me out. A bird couldn't just be a bird anymore. They were all potential spies, and they might not all be spying for someone with my best interests at heart.

A strange wail rose deep in the woods, almost like a siren at first, but it ended in a howl that definitely sounded as though it came from the throat of something I didn't want to meet. In front of me, the Hawk's shoulders tensed as he glanced in the direction of the sound. His face seemed flushed, and there were beads of sweat on his forehead.

"Was that a wolf?" I asked, nervously.

"We should be so lucky," he said, still scanning that side of the path.

"So that's a no, then?"

"No, Allegra, that was not a wolf." He drew his sword from thin air again, but the trick didn't impress me as much now I knew he had it concealed with an Aversion. Besides, I was far too worried that he might have to use it, and uneasy about what he might be using it against. Another howl rent the night, but this one came from the other side of the path. I drew a shaky breath. Were the bastards talking to each other?

"How far is it to this hidden Way?" I asked as the Hawk pushed to the front of our little line, staggering a little as he did so. Was there something wrong with him? He normally moved with the grace and assurance of the warrior he was. But I had no time to worry about him now.

I kept close to Edgar's back, my eyes darting from one side of the path to the other, my hand on my dagger. Not that a dagger would do much against whatever was out there. They sounded big, and if the Hawk was worried, then I was, too.

"Not much further," Edgar said, his walking stick making its regular thump-thump-thump on the detritus of the forest floor.

Good. As long as we stayed on the path, we should be fine. I'd never heard of anyone being attacked as long as they kept to the Way. Of course, the Greenways had a reputation for trickery. If the path disappeared, or Edgar's charm didn't prove up to the job of leading us in the right direction, we could have a problem.

Up ahead, the tip of the Hawk's sword swayed drunkenly, and cold fear ran through me as I realised the man that held it was swaying, too. I opened my mouth to ask him what was wrong, when Edgar stopped, his arm drawing back with a speed I hadn't imagined possible from the old man. Before I quite understood what he was about, he slammed the walking stick down on the Hawk's sword hand, and shoved him violently in the middle of the back.

The Hawk dropped Ecfirrith, and it flashed bright silver as it tumbled into the undergrowth. He snarled an oath as he went staggering to one side, unable to keep his footing.

"What the hell?" I shouted, reaching uselessly for the knight as his foot caught on something in the dark and he fell.

The bushes shivered. Suddenly, the night was full of the flapping of wings.

"If you run, you might make it. I'll tell them you got away," Edgar said, his expression unreadable in the dark. "I'm sorry, Allegra."

"You're *sorry*? What is *wrong* with you?"

In the moment I had taken my eyes off him to glare at Edgar, the Hawk had disappeared. He'd been lying right there, sprawled next to the path, but now there was no sign of him.

Next to the path. Oh, shit. A howl rose from the dark forest, nearer than before, sending shivers of dread creeping over my skin. The Hawk had left the path.

What did I do now? I clutched my dagger in a fist suddenly clammy with fear. I couldn't just leave him—but those things were still out there.

"Fuck," I muttered, clenching the dagger tighter, and plunged into the darkness under the trees.

19

Silver bloody *Tree*! My pulse pounded in my ears, my insides tangled into one big knot of terror.

"Hawk? Hawk!" I screamed, my voice coming out in a strangled squeak. Where was he? What had Edgar done? His betrayal was a shaft of pain lodged in my chest. I couldn't believe it, though I'd seen him shove the Hawk off the path with my own eyes. Was he possessed? "Hawk!"

My last scream ended in a muffled shriek of terror as a hand closed over my mouth from behind. A strong body pressed against my back, and I sagged against him in relief as the Hawk's voice whispered in my ear.

"Hush—you will summon them."

I drew a deep breath. More than anything in my life, I wished not to find out what was howling out there. I clenched my fists to keep them from trembling, so hard that the hilt of the dagger ground against my bones. I had a very bad feeling that I wasn't going to get my wish.

"What happened to you? Are you ill?" He was a Knight

of the Realms. How could one frail old man have bested him so easily?

"Not any longer." His voice was an angry growl. "I suspect the charm on your friend's walking stick was aimed at destroying my strength. I could barely walk. This betrayal was well planned."

And now we were lost in the Wilds while something out there hunted us. Howling reverberated all around us. Make that some*things*. It sounded like there were at least three of them, and they were getting closer.

"Did he push you, too?" he asked.

"No. I came after you."

His eyes widened in surprise. "That was brave. But a little stupid. Do you have any weapons?"

"Just this."

He held his hand out, and I offered him the dagger, hilt first. Then he took my hand and drew me after him into the woods.

"Do you have any idea where you're going?" It all looked the same to me. Trees loomed out of the dark, their branches twisted into the shapes of gnarled arms, their twiggy fingers reaching for us, snaring my hair and clothes as we pushed our way through the undergrowth. "Can the gate glyph help us?"

"No," he said. "Now, hush."

I stopped talking, my ears straining for any hint that the howlers were getting closer, but the forest was full of sounds. Leaves and grasses rustled, insects chirped, and the faint scurryings of small creatures sounded in the fallen leaves. Nothing bigger. Yet.

He scanned the dark forest, searching for something. I soon discovered what when he stopped by a straight sapling and put his foot against its base. Grunting with effort, he bent and twisted the young tree until it broke off at the base, then he ripped off its few thin branches, using my knife to help him as needed. In a remarkably short time, he had a staff as tall as himself, and he handed the knife back to me. I didn't bother sheathing it. I had a feeling I'd be needing it soon.

The staff-cutting had made a lot of noise, of course. I spent the whole time he was working watching the darkness around us for signs of the howlers, expecting something to leap out at us any second. The trees grew so close together that visibility was very limited, and their entwined branches overhead stopped all but the barest amount of light from leaking through. I breathed a little easier once we were moving again, though, in truth, we were no safer.

A raven fluttered to a low-hanging branch directly in our path and croaked softly. It had only one eye, like a tiny black pearl nestled among its feathers. As we approached, it flew at us, and the Hawk raised his staff, but the bird banked away and landed on another branch a little further away, watching us expectantly.

The Hawk paused, watching it right back. What would have been unusual behaviour in the mortal world was not so odd here in the Wilds of the Realms. Here, animals sometimes spoke, or guided a hero, just as in fairy tales.

"You said a one-eyed raven saved you from the explosion," he murmured, still watching the bird, which was hopping from foot to foot impatiently. "Is this the same one?"

About to say no, I hesitated. It had a black eye, as all ravens in the Realms did, whereas Thing One's eye had been white, but the way it danced from foot to foot was very familiar. Thing One had done that every morning, waiting for his cabanossi. If I was prepared to believe that a bird could be watching me on behalf of some unknown benefactor, and smart enough to intervene when my life was in danger, it was no great leap to imagine that the colour of its eye could be changed to suit its surrounds. And how many one-eyed ravens were there, anyway? "It could be. I think it wants us to follow it."

The Hawk changed course, leading me toward the raven. Once it was satisfied that we were truly altering course, it flapped a little further away, alighting on another branch and looking back expectantly. Where was it taking us? Somewhere with high, sheltering walls would be pretty sweet right now. Or even back to the path. Was it possible that the bird was unaffected by the disorienting magic that imbued the Wilds, making it impossible for people to find their way back to the path once lost? I held tight to the Hawk's hand and prayed.

A long, mournful howl sounded from the direction the bird was leading us, making me doubt our raven guide until answering howls sounded behind us, appallingly close. I threw a frightened glance over my shoulder, but there was nothing to see but the dark forest. We moved faster, almost running after the bird, since the creatures that hunted us were so close, now, that our silence made no difference.

We entered a tiny clearing, not big enough to show us sky but large enough perhaps to make fighting our pursuers a little easier. The raven landed on the lowest branch of a huge tree. It was this tree that had formed the small space, since its mighty branches had choked out any other trees that might have taken root, cut off from the light.

"Hurry," said the Hawk. "Get into the tree. I'll boost you up."

I lunged for the lowest branch, his warm hands on my thighs boosting me skyward. For a moment, I dangled awkwardly before I managed to haul myself onto the branch, scraping both forearms in the process. The raven hopped impatiently right next to my head during this manoeuvre.

"Will you fly up?"

He shook his head. "No. Then we'd both be trapped in the tree—the branches grow too close here for me to gain the sky." True. His wingspan was enormous. He would need a lot of room to get airborne. "We have to kill them. It's the only way."

He meant *he* had to kill them. And all he had was a wooden staff.

"Take my knife."

He ignored the outstretched knife. "Climb as high as you can. Hide in the topmost branches while I lead them away."

I stared down into his honey-coloured eyes, willing him to take the knife. He wanted me to keep it because he thought he would fail, and he didn't want to leave me weaponless. My heart rebelled, horrified. I shook the knife at him. "Take it, damn you."

"Climb!" he said. "Hurry."

As he turned away, a black shape detached itself from the shadows and I drew back against the tree's rough trunk in disbelief. It was like a dog, but no kind of dog I'd ever seen—its long legs were built for speed, but it had a heavy barrel chest and a strange ruff of fur all around its thick neck. It was also nearly as big as the Hawk, and my heart sank. Its lips skinned back, revealing long, sharp teeth. He would have to fight this thing with a *stick*?

Two more entered the tiny clearing, each as black as the first. Their eyes glowed, and at first, I thought they were catching what little light there was, but then I saw with a sick kind of horror that they actually glowed red, as if they were goddamn cyborgs. One of them looked straight at me, and its mouth contorted into something that looked like a grin. Sick bastard. I shrank back against the tree trunk, debating whether to climb higher as the Hawk had ordered. How high could these things jump?

I hesitated, not liking to leave him. I still had the knife clenched in my fist—if all else failed, I could drop out of the tree and drive it into one of those horrible red eyes. The dog that was looking at me shook its neck ruff, which rattled like cutlery in a drawer. Obviously not fur, then, though it was as black as the rest of the monster. Then it transferred its attention to the Hawk, backed against the tree trunk directly below me.

The three of them stalked forward, moving slowly, hugging the uneven ground. Their eerie red eyes focused like lasers on their prey. The Hawk held his staff loosely, watching them all with a calmness I could not have shown in his situation. Sweat trickled down between my breasts though the night was cool. I was a mass of nerves. I transferred the knife to my other hand, wiping the first on the leg of my jeans. My palms were so clammy with fear, I was afraid I'd drop the knife before I ever got to use it.

The first dog chose that very moment to leap at the Hawk, and it was so fast that I almost did lose my grip on the knife from the shock. Fortunately, the Hawk wasn't caught off-guard—he swung the staff and caught the huge animal a massive blow, hurling it against a tree. There was an ugly cracking sound, and the hound tumbled into the bracken at the tree's foot and didn't rise again. From the odd angle of its head, I judged that its neck had been broken by the force of its collision with the tree.

I shouldn't have been surprised. The dog must have weighed as much as the Hawk himself, but I knew how strong the fae were. No one but a fae could have delivered such a blow. He was lucky he hadn't broken his staff.

He resumed his ready stance at the foot of the tree, facing the other two hounds. A raven dived at the head of one dog, and then it seemed the air was full of whirring black wings as a whole flock of them appeared out of the depths of the forest. On a branch above my head, the one-eyed raven cawed loudly, as if egging his brethren on.

Where had they all come from? They dive-bombed the

dogs mercilessly, claws and beaks seeking those glowing red eyes. The dogs snarled and snapped, dragging birds out of the air, then a glance passed between them.

As one, they leapt at the Hawk, as if they had decided in that moment to use the weight of their heavy bodies to end the fight before the birds succeeded in blinding them. Blood gleamed black on dark fur and the Hawk shouted as his staff swept out to meet them, but he couldn't fight them both at once. One caught a blow to the leg mid-leap and fell aside with a yelp, but the other knocked the Hawk to the ground, where they rolled together, the Hawk straining to keep those massive jaws from his throat.

Birds dived at the hound as the combatants writhed across the ground. My heart was in my mouth, watching the Hawk's arms shake with desperate strength. The dog's claws raked his chest, and I shuddered to think what damage they might do.

The dog, unable to do anything about the birds that plagued it, changed tack and lunged at one of the Hawk's straining arms instead. Then he backed up, dragging the Hawk across the forest floor. The other dog got up, limping on three legs, and came to help. A chill ran down my spine at the intelligence of these monsters. They meant to drag the Hawk away from the clearing to somewhere where the birds would find it harder to attack them.

He kicked out at the limping dog and caught it on its injured leg. It yelped and fell back, thinking better of any further involvement. But that still left the other animal, who'd managed to drag the Hawk almost to the cover of the surrounding trees, despite the ravens' best efforts to hinder its progress.

By some desperate acrobatics, the Hawk managed to get his feet under him and lever himself upright. As soon as he was standing, the magnificent wings that I'd only glimpsed before sprouted from his back. They were dark as his hair, but the ends of the feathers were tipped in gold.

With a mighty downbeat, he hurled himself into the air, with the dog still hanging off his upper arm. There was nowhere really to go, as the branches of the massive tree I clung to cut off his access to the open sky, and a seesawing, limping flight was all he could manage. The dog clung on, its claws scrabbling for purchase and its bladed ruff slicing at him as it writhed around. Equally determined, he flew as close as he could to the surrounding tree trunks in an effort to dislodge the monster. I could hardly bear to watch as the dog's body swung like an unholy pendulum, suspended only by its teeth. If he did manage to dislodge it, the mongrel would probably take half his bloody arm with it.

At last, he managed to slam the hound into a tree branch and it fell, senseless, to the forest floor. Leaves kicked up as its heavy body slammed into the ground. Above, the Hawk's vast wings brushed the branches as he fought to stay aloft. His arm was a sheet of blood, and looking at it sickened me. His shirt hung in ribbons, his chest bleeding freely from more scratches than I could count.

He lurched in mid-air, and I gasped. If he could make it to the branch beside me, he'd be safe. My heart hammered as I watched. Fae healing was spectacular, but it wasn't instantaneous. Blood literally dripped from him, pattering onto the leaves below in a deadly rain. Much more of that and he would lose consciousness.

No sooner had I thought it than his head lolled to one side, his wings folded, and he dropped like a stone. But before I could do more than draw breath to scream, the ravens converged—dozens of them, hundreds, maybe—forming a dense, black blanket that caught his unconscious form and carried it away through the trees.

I stared after them, my mouth open in shock. If I had needed any further proof that these weren't ordinary birds, I'd just received it.

"Holy *shit*," I murmured, and beside me on the branch, my one-eyed companion croaked softly in satisfaction.

20

Worry for the Hawk gnawed at me, but at least he was
out of danger for the moment. I couldn't say the
same for myself. The monster with the injured leg still
waited in the clearing, its baleful red eyes fixed on me. Just
because it couldn't run as fast on three legs didn't mean it
was no longer a threat.

As if it had heard my thought, it got up and limped over
to the foot of the tree and planted itself right beneath us.
Lady take the damn thing. I couldn't stay in this tree
forever, but how could I get down without becoming a
monster chew toy? Frustrated, I stared down at the beast,
and it stared right back, unflinching. It held itself stock still,
fixated on me, as if it had all the time in the world to wait.

Time was the one thing I didn't have. Every moment I
was trapped here was another minute for the other denizens
of the Wild to find me. I almost laughed as a picture of a
whole clearing full of monsters arranged around the tree,
waiting for me to fall, popped into my head. And besides,

I needed to go after the Hawk. Every moment, the ravens were bearing him further away, and my chances of ever finding him again decreased.

I eyed the one-eyed raven perched by my head consideringly. "I don't suppose you know where your mates were taking the Hawk, do you?"

The raven's beady eye glittered as it stared at me, but it made no response. I sighed. Looked like I was on my own.

I met the glowing red eyes of the gigantic dog. I could probably outrun it, given its injury, although even that wasn't certain, considering I'd be dodging trees and obstacles in the dark. But if the raven *could* help me find the injured Hawk, the last thing I wanted was to lead the monster straight to him.

The dog's unnatural stillness and those damn cyborg eyes freaked me out. Even though I'd lived in the Realms for most of my life, I'd seen very little magic. The Fae didn't go in for big, splashy displays in their everyday lives, which were surprisingly simple, at least in my little corner of Autumn. I'd certainly never come across a monster like this before. Of course, I'd never managed to get myself lost in the Wilds before, either. A pang of homesickness for the bright, airy forests of Autumn struck me.

I took a deep breath, centring myself. No time now for homesickness or feeling sorry for myself while the big, scary dog stared at me as if I was the tastiest thing he'd seen in days. If I was really quick, I could probably scramble down the far side of the tree trunk before the dog attacked, but what then? The bloody thing was still bigger than me—

shit, he was bigger than the Hawk, and I was no knight—and all I had was a knife. The Hawk's insistence on leaving it with me didn't seem like such a bad idea now.

Tightening my grip on the knife, I eyed the bird again. It had to be Thing One—the way it had danced on the branch, the fact it was following me around at all—it was just too much coincidence to swallow.

"I'm not sure if you can understand me," I whispered, "but if you can, I could use a distraction right now."

It shifted its claws on the branch and fluttered its wings as I tensed my leg muscles, my grip on the knife firm and sure. The bird leapt from the branch a mere heartbeat before I did, in a beautifully timed swoop at the monstrous dog's head.

Distracted, the beast snapped at Thing One as I landed on its back and drew my knife across its black neck in a vicious slice, angling my blade underneath the protective ruff. Warm blood spurted over my hand as the creature convulsed under me. Its great jaws snapped at me, but I was already rolling away, gore-covered knife still firmly clenched in my fist.

It thrashed around in panic, its ruff clattering as blood poured over it, and made a half-hearted attempt to go after me, but it was already dead—it was just taking a while for its brain to catch on. A moment later, the baleful red light faded from its eyes, and it collapsed, its face still turned toward me, determined to the last not to let me out of its sight.

I stood for a moment, breathing hard. It was certainly

not the first beast I'd killed, but this was no sunlit hunt through the forests of Autumn. I could have wiped the knife clean on the beast's black hide, but I wasn't going near the thing again, even if it was dead. Instead, I did the best I could, wiping the knife on the grass. Not a perfect job, but it would do for now.

Thing One cawed his approval and fluttered to a tree on the other side of the clearing. That was the direction the rest of the flock had taken the Hawk. He gave me a look that said, more clearly than words, "what are you waiting for?" before swooping away into the darkness. With no better options, I hurried after him. At least there was some hope he was leading me towards my companion. He'd helped me already, and I trusted him more than anything else in this benighted forest.

He made sure I never lost sight of him, but he moved fast, and soon my blood was pumping as I forced my way through thickets and stumbled around outcroppings of rocks or fallen trees. I was making more noise than I liked, but it couldn't be helped. As I walked, my ears were pricked for a howl that would signal more of the black dogs on my trail. The forest was full of noises, none of them particularly reassuring—rustles and rattles; odd calls of night birds I'd never heard before, punctuated by the occasional shriek as some small prey thrashed in the bushes, its life ended by some nocturnal hunter.

Where was the Hawk in all of this malignant wood? I heard no raven calls, apart from the occasional croak from my guide. It was as if he had been swallowed up by the

Wilds, and my heart hammered from fear just as much as from the fast pace Thing One was setting.

His chosen path forced me through some particularly spiky bushes. As I pushed my way through, collecting an impressive number of scratches, I couldn't help a resentful glance skyward. It was so easy for him, flying above it all.

As a result, I nearly tripped right over the body on the ground as I fought my way free of the thorns at last. For a heart-stopping moment, I thought it was the Hawk. I dropped to my knees, hand reaching helplessly for the knife protruding from the body's back, but as soon as I touched him, I realised it couldn't be the Hawk. His arms were thin, the flesh hanging from them, not the strong, muscled arms of the knight.

Gently, I rolled the body so I could see the face. Though it was no real surprise, a pang of grief pierced me as I recognised Edgar.

I'd thought him already dead, but he groaned, and his eyes fluttered open. "Susie?" he murmured, his voice a bubbling sigh.

"It's me, Allegra," I said, finding his hand and clasping it between both of mine. It was icy cold. I had no idea who Susie was—a lover? A friend? Perhaps even the mother of his son? "Let me help you."

I slipped an arm beneath his shoulders, trying to help him up, but he moaned in pain, so I let him lie, turning him slightly so that at least the hilt of the knife wasn't banging on the ground. Should I take the knife out? But I had no bandages, nothing to stop the bleeding except the shirt I was wearing. The ground beneath him was already soggy with blood. He'd probably bleed out in moments if I removed the knife.

Perhaps that would be kinder.

"Allegra," he wheezed. "Don't fuss. Nothing you can do will make a difference. I'm dying."

"Edgar." I squeezed his cold hand tighter as hot tears prickled at my eyes.

"Don't … waste your tears on me, girl. I betrayed you. And now, I am betrayed in turn." He wheezed a kind of laugh, full of gurgles and rattles, and bubbles of blood appeared on his lips. "It's ironic, really. Could be … one of those teaching fables. I did it because I didn't want to die. Now … dying."

He laughed that horrible bubbling laugh again, then gasped for breath, his lungs filling with blood. One of my tears splashed onto his face, and I wiped it off, but he didn't notice. His eyes were gazing off into some distance that I couldn't see.

"You hate me now," he said. "But you'll feel differently when it's your turn to face death."

"I don't hate you," I said, and it was true. I was hurt and confused by his betrayal, but there was too much history between us for hate. "But I don't understand. Why did you lure us here?"

"Same reason … you jump every time … Eldric whistles," he gasped. "You would have … done the same, if he'd offered the Realms. We all want to go home, don't we?

And now I've … lost my chance. Lost my son. Only … darkness awaits."

He coughed, and blood burst from his lips, covering his chin. I clutched his hand tighter, helpless. *We all want to go home?* Someone had promised him every changeling's dream in return for leading us to our deaths in the Wild. No other reward could have induced him to turn on me like this.

"Who are you working for?" Who wanted me dead so badly? And why? Or were they after the knight, and I was just collateral damage?

No. No one had blown up the Hawk's house.

"All discarded now. Like … pawns in the Lords' great game … of chess."

"Edgar? Who are you working for?"

But he only coughed up more blood, his eyelids sagging shut. He made such an incongruous picture, in his handknitted vest and neatly pressed trousers, a little old man sprawled painfully on the forest floor. It wasn't right.

"Edgar?" I leaned closer, gently squeezing his hand. "Who did this?"

His eyes opened again, but it was as if he couldn't hear me. "Ally?" he gasped. "Hold my hand?"

Another tear trickled free. I already was, but he couldn't feel it. I brought our clasped hands up where he could see them. "It's okay, Edgar. I won't leave you."

I leaned forward to kiss his forehead, my heart bursting with conflicting emotions: pain and confusion at his betrayal, grief at his dying. He'd been my first friend in the mortal world, like an uncle to a lost and frightened girl. When I sat back again, his eyes stared sightlessly up at the dark canopy of trees.

I bowed my head and let the tears come.

21

I jumped when Thing One fluttered to the ground at my side. Wrapped up in my grief, I'd forgotten where I was, and that was a sure way to end up dead. The Wilds didn't care that I'd just lost someone dear to me. So I scrubbed the tears from my face and closed Edgar's staring eyes.

Thing One croaked softly and hopped closer.

"Don't touch him," I said, shooing him away, afraid that those sightless eyes looked like a tasty snack to the bird. He gave me an aggrieved look and fluttered a little further away, as if the thought had never crossed his mind.

Now that it couldn't hurt Edgar, I tugged the knife free from his back. The blade was long and slightly curved, like a skinning knife, though the hilt was far more decorative than most hunting knives. An enormous black opal was embedded in it, amidst swirling silver leaves. Red fire glinted in the depths of the opal, reminding me uncomfortably of the eyes of the dog I'd killed.

It looked a hell of a lot like the knife Dansen Arbre had been toying with at Eldric's table the night I met him.

Thing One squawked his impatience at me.

"I'm coming," I said, rising to my feet.

I hated to leave Edgar just lying there, like a piece of discarded trash, but I could hardly carry him. Nor could I bury him, with nothing but my bare hands and the ground full of tree roots. I arranged his frail old body into a more dignified pose, with his hands crossed on his chest, and stood over him for a moment.

"Thank you for everything you did for me over the years," I told him. "I'll try to forgive you for turning on me at the end."

That might depend on whether I lived long enough. With a sigh, I turned away, leaving him there in the shadow of the spiky thorn bushes. The Wilds would swallow him, and eventually he'd become part of the Realms he so loved. Not such a bad fate for a changeling.

Nevertheless, I wasn't ready to meet the same fate myself. I was putting a lot of faith in Thing One, but I didn't see any other option but to follow the bird and hope he could lead me to the Hawk. I was worried about the knight's condition. Aided by their magic, fae healed a lot faster than humans did, but his arm had been a mess. I hated to think of him, alone and unconscious, unable to defend himself, with only the ravens to take care of him.

Thing One resumed his guide duties, flying ahead of me from branch to branch, looking back now and then to make sure I was keeping up. There was no path, and I could see no landmarks—just trees, trees, and more trees in the unrelenting blackness of the night. There didn't seem any way that he could tell where he was going, but he led on with such confidence that I followed anyway, though my aching body cried out for rest. I might have been walking for hours or days—I couldn't tell. Time moved differently in the Wilds.

Several times, I tripped in the dark, so I fell into a routine of checking where Thing One had landed, then watching my feet as I headed in his direction, only looking up when I heard the flutter of his wings as he flew to his next landing place. I was plodding along, putting one foot in front of the other in a kind of walking dream, when I realised that the ground beneath my feet was blessedly flat all of a sudden.

When I looked more closely, I realised it was a path. *The* path. That beautiful bloody bird had led me back to the Greenway.

The shout of triumph died on my lips as I looked up and discovered a man standing not three steps away. The opal-studded knife was still in my hand; reflexively, I brought it up in a defensive move.

"No need for that," the stranger said. "I'm not here to assault your person or your virtue." One side of his mouth curled in a sardonic smile as he looked me over. "Though I could be persuaded, if you were so inclined."

I stepped back, putting some more distance between us, though I was careful to remain on the path. After what I'd been through, there was no way I was stepping off this sucker again.

He was clearly fae. That much would have been obvious from his impossible beauty, even if he weren't standing in the middle of the Wilds in the dead of night with no more concern than if he were taking a stroll in his own garden.

"What are you doing here?" I was too much of a sceptic to believe that he could be standing right here, on the very stretch of path Thing One had led me to, by coincidence. The only real question was whether he was friend or foe, but I wasn't likely to get a straight answer. Was it on his instructions that Edgar had led us into the Wilds and abandoned us?

"I could ask you the same thing."

Perhaps he was the owner of the dogs that had attacked us, or some kind of monster in disguise. Not everything in the Realms that looked fair actually was. Though he *was* on the path—that was a point in his favour. The Greenways didn't suffer monsters gladly.

While I was still debating with myself, Thing One swooped down and landed on his shoulder. The stranger reached up to stroke the soft feathers of his breast, and Thing One rubbed his head against the man's cheek with obvious affection.

I lowered the knife, reassured by this display. Thing One hadn't led me wrong so far. If he trusted the strange fae, I could afford to relax a little.

"Who are you?" I asked.

"Call me Raven," he answered, with an indirectness typical of the fae. It was said that they couldn't lie, but they could sure as hell twist the truth into unrecognisable pretzels. Not giving a straight answer to a simple question was one of their superpowers.

"Thing One is your pet? Your servant?"

A frown of confusion ruffled that perfect brow. "Thing One?"

I nodded at the bird still perched on his shoulder. "The raven."

Raven's hair was as dark as Thing One's feathers, and his eyes—at least in this dim light—appeared coal black as well. If I'd tried to imagine what a raven would look like in human form, this would have been pretty close to what I'd pictured. He looked young, no older than me, though among the fae that meant nothing. He could have been anything from decades to centuries older than he appeared. He smiled. "What an odd name. He is my friend."

"But he's not an ordinary bird, is he?"

He nodded. "He and his flock mates have been … modified to better suit our needs."

He didn't specify who the "our" referred to, and I didn't ask. Now that I seemed to have found relative safety, my exhaustion hit me all at once, and I sagged.

Raven frowned. "I smell blood. Are you hurt?"

"No, it's not mine. Are you the one who's been helping me? Do you know what happened to my friend? The ravens carried him away."

"He is safe. You should go home while you still can."

"Are you threatening me?"

"So touchy! Just giving you some friendly advice. This game is too dangerous for you—you should bow out before you are taken out. And to aid in your escape, I have something for you." From his pocket, he pulled a handful of black feathers and held them out to me.

Doubtfully, I took them and discovered they were attached to some gossamer-light fabric. It slid through my fingers like a whisper of air. "What is it?"

"A cape. Put it on and I'll take you home. There are watchers along the path."

Did I look stupid? He seemed friendly enough, but I wasn't about to accept a gift from a random fae. Who knew what that would bind me to? "I'm not going home. I want to see the Hawk."

When I made no move to put the cape on, he made a noise of impatience. "I swear to you that this gift, freely given, will not harm you in any way, nor will you owe me anything in return."

I crushed the feathered thing in my fist. "Good. Will you take me to the Hawk?"

He sighed. "If I do, will you wear the cloak? Otherwise you risk bringing his enemies down on him."

"Fine, then."

"Allow me." He took the bunch of feathers and shook them out, then whirled the tiny cape around my shoulders with a flourish. There was no clasp, but it clung like a second skin. The feathers rippled, and I disappeared.

"What the—?" It was the weirdest feeling. I held out my arms, but they were as invisible as the rest of me. I could see the ground underneath my feet, as if I didn't exist. I staggered a little, disoriented.

"It's a cloak of shadows," he said. "It won't hide you completely during daylight, but at night, you can pass unseen even by the keenest eyes."

"Sick," I murmured. As long as I ignored the fact that I couldn't see my own body, and kept my eyes on something else, the dizziness faded.

"Come," he said, turning away. He raised his arms in an odd, dance-like movement, and the arms suddenly became wings. In the blink of an eye, two ravens soared where only one had been before. He was bigger and glossier than his one-eyed companion, with a blue-black sheen on his feathers so that they glistened as if wet in the soft moonlight that shone over the Greenway.

My mouth fell open with surprise. Once I'd managed to pull my scattered wits back together, I asked, "Where are we going?" God, I hoped it was somewhere close by. I was sick of walking tonight.

I didn't actually expect a reply, but the bird that had been a man scant moments earlier croaked at me. Though the sound wasn't like a human voice, I could understand what it said: "Where you want to go. Now be silent, or the cloak will not hide you."

The Realms, where men could turn into birds and still form human speech. How I had missed this place.

Then the two of them took off, leaving me to follow beneath.

At least now I was on the Greenway, not stumbling around among the fallen branches and tree roots with brambles catching at my clothes every second step. That made it easier to move silently. The birds didn't move from branch to branch as Thing One had done when he led me through the Wilds. That probably would have looked suspicious to the hidden watchers, wherever they were. Instead, they disappeared for long stretches of time, only reappearing now and then as if to check on me, swooping out of the trees apparently at random. At least, I hoped the hidden watchers would think it was random.

I moved as quietly as I could, controlling my breathing though my heart pounded with nerves. I was lucky I hadn't had an asthma attack. That would be all I needed to make this monumentally shitty night complete, and the wheezing would give me away, cloak or no cloak.

Raven was surely the mysterious benefactor who'd sent Thing One and Thing Two to watch over me in the mortal world. Judging by Thing One's behaviour around him, he wouldn't take orders from anyone else. I watched the two of them swoop and soar, and a smile tugged at my mouth as I tried to imagine feeding Raven cabanossi. I was completely in his power now, so the joke was well and truly on me if he turned out to be a bad guy, but I didn't think he was. Of course, he might not be precisely a good guy either. Things were rarely black and white in the Realms. Forget fifty shades of grey—more like fifty thousand. But if he had saved my life twice already, surely I had nothing to fear?

I was dead on my invisible feet and probably making more noise in my tiredness than was safe when an archway of black stone appeared across the path. Mist swirled around its dark form, and it was impossible to see what was on the other side. The two ravens burst out of the forest and swooped through the black arch, but my steps slowed. Where were they taking me? Raven never had answered that question. I didn't consider "where you want to go" to be an acceptable answer. The Hawk had better be here, wherever "here" was.

Beyond the archway, another world awaited me. It was still dark, but this darkness wasn't as intimidating as the brooding woods of the Wilds, where you just knew that something nasty was waiting to pounce. Here, the darkness was relieved and enhanced by a succession of lights in warm golds and oranges, glowing atop lamp posts and hanging on silver chains from trees that hung gracefully over the path. The path was wider, too, and led to double gates in a high wall. Through the gates, a building of the same black stone as the archway stood, but its many windows blazed with welcoming lights. It was a large house, or maybe a small castle, and the forest snuggled right up against its black walls.

Raven was waiting at the gates, a man again. A breeze that carried the scent of the sea stirred my hair as I closed the distance between us.

"Welcome to my home," he said, smiling.

"Is the Hawk here?"

His smile broadened. "Does he realise you're so obsessed with him?"

"I'm not obsessed. Just concerned."

"He is well." He reached out and took my hand,

drawing me with him through the gates. "The healers will take good care of him. You can take off your cloak now. It's safe here."

I'd forgotten I had it on, too busy gawking at my surroundings. Strange that Raven had taken my hand so unerringly. Clearly, he could see through the cloak's magic. But I was too tired to puzzle over it now. The stress of the long journey through the Wilds had completely drained me. If the breeze got any stronger, I was sure it would blow me away like a leaf.

Inside, I got a quick impression of high, arched ceilings; warmth and luxury. A fire burned in a huge fireplace, but Raven drew me on towards a sweeping staircase.

"Come upstairs—you're exhausted. Let me show you to a bedroom. You need sleep."

I tried to tug my hand away, but he wouldn't let go. "I can't stay. My friends will be worried about me. Just let me see the Hawk first."

"Sleep," he insisted, and the word wound through my head, its siren song irresistible. My eyelids sagged closed between one step and the next. I was about to tumble straight back down the stairs, and I couldn't work up the energy to even care. All my limbs were impossibly heavy.

I felt him catch me and scoop me up into his arms as sleep claimed me.

22

The sun streaming in the window woke me, its light warm on my face. I blinked, shaded my eyes, rolled over.

I had never seen this room before. Its black stone walls were relieved by colourful tapestries of wooded vistas, which made the room feel light and airy. The bed I lay in was big enough for me and a couple of friends, the pillow so soft it felt as though my head were sinking into the clouds. I sat up and sank my feet into a deep green carpet that was as soft as it looked. Someone had cleaned my clothes in the night; they lay neatly folded on a chair by the bed, with the cloak of shadows Raven had given me on top. I was wearing a soft, white nightgown that hung modestly to the floor. I wondered who had changed my clothes and decided it was probably better not to know—then I wouldn't have to squirm with embarrassment every time I saw them.

I dressed quickly and wandered over to the window. Below me, a garden spread out, bursting with coloured blooms that turned their pretty faces up to the sun. The black wall beyond them made a striking backdrop for all their colour.

My stomach rumbled, reminding me how long it was since I'd eaten, and my bladder also put its hand up to be noticed. Fortunately, there was a clean, modern bathroom behind a discreet door, so I quickly took care of that.

Feeling more human, I left my room and found my way down the hall back to the staircase where I'd so quickly fallen unconscious last night. That had been magic at work. Sure, I'd been tired, but I'd never fallen asleep between one step and the next like that before, and I was pissed that Raven had done that to me.

The fire still burned in the gigantic fireplace in the entry hall, but I kept walking, looking for the master of the house. I found him in a dining room that overlooked the same garden I'd seen from my room, seated at the head of a long table. The dagger that had killed Edgar lay on the table next to his place setting. The table was loaded with fruits, bread, little cakes, and a silver pot from which the unmistakable scent of coffee rose.

"Good morning." He was still dressed all in black today, but his shirt had a silver collar and tiny silver buttons. "Are you hungry? Have a seat."

I grabbed a banana and tore into it, but remained standing. "You put me to sleep last night."

"Yes," he said cheerfully. "You needed it. You feel better now, don't you?"

"That's not the point." I stabbed the banana at him.

"You had no right to put me to sleep without my consent. I'm not a child."

A piece of banana fell off and plopped onto the table. He picked it up and ate it, eyes gleaming with amusement. "I apologise."

"Oh." I'd been working up to a fine denouncement of the fae and their high-handed ways, but this took the wind out of my sails. "Good. Don't do it again."

"Won't you sit down, now?" He stood and pulled out the chair on his right. "I know I have no right to force you to eat, but I'm sure you must be hungry."

Was he taking the piss? His face held only an expression of polite concern, but I suspected he was laughing at me. I was starving, but sitting down felt like letting him win. I compromised by grabbing another piece of fruit. "Have you seen that dagger before?"

"No." He picked it up, admiring the silverwork around the huge black opal. "Have you?"

I nodded. "It belongs to Dansen Arbre."

"Are you sure?"

"Pretty sure. I saw him playing with it only last week."

"*Pretty sure* isn't the same as absolutely certain. You can't go accusing Summer's right-hand man of murder without more than *pretty sure*."

"Is Arbre a friend of yours? You sound like you're on his side. He murdered Edgar."

He laid the dagger down again, sighing. "But you don't know that, do you? You didn't witness it. Someone could have stolen it from him. Or it may not be the same dagger.

Perhaps his has five leaves around the stone, where this one has seven. How can you be certain it was him?"

I glared at him, then looked at the dagger again. I *had* only seen it for a few moments. It sure looked like the same one, but I could be wrong. For the first time, I wondered why Dansen Arbre would be trying to stop us discovering who had stolen the drake skins, when he was the one who'd given us the task of investigating in the first place.

"You're right." It nearly killed me to admit it. "I can't be certain."

He smiled. "Now, won't you please sit down and eat?"

"I'd like to see the Hawk first."

"So devoted." He dropped gracefully into his chair again and helped himself to one of the little iced cakes. Dark eyes watched me over the top of the delicacy. "You know he doesn't feel the same way about you, right?"

"Sorry?"

He waved the cake at me. "This crush of yours. Understandable, I suppose, but he's a Knight of the Realms. He can have any woman he wants. You really should have a little more pride."

"I don't—I'm not—" Heat roared into my cheeks. "We're just working together."

"Sure you are. That's why you refused to go home without seeing him. Because you're *working together*."

I had to remind myself that this guy had saved my life twice before I let him have a piece of my mind. "I'm perfectly happy to go home. But I want to say goodbye to the Hawk first, and make sure he's all right."

"I'm thinking of your own good, you know. You really shouldn't see him again."

"Where is he?"

"Upstairs. His room is next to yours."

I took two of the pretty pink iced cakes and left, glad to escape the humiliating conversation. They were good, light and flavoured with lemon, but I took little pleasure in them. Where had Raven gotten the idea that I was all starry-eyed over the Hawk? Was that what *the Hawk* thought? I paused outside his door long enough to wipe the crumbs off on the seat of my pants, horrified at the idea.

Maybe I should have knocked, but I'd assumed the Hawk would be in bed, perhaps even still unconscious after what he'd been through. Raven had said his healer would take care of the knight, but I'd fully expected the Hawk to be fighting off infection from that bite for days, even knowing how fast the fae healed compared to humans.

Instead, I found him standing next to the bed, struggling to pull up a pair of pants with only one hand, and swearing a blue streak.

"Oh!" About to close the door and beat a hasty retreat, I noticed how pale his face was—and then he swayed and sort of sagged against the bed post for a moment, so I marched right in. "What are you doing? You should be in bed."

His tawny eyes were huge in his ashen face, circles of pain and fatigue beneath them, but they lit up at the sight of me. Then he closed them, and a sigh of sheer relief escaped him. "Allegra. Thank the Lady. You're alive."

I stalked across the carpet to him. His bedroom was furnished in a similar style to mine, and the carpet was just as soft and luxurious, though his was blue and not green. He straightened at my approach and tried to pretend he hadn't just been about to pass out. Deep scratches on his chest were scabbed and healing, except for one which was crisscrossed with tiny stitches and oozed a pinkish fluid. His left arm was heavily bandaged from the shoulder to below his elbow, and he held it straight and stiff by his side.

With his other arm, he jerked me roughly against him and pressed his face into my hair. "I thought I'd failed you, that you were lost in the Wilds."

"I'm fine." I looked up into his gold-flecked eyes, now gazing down at me with such intensity, and forgot all about the conversation with Raven. Up close, he was overwhelming. His bare skin was warm, his arm around me possessive, and I melted against him, careful to avoid the worst of the scratches. For a long moment, he stared at me as if he were drinking in the sight of me, and then he sighed and leaned against the bedpost again.

"Do this up for me, would you?" He indicated the button of his jeans. He'd managed to get the zipper done up, but the stiff button had eluded him.

"I most certainly will not." That was one I'd never been asked before. "Why are you getting dressed at all? Did the healer say you could get up?"

In between the scratches, his chest was lightly covered with hair, and a line of it trailed down the centre of his firm torso and disappeared into the jeans, which were hanging off his hips as if he were an underwear model—although I was pretty certain he wasn't wearing any underwear. With some difficulty, I resisted the urge to run my hand across his bare flesh, and put some space between us instead.

He tucked a strand of my hair behind my ear, his fingers trembling. "Damn the healer. I couldn't lie here thinking that you were still out there. I was supposed to protect you."

"You did. You saved us both." I laid a comforting hand on his muscled shoulder, and realised he was still shaking. He was *not* well enough to be out of bed. Only strength of will was keeping him upright. "So you can relax. Get back into bed—you look like you're about to pass out."

Clearly, that was the wrong thing to say to a man who prided himself on his physical prowess.

He scowled. "I don't have time for this."

"Time for what? To recover from a terrible wound?"

"I have things to do."

"They'll have to wait. You're in no fit state—"

"The king needs me."

"The king needs you alive. Not dead from blood poisoning."

We were practically nose to nose, or at least nose to collarbone, given the disparity in our heights, when his eyes rolled back in his head and he collapsed against me without warning. I managed to guide our fall so that we hit the bed instead of the floor, but that was the best I could do; I had no hope of catching him.

A wall of solid muscle pinned me to the bed. His dark head was pillowed on my chest, and I threw my arms around him, worried that he'd slip off onto the floor and hurt himself even further.

For a moment, he was a dead weight—then he came to and began to struggle. I tried to help him, but it was an awkward position, and he only had one working arm. By the time we were both upright again, the bandage on his upper arm had blood soaking through it and his face was tight with pain.

I pushed him back against the pillow and helped him get his legs back on the bed. He was clearly in too much pain to protest at being bundled back into bed.

"Let me get someone to change that bandage for you," I said.

He caught at my hand with his good one, his grip still strong. "Stay. Just let me rest a moment."

Returning the pressure of his hand, I sat on the side of the bed. There were several rolls of clean bandage in a bowl on the table next to it. "You need to rest for more than a moment."

I unfastened the blood-soaked bandage and began to unwrap it. He lay back against the pillow, his eyes shut, and made no further protest. I tried to be as gentle as I could, but the expression on his face told me that even this was hurting him. As the bandage came off, I could see why.

The damage was as bad as I had feared. His arm was like a hunk of raw meat. The healer had done the best she could to sew it back together, and her stitches were neat, but there were a couple of sections where all the stitches in the world couldn't make any difference. The monster's bite had ripped away chunks of flesh. The wounds were packed with healing herbs, but it would take a while for him to regenerate the missing flesh. He might even end up with permanent scarring. Fae healing could only do so much. I just hoped his arm still functioned properly. At least it wasn't his sword arm.

He didn't speak or move until I'd finished, his body taut with pain. A jug stood next to the bowl of bandages, containing a dark green liquid. I sniffed experimentally at it.

"What's this?"

He opened his eyes to check. "Draught for the pain."

I'd thought so. Anything that smelled that bad had to be good for you. I poured some into a glass and offered it to him.

"You don't have to play nurse for me." But he took the glass and downed it in one gulp.

"Why not? You're not Robinson Crusoe."

His long lashes lay against cheeks much paler than normal and beads of sweat had gathered on his brow. He looked exhausted, and an unexpected wave of tenderness washed over me at his unfamiliar vulnerability. He'd nearly died to save me. I would have taken his pain for myself if I could. "Who is Robinson Crusoe?"

"A guy from a famous novel." It didn't surprise me that the Hawk hadn't heard of him. The fae weren't much interested in human culture, except for the odd enthusiast like Rowan. I wouldn't have heard of him myself if it hadn't been for Edgar's well-stocked book shelves. He'd given me armfuls of books to read in the first year or two of my arrival in the mortal world, things he thought I should understand to enable me to better pass as a regular human, like the Bible, and many works that human children read as part of their education. I'd found TV more useful as a guide to the current culture and to learn the way that humans talked, but Edgar's books had given me a background into the human psyche and what they thought was important. "He was cast away on a desert island and lived all alone for years."

"Sounds riveting."

"It was surprisingly interesting." Especially to a girl with no exposure to the human world. Robinson Crusoe's resourcefulness reminded me of the life I'd lost. There were no big supermarkets or hardware stores in the forests of Autumn. We traded with others or made things ourselves, so I felt almost a kindred spirit to Crusoe on his island. "But the point is, being alone, cut off from other people, was the greatest hardship Robinson Crusoe had to face. I'll never forget how excited he was the day he found a set of footprints on the beach that weren't his. No man is an island."

"No man is an island," he repeated.

"Yes. No one can thrive when they are cut off from other people."

"And you think I am cut off from other people?"

The tone of his voice might have warned me, but I was on a roll. "Well, aren't you? You've been on this one-man quest to find the king for years. Do you have a wife? Family? Who are your friends?"

He stared at me without speaking, and I suddenly remembered I was supposed to be getting on this guy's good side, not telling him he was a loser who had no friends. And he could have had bucketloads of them, for all I knew. We'd only known each other a little while. Just because I hadn't seen any sign of a social life in that time didn't meant it didn't exist.

"I mean, you don't have to answer that. It's just, you don't have to be so independent, you know? I'm happy to help. There's nothing wrong with needing a bit of help when you've been injured. You're not invincible."

Just shut up, Al. I'd let my mouth run away with me again. Not only was he a loser with no friends, I'd just reminded him that he'd been bested by a dog. Way to go. The silence stretched.

"I am fae," he said at last. "Not a weak human."

Ouch. Well, that put me in my place. I looked down at my hands, determined not to dig myself any deeper into the hole by speaking.

"And even among fae, I am exceptional," he continued. "I have not always been the Hawk. It was a title bestowed on me after I had proved myself the best of the best, worthy of the honour of becoming a knight of the king."

Lady save me, he was really pissed. Why couldn't I learn to keep my mouth shut?

"But you are right."

I looked up in shock.

His face was stern, but not angry. "Thank you for your assistance. I'm sorry I accepted it with such bad grace."

"That's okay," I faltered. "You're welcome."

He reached out and took my hand in his large one. "And I do have at least one friend, I hope." Then he raised my hand to his lips and kissed it, his gaze never leaving mine.

I felt my cheeks warm and stood up, unaccountably flustered by the steady regard of those tawny eyes. Were we friends? How strange. "Yes. You do. But I'd better leave you to rest, or I'll be a bad friend."

Out in the hallway again, I took a deep breath, my emotions churning. Something in that hypnotic gaze of his made me feel we were more than friends, and my stupid heart was leaping at the idea—despite all my promises not to get involved. But this time, it felt different. It wasn't just about his looks.

I'm sorry. I wondered how many years it had been since the proud knight had uttered those two little words. He made a pretty sweet apology when he got around to it. I could still feel his lips on my skin.

It occurred to me that he was the second fae who'd apologised to me this morning. That had to be some kind of record.

23

When I got back to the dining room, Raven was gone, but the food was still there, so I sat down and helped myself. The coffee was divine, rich and strong with a hint of hazelnut, and I downed two cups. Coffee was one of the few human inventions that the fae had adopted wholeheartedly. Even magic couldn't wake you up in the morning the way coffee could.

Hunger satisfied, I went looking for the master of the house and eventually found him in the stables, talking to a man who was grooming an enormous black horse. He broke off his conversation when I came in, and walked me back out into the sunshine, stroking the soft velvet nose of each horse he passed on the way.

"I trust you found our friend the knight in good condition?" he asked.

No more digs about my supposed infatuation, even though I felt that infatuation might well be clear on my face. But I tried to sound casual. "Our friend the knight is a little too impatient to be up and moving again. He needs to rest and allow himself time to heal."

"I can assure you that my healer will take good care of him. She won't allow him to push himself before he is ready." His hair gleamed blue-black in the sunlight, reminding me of his raven feathers. He'd saved my life twice, now, and I knew nothing about him. Who was this man?

"Thank you for helping us. It was you who sent the birds, wasn't it?"

He shrugged. "I do what I can."

"Why?" The fae were not Boy Scouts. They didn't help people for the sheer joy of doing good. "Why have you been watching me?"

"I haven't," he said, neatly sidestepping the question.

Talking to the fae could be an exercise in frustration. Technically, Thing One and Thing Two had been watching me, so he wasn't lying, but he'd chosen his words carefully. I needed to be just as careful with my questions, or he'd give me the run-around all day.

"Why are you protecting me?"

"You have powerful enemies. I am helping even up the scales."

Enemies? As in, more than one? I stopped walking to stare at him. That was incomprehensible to me. What had I ever done to earn powerful enemies? "Who? Who are my enemies? Why does anyone care about me? I'm a nobody."

There was sympathy in his coal-black gaze. "It would be safer for you to assume that everyone is your enemy and keep out of this business with the Hawk."

I couldn't do that, not unless I wanted to lose any chance of ever being allowed back into the Realms. I could just imagine how well Eldric would take it if I chucked his gate glyph back in his face and told him to go find his own drake skins.

"Everyone is my enemy?" I echoed. "What, even my friends? I can't go around distrusting *everyone*."

"The man who led you into the Wilds to die was your friend," he pointed out.

Dammit. He had a point there. "That's true, but I'd trust Sage and Willow with my life." In fact, I did, since I slept in their house every night. If they were out to kill me, they'd had plenty of opportunities. "And Rowan. And they'll be worried sick about me. I need to get back to them."

"Then go. The Hawk will be safe enough here. Better for you to stay out of this business, now. But wear the cloak I gave you until you are safely through the Wilds."

It was good advice, and I took it, though the cloak didn't make me completely invisible, since it was daylight. A shimmer in the air, like a heat haze, might have alerted any watchers that someone passed, but they could not have told who it was. They might not even have been sure that what they were seeing was anything more than a trick of the eye, or the movement of the wind in the trees. It helped that, for most of the way, the trees crowded close to the path, casting deep shadows on it. The power of the gate glyph didn't fail me and, much faster than I had arrived, I found myself back in the mortal world, the tall trees of Hyde Park welcoming me home.

I caught the train from Museum station, and in less than an hour, I was back at Willow's sith. I'd expected to find them both asleep at this time of day, but the sound of my footsteps down the long hallway to my bedroom brought them running.

"Where have you been?" Sage asked. "We were worried sick when you didn't come home."

Willow stood behind her, arms crossed and a thunderous scowl on her face, looking for all the world like a mother about to berate her teen daughter for sneaking in after curfew.

"It's a long story," I said. I sighed as I thought of Edgar and what I had to tell them. "And not an altogether happy one."

"Where is the Hawk?" Willow asked. "Was he with you?"

"He was, but he's been hurt. I left him with ..." Who? A friend? A random stranger I'd only just met? How exactly did I describe Raven? My friends would probably think I was crazy for trusting him, especially since I couldn't really explain why I did, other than that he appeared to be looking out for me. But we all knew altruism was not a fae characteristic. Raven wanted something, no doubt, and one day, the bill for his help would fall due. I just hoped it wouldn't be too hard to pay.

We went out into the garden, and I lay back in a hammock, staring up at the leaves overhead while I filled them in on all that had happened. Sage was fascinated by the battle with the monster dogs, and made me go over every gory detail two or three times before she would let me move on with the story. They were both as suspicious of Raven as I'd expected, though they grudgingly agreed that the fact that he was clearly behind Things One and Two saving me from getting blown up was a point in his favour.

"The raven folk are usually from Night, aren't they?" Sage asked Willow.

"Usually. Though there are some in Winter and Air, too."

"What is his interest in you, then?" Sage frowned at me. "They have no alliance with Autumn."

"What is anyone's interest in her?" Willow asked. She gave me a frank look. "No offence, but you're a changeling, and one who has been outcast. As far as the Realms go, you don't exist."

"I know," I said, though hearing her state it so baldly still smarted. "Raven's right. It must be because I've been helping the Hawk with this investigation. Someone *really* doesn't want us to find these drake skins."

"Then why don't they blow up the Hawk's house?" Sage muttered. "He won't stop looking just because *you* die. He barely even knows you."

That was true, though perhaps I knew him a little better than she realised, now. I didn't believe that he'd taken many people to Oldriss, or shared with them the story of how Oldriss had hidden him for seven years after the attack on the king. Not lately, anyway, since his story had been laughed out of Court the first time. No wonder the poor bastard was standoffish. "The Hawk's convinced the people behind this are the same ones who took the king, so nothing short of death will stop him. He's obsessed with finding the king."

"So, do we assume these mysterious king-killing enemies are from Summer, since Edgar was a Summer changeling?" Willow asked.

"The Hawk doesn't believe the king is dead," I said, but Willow just rolled her eyes. "The other Realms wouldn't even have known who Edgar was, so it would make sense that it was someone from Summer. And it sure as hell looked like Dansen Arbre's knife."

"No," Sage objected, "it doesn't make *any* sense. Why would Summer be stealing drake skins from the queen? She's from Summer herself. And Dansen Arbre was the one who told you to go look for the bloody things!"

"It may not have been someone from the noble House," Willow pointed out. "Summer's a big place. You're assuming all plots must come from the ruling Houses, but I assure you that every fae is born with the backstabbing gene firmly in place."

"That's a little harsh," I muttered, thinking of the Hawk.

"The real question is, why the sudden interest in drug-dealing? What possible interest does any fae have in human money?"

"There are plenty of fae living right here in the human world who might fancy growing rich on the proceeds of crime," I pointed out.

"Yes, but do those fae have access to the royal palace? Or

the Lord of Autumn's halls? Those drake skins aren't lying around waiting for any light-fingered fae to pick up. The kind of fae living here aren't usually the kind with the right connections for this kind of crime."

"So you're saying it *is* someone from the noble Houses, then," Sage said. "Make up your mind."

Willow cast Sage a scathing glance. "I'm just thinking aloud. It could be a network of people, I suppose, but I wouldn't have thought it would be worth going to that much trouble. Drake skins are rare. There's not much point setting up a whole operation to deal drake skins to humans when you're going to run out of product very soon."

"And if they're so difficult to get, wouldn't you be charging a premium, and only flogging them to rich people?" I added. "Someone like Edgar's son couldn't have had that much money to spend on drugs."

We all fell silent, pondering the problem.

"Okaaay," Willow said, drawing out the word as she thought. "What if the drugs aren't being paid for by the humans at all? What if the drugs themselves are payment for some kind of service the humans are performing for the fae?"

Sage snorted. "What could a nurse at an old people's home do for someone in the Realms?"

"I don't know. Use your imagination. Maybe he's a hired killer."

"Again, we come back to the fact that most fae don't give two shits about what happens in the human world," I said. "They wouldn't be assassinating humans because they couldn't care less what happens to any of us."

Willow shot me a sympathetic glance. "Careful, the chip on your shoulder is showing there, hon."

"Whatever. I don't think we can figure this out without more information. I'd love to get a better look at that nursing home. Maybe Peter kept a stash there."

"And maybe he'd used everything he had, and there's nothing there to see," Sage said. "I, for one, am not going back to that place. It was horrible. Like a prison."

I had to agree. That poor, confused old man who'd appeared as we were leaving had nearly broken my heart. "Remember the guy who wanted us to take him home?"

Sage shuddered. "It was so sad. He wanted his mum to sing to him about the crystal cliffs again."

Willow sat bolt upright. "The crystal cliffs? Are you sure? What else did he say?"

"Um … nothing?" Sage looked at me for confirmation, confused. "We only saw him for a moment. He asked us if we'd come to take him home, then he mentioned the song about the crystal cliffs. Why?"

"The Crystal Cliffs was the old name for Whitehaven, before the king built his palace there." Her eyes were huge. "Guys, what if that old man is the king?"

I had the afternoon shift at work, from two until ten, and it passed in a haze of speculation about the king. It was possible that we were connecting things that had no business being connected, but I felt in my bones that we were right, and the king of all the Realms was trapped in a dementia ward in the human world, not dead as everyone had supposed.

Well, everyone but the Hawk. I'd been awed by his dedication before, but the awe had been tinged with pity that he was wasting his life on a dream. Now, it appeared that it had not been a dream, but a deadly reality: someone had kidnapped the king, and done it in such a way that the Hawk was the only one looking for him. In a weird way, it made me proud of the Hawk for not giving up in the face of such disbelief and, from some, outright contempt. Hopefully, his dedication would soon be rewarded.

Plan A had been for Willow to sneak in to the nursing home using my cloak of shadows. With her fae magic, she would be able to tell if the person we thought was the king was disguised with a Glamour. We figured we needed to know for sure before we went to the Hawk with the news. But that idea had failed when it became apparent that the cloak would only work for me. Every time Willow tried to put it on, it fell right off her. So we'd moved on to Plan B.

Ricky came in to start his shift a few minutes before mine ended. "You not going out partying tonight?" he asked as he took in the dark shirt and jeans I was wearing.

"Not tonight. A girl needs to catch up on her beauty sleep sometimes."

"Not you, sweetheart. You're beautiful enough already. How did you go with that old boss of yours? Did you knock him dead?"

I'd forgotten that I'd been on my way to see Eldric last time I'd spoken to Ricky. So much had happened since then that it seemed a long time ago. "Yeah, it went pretty well."

"Good. But you're still not leaving me, right?"

I laughed as I grabbed my jacket. "Never, Ricky. You're the sunshine in my life."

He was still chuckling as the automatic doors swooshed shut behind me. Willow's big Mazda was waiting on the street outside, and I slid into the back seat.

Plan B was for me to go in with the cloak and see if there were any other fae there, working on the assumption that the job of guarding such an important prisoner wouldn't be entrusted to mere humans. According to Willow, if the king was there, he was bound to have some fae guards.

Sitting in the back seat, clutching the feathered cape as Willow drove through the dark streets to Alder Grove, I wasn't as confident.

"How will simply seeing a fae in the vicinity tell me for sure that the king is there? There could be fae working there for perfectly legitimate reasons. People have to earn a living."

Sage snorted. "You're thinking of people like Jamison and Randall. You'll note that they both work for themselves." Jamison ran the pharmacy, and Randall the pub. "Fae living in the mortal world might need money as much as the next person, but if you think any fae is going to take on a job where he has to answer to humans, you've got rocks in your head. And a job where he might have to *minister* to humans? Not happening. I mean, can you imagine any fae you know wiping some old guy's butt in a nursing home? If there are fae there, you can bet your sweet bippy that they aren't part of the nursing staff."

That made sense. Which meant I didn't need to see the king to know he was there.

"Bet your sweet *bippy*?" Willow repeated, diverted, as she always was, by creative human slang. "You made that up."

"Did not. It's historical. Ask Randall—he said it the other night."

Randall had been living among the humans longer than any of the fae in our circle of friends. He'd seen the Great Depression and both World Wars. He tried to keep up with modern usage, but occasionally, something from a previous age slipped out.

"Historical doesn't count. This is supposed to be an assimilation project. You can't assimilate if you sound like someone's grandmother."

"I don't care; I like it."

"What does bippy even mean?"

"Arse."

Willow rolled her eyes. "Of course it does. Why not just say arse, then?"

Sage shrugged. "I don't know. 'Cause humans are weird? They have more cutesy names for certain body parts than you can poke a stick at."

Willow's mouth twitched. *More somethings than you can poke a stick at* was one of her favourites. She delighted in the more outlandish expressions, and Australians certainly delivered on those. She and Sage had fallen about laughing the night they'd watched *Crocodile Dundee*, and afterwards, I'd seen her making notes of her favourites.

We pulled up around the corner from the nursing home, and I took a deep breath to quiet the sudden flutter of nerves in my stomach. Whoever was holding the king was determined he not be found. I had no illusions about what would happen to me if I were discovered. There was no curse of the Brenfells protecting *my* life. "You guys don't have to stay, you know. If all you're going to do is wait in the car, I can just as easily take the train back and you can go home and watch TV."

Sage turned around from the passenger seat and gave me the *don't be stupid* frown. "It won't hurt to have back-up. Just in case."

"I'll be invisible. It'll be a piece of cake."

She flinched dramatically. "Don't *say* that. Have you learnt nothing from all the movies you've watched? As soon as someone says that, it all falls to shit."

Willow caught my eye in the rear-vision mirror and grinned. "B-grade movies: every girl's guide to navigating real life."

Sage turned back to face front huffily. "Laugh all you want. You'll thank me one day. If you live that long."

"Be careful," Willow said as I got out of the car.

"Always."

I checked that there was no one in sight before donning the cloak, then I walked, invisible, around the corner and up the driveway to the nursing home. I took my time, moving noiselessly in my sneakers, careful not to step on anything that might crackle or snap and give me away, a skill I'd perfected in the forests of Autumn.

At this time of night, there were only a handful of cars in the parking lot. Presumably, they belonged to staff. I pushed on the door to the dementia unit, but it was locked. Not all that surprising, I guessed. No one wanted the residents wandering the streets at this time of night.

I prowled up the driveway beside the building, past the little paved area where we'd seen the old man. There were no windows, which seemed strange. I circled around the building, hoping to find another means of entry. There'd have to be a delivery entrance somewhere, right? I did find a door marked Private around the back, but it was locked. On the opposite side from the driveway, the fence ran close to the building, leaving only a narrow concrete passageway. That side had plenty of windows, spaced at regular intervals, which looked as though they belonged to individual rooms, but the only view they had was the silvered palings of the boundary fence.

I came back around to the main doors, pondering my options. They were glass, and showed me a small reception area and the beginnings of a hallway that turned out of sight. In deference to the late hour, the place was lit only dimly. A faint clanging came from somewhere inside, as if someone was tapping a pot lid with a metal spoon.

I could pick a room that seemed unoccupied and break a window to get in, but that might put the king's guards on high alert. The Hawk wouldn't thank me for that when it came time to break the king out of there. I could stand in the driveway and shout, "Fire!" and wait until someone opened the door to investigate, but that might also be suspicious. Or I could just wait here and see what happened.

I pulled my phone out of my pocket to call Sage and Willow and give them an update. It was as invisible as I was, which was the weirdest experience. Trying to type in a number when you can't see the keys is a little tricky, but I got through on the third attempt.

Sage's voice answered. "Well?"

"Nothing to report yet. I'm still outside. I'll wait and see if an opportunity to get in comes up."

"Okay. Leave this call connected so we can hear if anything happens."

"Okay." I slipped the phone back into my pocket without ending the call and settled in to wait.

My opportunity came about ten minutes later. A harried-looking nurse came around the corner from the hallway, heading straight for the door. I jumped reflexively and looked around for somewhere to hide before remembering that I was invisible.

She walked briskly to the door and waved her key card over the sensor. The doors slid open and I slipped inside as she went out, fumbling in her pocket for cigarettes and a lighter.

Inside, I examined the sensor. Getting out again could be a problem. She'd worn her card on a lanyard around her neck. Maybe some kind nurse would leave one lying around where I could borrow it. I gave a mental shrug and turned down the hallway. That was a problem for later. I was in, and that was the main thing for now.

The clanging was louder now I was inside. It was coming from somewhere down the end of the hallway. I rounded the corner and headed in that direction, since that was where I wanted to be anyway. The door that the king had come out of was down there, somewhere on the left.

I passed doors at regular intervals, all marked with the names of the residents who slept inside. Most were closed, but some were open, showing glimpses of shadowy bedrooms. At least here they only seemed to sleep one resident per room, unlike the building that Sage and I had visited the other day. The doorways marched down both sides of the hallway until partway along, when the hall opened out into a large area with lounge chairs on one side and a dining room on the other. A door that presumably led to the kitchen on the dining side was closed now. The windows of the lounge room looked out onto the tiny paved area.

The hall continued on past the communal areas, but there were no more doors or windows on the left-hand side, only on the right. It was as if there was nothing on the left-hand side, but I knew from the shape of the building that there must be more rooms there. Only one door in this hallway didn't have a resident's name on it, and that door faced me at the end of the hallway. Surely this door must lead to the missing rooms?

I was standing close enough to touch it when it suddenly opened. I barely managed to leap aside in time before a huge guy came out. He was wearing a nurse's uniform and a frown that could have stopped traffic, and if he wasn't a troll then I would hand in my changeling badge. I would have bet my sweet bippy on it.

He paused, as if sensing a disturbance in the air when I'd moved, and I froze against the wall as his head swung from side to side, taking in the whole corridor. The door clicked closed behind him, and I cursed myself for not taking a peek inside while I still could, but Mr Tall and Granite-Faced had given me such a scare I was surprised he couldn't hear my heart pounding. I certainly hadn't had the presence of mind to scope out the room behind him. I consoled myself with the thought that his shoulders were so broad he'd probably completely blocked the view anyway.

He turned around and went back inside, thereby

proving that my theory was correct—he blocked any view of the room. I'd just started to back away when he reappeared with another, equally massive, friend. I was at the door of the nearest room, which was open, so I slipped inside, afraid that he'd only gone for backup to search for the source of whatever had disturbed him.

According to the sign on the door, this room belonged to Mrs Gladys Phipps. I sidled in, only belatedly realising that this room was the source of the clanging noise. Gladys was sitting up in bed in the dark, and she was bashing the end of her bed with her walking stick. Both were made of metal, hence the noise.

"Who's there?" she demanded, squinting suspiciously into the dark. I froze against the wall again. Did everyone in this place have some kind of sixth sense? Was the cloak not concealing me as well as it should have? I checked myself out but, as far as I could tell, I was completely invisible. After a moment, she started up her banging again. She must have heard the troll opening and closing doors.

I stood against the wall, out of the way, watching the corridor. It was probably only coincidence that the troll had gone back for reinforcements. Maybe they were both going for a smoke. There was no reason to doubt Raven's gift, and trolls were not known for their sense of smell—I was just feeling jittery.

Nevertheless, a moment later, the first troll appeared in Gladys's doorway and my stomach clenched with nerves. I held my breath as he lumbered into the room. Gladys saw him but didn't seem surprised to find such a huge man in her room in the middle of the night.

"Shut up, old woman," he growled, in a voice like rocks tumbling together.

Deliberately, she banged the walking stick against the bed a little harder, staring at him with unmistakeable defiance. I wondered what Sage and Willow were making of this, if the phone was even picking any of it up through the thick denim of my pocket.

He growled again, and she pointed the walking stick at him. It was one of those ones that could stand up by itself, ending in four little legs with rubber feet for stability. She must have some pretty decent arm muscles for an old girl, considering how long she'd been banging that stick against the foot of the bed.

"Don't you take my chocolates. They're not for you. They're *mine*."

He made a noise of disgust and moved closer.

"I'll hit you with my walking stick," she said, adding another couple of bangs for emphasis.

A woman appeared in the doorway. The carpet had muffled the noise of her footsteps approaching. She eyed the troll with suspicion. "What are you doing?"

"She won't stop making that noise. How is anyone supposed to sleep around here with that racket going on?"

"Most of the residents are deaf anyway," the woman replied, bustling into the room. She wore light blue scrubs, the same as the troll. "And you're not supposed to be interfering with the general residents."

"I didn't go anywhere near her."

He made room for the nurse, bringing him a little closer

to where I stood, hardly daring to breathe. Only Raven's cloak stood between me and discovery. Out of the corner of my eye, I watched him, and in a moment, I was rewarded with a glimpse of his true, towering form. Yep. He was a troll, all right.

He glared at poor old Gladys with such ferocity that I would have been cowering in my boots, but Gladys had no fear. She banged the stick against the end of her bed once more, daring him to do anything about it.

Another noise, very faint, entered the room. For a moment, I couldn't place it. Then I realised with horror that it was coming from my back pocket.

"What's that?" the troll asked.

Why the hell did this guy have to have the hearing of a bat? I pressed my butt up against the wall, hoping to muffle the sound, but it made no difference. Far off in the distance, I heard the wail of a siren, and I suddenly realised that was what I was hearing from my phone, too. Willow and Sage must be much closer to the sound than I was, and the phone was picking it up. Shit.

"What's what?" the nurse asked impatiently as the troll took another step closer to me, staring suspiciously into the corner of the room. Nothing more offensive than a TV on a little cabinet sat there. I backed up toward it as quietly as I could, fumbling in my pocket all the while for the phone. Sweat was breaking out all over me. I really wasn't cut out for this. I'd be a dead loss as a spy.

Fortunately, I managed to end the call, cutting off the faint echo of the siren.

"You should get back to your patient," the nurse said, fixing the troll with a stern look. He turned back to her, and I sent up a silent prayer of thanks as he moved away. The nurse wasn't at all daunted by having him loom over her. She had the air of someone who was used to being obeyed. The troll glared at her, but he must have decided it wasn't worth pushing the issue.

"Keep her quiet, then," he threw over his shoulder as he walked out. "She's disturbing my patient." I heard the door at the end of the corridor open and close. I stared sideways at the nurse, but I couldn't see any sign of a true form underneath her human exterior. She was no more than she appeared to be—just a nurse who was used to dealing with troublesome people.

"Gladys, what's the problem, lovey?" She laid a firm hand on the walking stick, stopping Gladys from banging it anymore. "Why don't I put this out of the way for you?"

Gladys surrendered the walking stick with surprisingly little fight. "He was going to take my chocolates," she said, bottom lip sticking out defiantly. "I said I'd hit him with my walking stick. Big ugly brute."

"No one is going to steal your chocolates," the nurse said. "You should be asleep. It's the middle of the night."

"That's when they come," the old woman said. "When they think you're asleep, that's when they come into your room and take your things."

The nurse helped Gladys lie down, pulling the blankets up over her shoulders. "Who does?"

"All of them. That's why I hid the chocolates under my pillow."

The nurse snorted and pulled a crushed box of chocolates out from under the pillow. The old lady made a noise of protest, but the nurse shoved them into the bottom drawer next to the bed. "They'll be safer in there, lovey. If you leave them under the pillow, they'll get ruined, and then no one will be able to eat them. Now go to sleep, and no more banging, all right?"

Gladys muttered something under her breath, which the nurse chose to take as agreement, though it sounded more like a complaint to me. Then the nurse left.

She'd barely cleared the door when Gladys propped herself up on one elbow, leaned over, and retrieved the chocolates from the drawer. She was shoving them back under the pillow as I followed the nurse out, grinning to myself a little. Maybe the old lady had once shared a house with friends like Sage and Willow. I'd hide the ice cream under my pillow if I could. It was the only way I would ever get any honey and macadamia before Willow ate it all.

The whole thing had taken very little time. I hurried back to the front door and only had to wait a few moments before my smoker came back in and I could slip out. I didn't remove the cloak until I was safely back in Willow's car, which had Sage swearing in fright when the back door opened to my invisible hand.

"Well?" Willow said, as she started the car and pulled out.

"There were two trolls there, guarding a locked door. I couldn't see what was inside, but there seems to be a large area of the building that's only accessible through that door."

"It's got to be him, then." Her eyes met mine in the rear vision mirror. "Congratulations. You've found the lost king of the Realms."

25

It nearly killed me to sit still for so long, but Willow was adamant that we should wait for the Hawk before attempting to rescue the king, and Sage all but locked me in the sith.

"There are people trying to kill you out there," she pointed out, when I objected to a virtual house arrest. "Why make it easy for them?"

So I cancelled my shifts at work, and the only time I left the sith was to go to a gig. I felt safe enough, with both Willow and Rowan on guard, but I kept a careful eye on the crowd just in case.

I was going stir crazy by the time my phone rang a week later, reduced to playing card games with Willow to pass the time. I'd tried texting the Hawk, but he must have still been in the Realms, as I got no reply. When I glanced at the display and saw who was ringing, I snatched the phone off the table so fast Willow raised her eyebrows and dropped her cards with the look of a woman who had every intention of eavesdropping shamelessly on the conversation.

"Hawk," I gasped, before he could speak, "where are you?"

"At my home in Sydney," he said. His voice was softer and full of warmth when he added, "And my name is Kyrrim."

That stopped me in my tracks. Even Eldric, Lord of Summer, had addressed him as the Hawk. How many people were allowed to call him by his name? I had the feeling it was a very small number. And now, I was one of them.

"Kyrrim, then." I felt oddly flustered at using his name, as if our relationship had reached some new, more intimate level. "Are you well? All healed?"

"Well enough." His deep voice was husky. "Raven told me that you killed one of the dharrigals. Not many could have brought down a monster like that armed only with a knife. You are a brave woman, Allegra. A true warrior."

"Umm ..." What did I say? *My pleasure* didn't sound quite right, though I'd been pretty happy that the damn thing was dead. "I couldn't really leave it to stalk us. I'm glad you're feeling better."

"I'm ready to resume the search, if you are."

"Yeah. About that ... we really need to talk."

"Then talk."

"Not over the phone. In person. Can you meet me at The Drunken Irishman?"

Willow shook her head. "Tell him to come here. It's

more private. You don't want people listening in to *that* conversation."

"Is someone else there?" he asked, a note of suspicion entering his deep voice.

"It's only Willow. I'm at her sith. She thinks it would be better if you met me here to discuss … what we have to discuss."

"Very well, then." He was better at hiding his curiosity than I was. In his place, I would have been busting to know what the big deal was. "I'm on my way."

Knowing he was coming, I felt an unaccountable desire to change my clothes, though the pair of jeans I was wearing was still mostly clean, and the T-shirt was a soft blue that brought out the vivid colour of my eyes. I stayed in my chair, refusing to give in to the urge, or even to check that my hair was tidy. This wasn't a social call. It was just business, and the Hawk's—*Kyrrim's*—interest in me was purely as a work colleague. There was absolutely no reason to doll myself up for him, or to feel a thrill of pleasure that he'd told me his name. Just as there was no reason to dwell on my mental image of him with his shirt off, or the feel of his strong body on top of mine on the bed in Raven's home.

No, what I should be thinking about was the king's dilemma, and how we could break him free of his jail. I'd only seen the two troll guards, but that didn't mean there weren't others, and perhaps magical defences to get through as well.

Maybe the Hawk would know what to do about those. That was kind of his job, after all. A thrill shot through me as I heard his voice at the door, but I took a deep breath and forced myself to stillness. A servant led him through to the dining room, where Willow and I were waiting.

I drank in the sight of him in the doorway. He also wore a blue shirt, though his was darker than mine, in a deep shade that brought out the russet highlights in his hair. It was also long-sleeved, hiding whatever damage the dharrigal had inflicted, but at least he seemed to be moving without pain, which was a definite step up from the last time I'd seen him. Although, last time, he *had* been half-naked, and that had certainly been a sight to treasure. But somehow, he seemed larger than I remembered and even more handsome, as if my memory couldn't do justice to the overwhelming reality.

His eyes sought mine as soon as he entered the room, and he smiled, drawing an answering smile from me. It was no use; I couldn't help myself. I felt like a giddy teenager.

Then he bowed to Willow. "Thank you for inviting me into your home."

She rose and went to greet him, offering her hand to be kissed. "May the peace of this home fill your heart and the hearts of all those who enter here."

It was the old fae offering of hospitality, and I'd never heard her extend it to anyone before. In the old days, it had been more than words—a calming spell had "filled the hearts" of visitors, to ensure that visits didn't end in bloodshed, and any host who broke the laws of hospitality suffered a backlash from their own magic. Basically, it had guaranteed good behaviour on both sides.

But no tingle of magic accompanied Willow's words today—she must just be feeling extra formal. Maybe it was a big deal to have one of the legendary knights of the kingdom enter your home. I'd stopped seeing him as someone awe-inspiring some time ago. Considering the power he had to affect my own goal of getting back into the Realms, that was a little odd. He was often irritating, and frequently inscrutable, but there was a closeness that came from facing danger together that made him feel more like a ...

Like a what? I could say "friend", but I knew that would be lying. He bent over my hand, too, and I gazed down on the top of his dark head with an unfamiliar feeling stirring inside. My heart hadn't leapt like that when Adam had taken my hand. I was in imminent danger of losing my heart to the winged knight, and that would never work.

Was it only wishful thinking, or did he linger longer over my hand than he had over Willow's? He straightened, but showed no sign of wanting to let go. Reluctantly, I withdrew my hand from his grip in a last-ditch attempt to be sensible. No more bad romantic decisions. I was done with men. Right? So why did I feel so bereft without the touch of his skin on mine?

Willow fussed around, taking her role as hostess very seriously, urging him into a chair and pressing refreshments onto him. He waved away all offers of food and drink, clearly eager to get to the reason for this meeting.

He sat opposite me, hands clasped on the table, gazing at me with an intensity that made it very hard to remember my good intentions. I hadn't realised how much I'd missed him until I saw him again. "So, what did you have to tell me?"

I glanced at Willow, suddenly nervous. What if we were wrong, after all? She jerked her head at the Hawk, as if to say, "go on!"

"We think we've found the king," I said baldly.

He didn't move, not even to blink, but suddenly, his attention felt laser-focused. "Where?"

"In a nursing home."

"Disguised as an old man," Willow added.

"They've done something to him. He acts as if he has dementia. And there are at least two trolls guarding him."

The Hawk's face could have been carved from stone as he stood up. "*Where?*"

"Whoa, there, hang on a minute." Willow stood, too, holding out her hands as if to calm an enraged animal. "Don't rush off. He's not in any immediate danger. He can stand to wait a little longer while we work out a plan."

"We don't know what other safeguards there are," I said. "I only got a brief look. But we've been thinking about the best way to do this."

The Hawk's tawny gaze swung from Willow to me. "You've been there? Tell me everything."

"Let's sit down again, shall we?"

He hesitated, still looking as though he was about to leap into action, but eventually, he sat, as if forcing himself to stillness by sheer willpower. I continued, telling him about the day Sage and I had seen the king, and how I'd gone back later and run up against the troll guard. I hadn't quite finished the story when Sage's voice sounded in the hallway.

"Hi, honey, I'm home!"

A moment later, she entered the room, dumping her bag on the floor by the door. She stopped at the sight of us, gathered in a tense circle at the dining table.

"Looks like your day was a lot more exciting than mine. What did I miss?"

"We're just talking about rescuing the king," I said.

"Cool. When do we do it?"

The Hawk looked at her, taken aback, then glanced at Willow and me. "You can't come. I am in your debt for this information, but I'll take it from here."

Sage dropped into the nearest chair, sitting back at her ease with one ankle resting on the opposite knee. "Why? Because you did such a good job out there in the Wilds?"

He glared at her, unused to being challenged. I could have told him he was wasting his time glaring at Sage— she'd been glared at by experts and wasn't easy to cow. "I was caught off guard in the Wilds by a man that Allegra had vouched for. That won't happen again."

"Don't be so quick to reject help," I said. "This is the king's life we're talking about. You need back up."

He locked gazes with me. I couldn't tell what he was thinking, but I hoped he was considering what I'd told him about no man being an island.

"We have skills that could be useful," Willow said, in her most persuasive tones. "And who else can you trust? It's not as if you can go to the other knights for help. Any of them could be in league with Summer."

He stiffened. "You have proof that Summer is behind this?"

"Not yet," I said. "But I bet you we can find some. And Raven still has the dagger that killed Edgar."

"It will be dangerous," he said.

Sage cast me a triumphant glance. Clearly, he was weakening.

"We know," I said. "But he's our king, too. We're coming, so let's figure out how we're going to get the king out and nail those Summer bastards to the wall at the same time."

26

At four o'clock in the morning, we parked Willow's car around the corner and walked quietly through the dark streets to Alder Grove. The entry was brightly lit, and lamp posts along the driveway illuminated the shabby concrete, but we ghosted across the grass, into the narrow laneway formed between the side of the building and the boundary fence. None of us spoke as I led the way into the darkness, passing the regularly spaced windows of the residents' rooms. The Hawk strode behind me, practically stepping on my heels in his eagerness, and Willow and Sage brought up the rear.

When we reached the last window, I stopped and listened. There was no metallic clanging tonight—Gladys must be asleep. Willow stepped up to the window and removed the fly screen, then laid her hand on the cold glass just above the latch.

A soft green glow rose around Willow's hand, and the scent of roses swelled briefly in the darkness, followed by a barely audible hiss as glass faded into sand and trickled away under Willow's magic touch. Even if she was awake, Gladys wouldn't have heard that.

Quietly, Willow reached through the hand-shaped hole and unlatched the window. The squeak as she pushed it up sounded loud to my ears, but I doubted anyone inside the building would have heard it, or thought anything of it if they had. Nevertheless, we waited for several moments, standing in silence by the open window, before the Hawk decided it was safe enough.

With an agility that belied his size, he climbed through the window with no more noise than a soft breeze stirring the curtains. I followed him in as fast as I could, leaving Willow and Sage to fight it out for who came next. The Hawk was already at the door that led into the corridor, which was ajar, listening intently for any movement.

I spared a glance for Gladys, who was on her back, snoring softly. Her walking stick stood within easy reach next to the bed on its little rubber-shod feet. Tonight, there was no sign of any chocolates.

Willow moved past me, to the door, where the Hawk made room for her. She closed her eyes and stood stock still. She didn't look as though she was doing anything, but we'd already discussed this, and I knew she was trying to feel for any enchantments in the corridor that might expose us before we were ready.

Sage's backpack caught on the windowsill as she climbed through, and she stumbled against the wheeled table that stood beside the bed. It banged against the metal leg of the bed with a noise that sounded like a bell tolling to my nervous ears.

"Oops," Sage said in an undertone.

My gaze flew to the sleeping figure in the bed. The snoring cut off abruptly. Old people had terrible hearing, right? She wouldn't wake up.

Like a woman possessed, Gladys jerked upright in the bed. For an old lady, she was certainly spry. She looked at us—four people frozen in place like guilty statues—and opened her mouth.

Fortunately, Sage had come prepared, having heard all about my previous visit.

"Chocolates?" she offered in a desperate voice, digging into the backpack.

"Who are you?" Gladys croaked in tones of deep suspicion. She was barely awake, but the mention of chocolate had caught her attention.

From the depths of the backpack, Sage pulled a large box of chocolates, while the rest of us watched, helpless. She deposited the box on the old lady's lap with an ingratiating smile. "I brought you these," she said brightly.

Gladys's gaze was drawn to the brightly coloured box like a magnet. When she looked up again, the suspicion was gone, replaced by a deep satisfaction. "They're my favourites."

"I know," Sage replied.

Willow whispered to the Hawk, and the two of them slipped out into the hallway. Evidently, the coast was clear. Torn between our mission and Sage's dilemma, I hesitated.

Would Gladys give us away? How could I shut her up if she did? She was an old lady; it wasn't as though I could *attack* her. But Sage seemed to have the situation in hand.

"Open them for me, dear," Gladys said, and Sage obliged, ripping off the plastic and presenting the open box for inspection. Lovingly, Gladys looked over the contents before choosing one and popping it into her mouth. "Strawberry cream," she mumbled blissfully around a mouthful of chocolate.

"They're the best," Sage said, apparently happy to chat all night.

"The orange creams used to be better," Gladys said, "but they stopped making them. Put in some more caramels. I mean, really! They already had two other caramels. How many did they need?"

Sage shook her head as she helped herself to a chocolate. "Terrible, isn't it?"

Gladys gave her an approving look. "Are you one of my granddaughters?"

I more than half-expected Sage to say she was, but she shook her head. "Just a friend."

The old lady apparently didn't see anything odd about having a friend drop by in the middle of the night. She waved the chocolate box in my direction. "Want one?"

"Ah … no, thanks. I've got to …" I waved my hand vaguely toward the door and slipped out into the corridor. A quick glance showed me it was empty except for the Hawk and Willow, who was standing in front of the door to the hidden apartments, eyes closed in concentration as she searched for enchantments on the door itself. The Hawk stood a little to the side, a naked blade in his hand— not Ecfirrith, which was still lost somewhere in the Wilds, but another one he'd found somewhere. He probably had a whole armoury full of them at his home.

I looked again down the corridor, nervous, now, as I hadn't been when we were breaking into Gladys's room. Anyone who saw the sword in the Hawk's hand would scream blue murder, and then the shit would really hit the fan. For a moment, I wished Raven were here with his handy-dandy   putting-people-to-sleep-against-their-will power, but only for a moment. I wasn't sure I trusted him enough for this.

It would have been a good skill to have, though. None of us had that kind of power. I, of course, could do nothing, and Sage had only the same few little tricks that any fae had, like summoning light or casting a simple Glamour. Willow's powers were mainly bound up in growth and decay, which was handy for encouraging your garden to grow, but not much use against armed trolls.

The knight was an unknown quantity. The battle skills of the Knights of the Realms were legendary, of course, but I'd never heard that they had that much in the way of magical power. What we needed was someone who could cast illusions to befuddle the mind, or who could use elemental power to break this place wide open. Maybe we should have invited Yriell on our little rescue mission.

Willow opened her eyes. "There's a powerful ward on this door. No amount of force could break it down or force it open. You could probably bulldoze the whole building and this door would still be standing."

"Can you open it?" the Hawk asked.

"It's beyond my skill, I'm afraid."

Sage came out of Gladys's room. "Is there another way in?"

I shrugged. "There were no windows along the driveway. That whole wall was blank."

"Probably covered by a Glamour," Willow said.

"And, presumably, also protected," Sage added, "even if we can find them."

I looked around the empty hallway. A metal trolley stood outside the closed door of a room partway along the corridor, the kind with locked drawers that nurses wheeled around when they were dispensing medicine. A white coat was draped over the top of it. I grabbed the trolley and brought it thumping and rattling back to the door, then shrugged into the coat.

"What are you doing?" Sage squeaked, her eyes wide. "You'll wake up the whole place."

Okay. Deep breath. I rapped on the door, trying to channel the commanding presence of the nurse I'd seen here the other night, the one who'd faced down the troll without flinching. "If we can't open it, we'll have to get them to do it for us."

The Hawk plastered himself against the wall beside the doorway. Obviously an old hand at rushing a fortified position. It took Willow and Sage a little longer to get with the program, but they quickly followed his lead on the other side, so that anyone opening the door would see only me, in my lame disguise. I guess I could have asked Willow to Glamour my black clothes to look more like a nurse's uniform, but I was reluctant to involve magic, in case they could sense it on me.

"It's four o'clock in the morning," Sage whispered. "You really think they're going to open the door?"

"Why not?" The troll had been happy enough to pop out in the middle of the night to chastise Gladys on my last visit. "I doubt they keep business hours."

And if they didn't open up, I could always borrow Gladys's walking stick and make such a racket that he came out again. When the door didn't open immediately, I rapped again, even more aggressively. My nerves were wound tight, and I wanted out of this corridor.

The door was wrenched open by a huge man in a blue nurse's uniform, who scowled at me. Troll, for sure.

"Hi!" I said brightly, favouring him with a dazzling smile, then I rammed the trolley into his gut with all my strength.

He grunted, but the trolley rebounded off the troll's hard body so fast it damn near winded me. My grand vision of mowing him down with the trolley and leaping, triumphant, into the room behind him would have died there and then, except the Hawk sprang to my aid, adding his considerable muscle to the job. Between us, we managed to shove the troll out of the doorway with the trolley, and Willow and Sage piled in behind us.

We found ourselves in a large sitting room, comfortably

but rather shabbily furnished. There was no time to check out the décor, however, as another troll hastily rose from one of the chairs—or as hastily as trolls ever did anything, which, considering their size, wasn't all that fast—and the one that we'd shoved had recovered his equilibrium, along with a club the size of a small tree. God knew where that had come from. It was all happening too fast to keep track of.

Sage slammed the door behind us as the club began a long arc through the air that was designed to end buried in the Hawk's skull. The Hawk didn't wait around, but leapt forward, shoving the trolley out of the way, his sword held high. The troll danced back with surprising agility, avoiding the first slash of the sword. The rest of us hugged the walls to avoid the combatants.

The second troll slammed his meaty hand against a button on the wall. It looked like a panic button, but no alarm sounded, though a light that I'd taken for a motion sensor up by the ceiling began to flash. Damn, that couldn't be good. Somewhere, the alarm was being raised. We needed to wrap this up before the cavalry arrived.

He reached out with his other hand and scooped up a club from where it had been leaning against the wall. Then he grinned at me, showing pointed teeth that didn't belong in any human mouth. He was deliberately letting his fae self bleed through the human disguise, hoping to scare us.

Well, I was plenty scared already. The Hawk was dancing around his larger opponent, who was now bleeding freely from a slice across his arm, but it hadn't affected his ability to swing that club. And now the other one was moving in on us.

Willow flicked her hand at a potted plant as the monster passed it. The plant suddenly burst into life, achieving a decade's growth in a split second, its branches catching at the troll. But it only slowed him down for a moment.

Still, a moment was all I needed to hurl a knife across the room. The blade entered his eye socket, and the troll roared in agony.

"You'll bring the whole nursing home down on us," Sage hissed.

"Sorry. Would you rather I let him hit you with that bloody tree trunk?" My heart hammered as I backed up against the door.

Consumed by pain, the troll I'd hit was out of the fight, which only left— No, scratch that. The Hawk's sword darted out again, and the first troll's head hit the floor with a sickening thud.

"Let's get the king." The Hawk strode to the door leading further into the apartments, his sword still out and dripping gore. I dropped my borrowed white coat and fell in behind him, avoiding the severed head and the rapidly pooling blood on the floor. The troll I'd hit with my knife was down, too, apparently unconscious, probably from shock.

I gestured at him. He seemed pretty done for, but I didn't like leaving an enemy behind us. Trolls had constitutions like oxen. "Should we—?"

"Let's not waste time."

Right. I glanced uneasily at the light that still flashed above the panic button. Reinforcements were probably on their way right now. The Hawk eased the door open, his stance alert. I figured, with the noise we'd made, anyone lurking back here would be well and truly on their guard.

But no one leapt out of hiding to challenge the knight. We found ourselves in a dimly lit corridor which stretched quite a long way, with doors opening off it on one side. Just as I'd thought, this whole side of the building, which had seemed only a blank wall from outside, was actually taken up by these hidden rooms. My certainty that we had indeed found the king grew a little more. Someone had gone to a great deal of trouble to hide this away.

We crept down the corridor, the Hawk in front, me behind him, and Willow and Sage bringing up the rear. It was deathly quiet in here, which made me wonder if this whole section was soundproofed. Perhaps our fight in the first room *hadn't* been heard.

That was too much to hope for, of course. That flashing light wasn't just for show. We'd barely advanced any distance at all when a pinpoint of light flashed into being at the opposite end of the corridor, becoming a ray of light that formed a line, and then another, as if someone were drawing in the air with a sparkler. The Hawk was striding down the corridor to meet this new threat before I realised where I'd seen this before. Someone was drawing a gate in the air, and we were about to have company.

"Find the king!" the Hawk barked over his shoulder.

His stride increased until he was practically running, but

the gateway was complete and a man with long, silver hair stepped out before he reached it.

Dansen Arbre.

In his hand, he carried a sword, and the blade rose to meet the Hawk's opening slash with a nonchalance as if he did this every day. Arbre drove forward to make room for two others to follow him through the gate—trolls again, neither of whom carried anything so basic as a club. The first one had a long staff, tipped with silver; the second, an axe. Fortunately, the narrow confines of the corridor prevented either of them attacking the Hawk or getting past him, but it was only a matter of time. Arbre was forcing the Hawk back towards us, step by step.

"Move!" the Hawk shouted.

I unfroze as I realised he was talking to us, and hurried to open the nearest door. Inside was a small but well-equipped kitchen. No king.

Quickly, I shut that door and moved on to the next. The Hawk and his opponent seemed fairly evenly matched. We needed to find the king and get the hell out of Dodge. Sage went past me, keeping a careful eye on the battle raging at the end of the corridor, and opened another. We were rapidly running out of time.

"In here!" Sage cried, and Willow and I hurried over to her door.

She was already inside, smiling her irresistible smile at an old man sitting in front of a TV. Hesitantly, he returned the smile, his eyes widening as Willow and I crowded into the room, too.

"Hello?" he said, his tentative tone making it a question.

"Hello!" Sage said brightly. "It's a lovely night for a walk. Come with us and we'll show you how pretty the moon is tonight."

The old man hesitated, looking from one to the other of us. "I'm not supposed to go outside."

"Full moon tonight," Sage said. "Special occasion."

She took his arm, and he let her help him up. He was stooped and frail, reminding me of Edgar for a painful instant. He clung to Sage's arm and shuffled toward the door.

He was nearly there when a strange hissing sounded from the corridor.

"What's that?"

Willow and I peeked out. Green mist was billowing up from the floor between us and the swordfight, as if someone had thrown a spell our way. Dansen Arbre was smirking as he traded blows with the Hawk, anticipating a quick end to his fight.

He was doomed to disappointment. Thank goodness for Yriell's potion.

"Will the king be all right?" Willow asked. "We've all drunk the potion, but what if it puts him to sleep?"

"Let's not hang around to find out."

The swordsman's smirk changed to a grimace as he realised that his green mist was having no effect on the Hawk. So much for his easy win. He shouted to the trolls as we brought the king out and began to retreat back the way we'd come. While he was distracted, the Hawk landed a heavy blow on his sword arm, which began to drip blood. Nice. Unless he was ambidextrous, he wouldn't be swinging that sword much longer.

He seemed to realise that, too, and shouted at the trolls again. The one with the axe turned and began to chop at the wall beside him, opening up a huge hole in no time. Then the swordsman fell back, leaving the Hawk to face the other troll, who brought his staff whistling down towards the knight's head. Fortunately, he didn't have enough room to allow him to swing freely, and the Hawk managed to block the blow.

Meanwhile, Dansen Arbre and the other troll had slipped through the hole in the wall that separated the hallway we were in from the main corridor of the nursing home.

"Shit," Willow said, taking the king's other side and urging him away from the battle. "They're coming around behind us."

I looked back the way we'd come. Any minute now, they'd appear there, trapping us between themselves and the Hawk.

And there was no way we could fight a troll on our own, not burdened with the king as we were, even if that swordsman was out of action.

"Stay with the king," I said.

I sprinted back up the hallway, hoping to head them off, though I had no idea how I was going to stop a troll and an expert swordsman. I needed the Hawk to finish off his opponent and join me.

This seemed like a good time to put on Raven's cloak of shadows, so I whipped it out of my jacket pocket and slapped it on just as I skidded into the sitting room we'd first entered. The troll appeared in the opposite doorway at the same moment, so he saw me wink out of existence.

Shit, he was big. And that axe was going to be a problem. He stood just inside the doorway, sweeping it through the air in front of him, knowing I was there but not exactly where.

Quietly, I grabbed a syringe from the abandoned trolley. It was enormous—big enough for a horse needle. But was it big enough for a troll? I needed to get in close, inside the reach of that deadly axe.

I hit the floor, rolling under the sweep of the axe, then leapt to my feet and plunged the hypodermic into his chest, aiming for the heart. People could be killed with injections of air bubbles, right? Sadly, I had no idea how much air was needed, or how long it took. Too bad if he keeled over twenty-four hours from now. I'd be well and truly screwed by then.

He hurled me aside and I slammed into the wall. Groggy, I tried to rise. This was no time to lie around. He couldn't see me, but there was nothing wrong with his ears, and he knew where I'd hit the wall. But my legs wouldn't seem to get the message. At the last minute, I managed to roll aside as the axe came crashing down.

There was still no sign of Dansen Arbre. Had he collapsed from blood loss or gone for reinforcements? Willow and Sage still huddled with the king, just inside the hallway, waiting for me to get rid of this troll—but how?

Shaking my head to clear it, I leapt up, wrapping my legs around his massive torso and my arms around his neck. Maybe I could cut off his air.

He roared and hurled himself against the wall with me clinging to his back like a baby koala. The impact drove all the air from my lungs, but I clung on grimly. There was a cord around his neck with a charm on it, which gave me another idea.

All fae wore warding charms of some kind, to protect themselves from iron, when they came into the mortal world. If I could get that off him, the metal cart might do some real damage to him. I hooked two fingers under the cord and twisted it like a garotte. Either it was coming off or he was choking to death. I'd be happy with either outcome.

He flailed over his head with the giant axe. It turned out to be a damned good thing it was so big—he couldn't hit me with it. Still, all he had to do was shorten his grip on the shaft and I'd be toast. I pulled harder on the cord around his neck, his gasping and choking sounds music to my ears.

Again, he smashed me against the wall, and I felt my grip loosening. If I lived through this, I'd be nothing but one giant bruise. He dropped the axe and scrabbled at me with his meaty fingers, trying to gouge out my eyes or get a grip on my own throat.

His reaching fingers scrabbled at the feathered cloak and ripped it off, bringing me popping back into view, then caught at the necklace around my throat—but if he'd hoped to choke me with it, he was out of luck.

The chain snapped straight away, sending the precious gate glyph it held flying. I sucked in a horrified breath, but there was nothing I could do about it now.

In his staggerings, he brought us to the door out into the main corridor. As the doorway flashed past in my gyrating field of view, I caught a glimpse of a figure out there—not Dansen Arbre as I'd feared, ready to literally stab me in the back, but Gladys.

The troll slashing his way through the wall into the corridor would have made enough noise in any other place to rouse every inhabitant, but these people were old, and their hearing was dodgy as all get out. Add that to the dementia, and it was a wonder anyone at all had been woken by our struggles. I wondered briefly where the nursing staff were— perhaps they'd had the sense to barricade themselves somewhere safe and call the cops. Only Gladys stood there, her sensible cotton nightie flapping around her wrinkly knees, leaning heavily on the infamous walking stick that had caused so much trouble last time I'd been here.

Two things happened in quick succession: the cord I was using to garotte the troll finally gave way, and the sudden release of pressure caused me to lose my grip and come flying off the troll's back and slam into the wall of the corridor, almost at Gladys's feet.

"You all right, there, dear?" Gladys asked, as if I were a toddler who'd bumped her knee and not a woman fighting for her life against a highly pissed-off troll.

The troll bent to regather both his breath and his weapon as I tried to find the energy to get off the floor. Gladys stepped over my legs and raised her walking stick. She slammed it down across the troll's back so hard that the metal actually snapped in half. The troll grunted in real pain and dropped to his knees.

Somehow, I managed to scramble up, my hand reaching for that beautiful piece of jagged metal. The troll heard me coming, but he was too winded to move fast, and I was driven by the very real fear of imminent death. If he got back to his feet, I was done. I had nothing left in the tank.

I drove that metal shaft into the troll's back like Neil Armstrong planting the flag on the moon, and that was one troll who was never getting back up again.

Sage and Willow hurried the king past the dead troll and out into the corridor, giving Gladys a wide berth. She didn't seem at all perturbed by the violence.

She gave me a sympathetic glance. "Did he steal your chocolates, too?"

27

The Hawk appeared, breathing hard. He must have finished off the other troll. Somehow, we'd all managed to make it through alive.

"Everyone all right?" he asked, but he was only looking at me, concern in his eyes.

I must look a sight. Going three rounds with a troll didn't do much for anyone's appearance. I smoothed my hair as best I could with shaking hands, grateful to find that everything still worked, more or less, though my back and shoulders were on fire.

"I could do with a massage, if you're offering," I said.

"I'll take it under advisement." He glanced at Gladys, who was wandering back towards her own room as if nothing had happened. "What was the old lady doing here?"

"Saving my bacon, as it happens." I indicated the broken walking stick with a fond smile. "Nothing like a good old metal spike to bring down a troll."

But then my gaze moved past the troll, and I gasped in horror, falling to my knees.

"What's wrong?" The Hawk was instantly alert, ready to take on anything that might threaten me. But there was nothing he could do about this.

"Oh, no—oh, no," I murmured as I picked up the broken gate glyph. The troll must have stomped on it as he was careering around the room with me on his back. The intricate silver knot work was unchanged, but the pretty green stone caught in its centre had been smashed to powdery fragments. Eldric was going to kill me. These things were irreplaceable. Had my chances of being allowed back into Autumn permanently just been crushed, too?

"It doesn't matter," the Hawk said. "Let's go."

It didn't matter? Easy for him to say. He already had a place in the Realms—at the very top of the hierarchy, too, especially if we could get the king back to safety. I couldn't really blame him for focusing on the mission at hand— Oh, who was I kidding? Of course I could blame him. My crushed dreams formed a lump of misery under my aching ribs. Just one more pain to add to the tally. This day was really not working out for me.

I gave his straight back a fierce glare, then rose to follow him, tucking the damaged glyph into my pocket and reclaiming the rumpled cloak of feathers. Maybe the stone could be replaced? Or perhaps the king himself would look kindly on my efforts on his behalf and reward me with permanent residence?

That was, if we managed to get him back to his true self.

Looking at him, sagging between Willow and Sage as they prodded and encouraged him down the hall ahead of us, the possibility seemed remote. But maybe the fae healers could work a miracle. I felt as though we were about due for one.

The Hawk quickly caught up with the other three and took point, but the nursing home was eerily silent. As we reached the front doors, I saw two frightened faces peeking out at us from the dark office behind reception: nurses who'd decided discretion was the better part of valour. I certainly didn't blame them. They weren't equipped to deal with swords and green mist and angry trolls. I felt a little sorry for the mess we were leaving them. They'd have paperwork up the wazoo after tonight's activities.

The glass doors refused to open without a card to scan, but the Hawk barely paused. He kicked them down, which shouldn't have been possible, but sometimes modern technology was no match for sheer fae cussedness, and the Hawk's blood was up tonight. We hurried out onto the long drive, the cool night air a welcome relief. I was hot and sweaty from the fighting, and I sighed with relief as the breeze lifted tendrils of damp hair from my forehead.

"Where to?" Willow asked as we urged the king down the driveway.

The Hawk's eyes were constantly moving, scanning our surroundings for danger. "The Realms. We have to get the king to the palace before Dansen Arbre gets back with reinforcements."

"I can't believe he really was involved," Sage said. "Why

would he ask you to look for the drake skins if he knew it might lead you to the king?"

"Because he didn't expect me to succeed," the Hawk said tightly. "He probably thought it was a great joke. He thinks me a fool."

"He doesn't think much of changelings, either," I said.

The Hawk smiled at me, warmth in his eyes. "That was his other mistake: underestimating you."

"But what's the connection between the king and the drake skins?" Sage asked. "Is there really one, or is this all a big coincidence?"

"I don't believe in coincidences," the Hawk said.

"But how will we get to the Realms?" Willow asked. "He's bound to be watching the Greenways. We'll be ambushed."

Damn. We kept moving, down the street, towards where we'd left the car, but she was right. Our options were severely limited. If the Hawk still had Ecfirrith, he could have opened a gateway directly to wherever we wanted to go in the Realms, but it was lost somewhere in the Wilds. So the only way in was the old slog-through-the-Wilds routine, and that was dangerous enough when everyone was fighting fit. When you were trying to manhandle a feeble and disoriented old man along those treacherous paths, while under attack from who knew what forces, the odds of making it to your destination were vanishingly small. I could tell from the Hawk's grim silence that he thought so, too.

"We could go back to the sith," Sage said. "We'd be safe there."

It was true; nothing could get in without Willow's permission, but there was a problem with that, and the Hawk saw it right away.

"Safe, but trapped," he said. "We don't want to be backed into a corner unless it's our very last resort."

"Where, then?" I racked my brains for a solution. "Could Yriell help?"

He shook his head. "Same thing. We'd be trapped in her house."

We arrived at the car. Sage helped the king into the back seat, and I got in on his other side. Up close, his hair smelled funny, as if were a long time since it had been washed, though his face was clean and he appeared well cared for otherwise. His hands were spotted with age, and shaking where they rested on his knees, so I took one in a firm grasp. This must all be so confusing for him.

Willow and the Hawk got in the front, and Willow started the car. "Where am I going?" she asked, as she pulled out.

"Yriell is strong, though," I argued. "She gave us the antidote to the green mist. She may have other things that could help us."

"She might be able to get a message to the palace for us," Sage said.

"Or even have a way to help us through the Wilds." It was probably a wild hope, but she'd told us once that the Wilds used to be part of the Earth Realm, before they were shoved out of the tamer Realms, and she was at home there. It didn't hurt to ask, at least.

"Yriell's it is, then." Willow chucked a U-turn and roared off down the street.

My whole body was throbbing, and I could feel my muscles stiffening up as I sat there, jammed up against the king in the back seat. I hoped no more fighting would be necessary tonight, but I had a bad feeling about that.

Sure enough, we weren't even halfway to the National Park when four motorcyclists appeared on our tail, roaring up behind us like the horsemen of the apocalypse.

Willow checked the rear-view mirror. "This doesn't look good, guys. Our friend Dansen is back."

I craned around to peer over my shoulder, ignoring the protest of my aching muscles. "With a few more trolls."

They were so big they looked like grown men sitting on kids' bikes, but I wasn't inclined to laugh. The prospect of imminent death had never particularly tickled my funny bone. One had a pair of swords sticking up over his shoulders, and the other two both carried axes. Damn. I did *not* want to face another axe-wielding troll tonight. I didn't even have Gladys to help. Now I wished I'd taken the broken walking stick from the first troll's back and brought it with me. Hindsight is always twenty-twenty vision.

"Dansen looks pretty good for a guy who was gushing blood twenty minutes ago," Sage said, peering over her shoulder.

Damn. Someone must have whacked him with a healing spell. He might be feeling lightheaded from loss of blood, but I bet he'd still be able to swing a sword.

"Hopefully he's run out of troll henchmen, now," I said. "This is really getting old."

No one pointed out that the three he had with him would be more than enough to finish us off if they caught us. The Hawk was a mighty warrior, but three trolls were like six ordinary guys. Not exactly a fair fight.

Willow floored it. Her car had plenty of grunt, and it flew through the dark streets at dangerous speeds. Grimly, I held onto the oh-shit bar and tried to steady the king with my other hand as we hurtled around corners, barely keeping all four tyres on the ground.

One of the trolls roared up beside us. He wasn't wearing a helmet, but trolls had hard skulls, so he probably didn't need one—if he could even have found one to fit. He grinned at me through the window, and I felt uncomfortably aware of how thin the glass was that separated us.

Suddenly, he launched himself from the bike, and the car rocked as he landed on the roof.

A moment later, an axe head came smashing through it. We all ducked reflexively, and I'm not ashamed to say I screamed. Willow spun the wheel hard, trying to dislodge him.

He held fast to his axe, using it as an anchor to hold himself in place while he hammered the roof with his fist. It was already sagging alarmingly from the weight of the troll on top. Willow tried again, fishtailing wildly down the road.

The troll's body slid from side to side, dangling with his legs almost on the road surface after the last manoeuvre. She veered close to a telegraph pole, and there was a mighty thud as the troll was wiped off the car against the pole.

After that, the other bikers were content to hang back, obviously happy to wait until we left the car, as they knew we would eventually.

"What's the plan?" Sage asked as we approached the National Park. "How are we going to shake these guys long enough to get to Yriell?"

We were still flying down the road, way faster than the speed limit. It was lucky we hadn't attracted the attention of the police yet. The entry to the park was dark, of course, the gates chained and padlocked closed for the night. Willow showed no sign of slowing as she approached. "Leave it to me."

"Stop!" I yelped. "You can't break through those. You'll get us all killed."

But I misjudged her. She slammed on the brakes at the very last moment, and the car came to rest with its bumper bar nuzzled up against the gate.

"Everybody out!" she yelled. "Get into the bush."

We hurried to obey, but the bikers were right behind us. The Hawk ran straight at Dansen Arbre, who was first off his bike, guarding our backs as we urged the king into the scrub at the side of the road.

"Now what?" I asked. "Have you got a tyre iron in the back?"

There was no way the Hawk could hold off all three on his own. I had to help him. But Willow caught at my arm when I would have gone to him.

"Hawk!" she called. "This way."

He fell back towards us, fighting all the way. It was just

as well he moved when he did, since the trolls had nearly encircled him. Sage was gone, leading the king further away, but I couldn't move, certain we were all about to be cut down.

But as Dansen Arbre entered the shadows under the trees where we sheltered, long strands of thick grass boiled out of the ground and curled up around his legs. He slashed at them, but as fast as he cut through them, more grew to take their place. One of the trolls was well caught, too, though the other hadn't ventured far enough off the road to become truly entangled yet.

"Go, go, go," Willow urged.

Sometimes it was bloody handy to have the heir of the Spring Court on your side. The magic of growth and decay was their thing, and Willow was good.

"Will you be all right?" Her magic came at a cost in this iron-laden world. She wouldn't be able to keep it up forever. Already, she had a drawn look around the eyes that I didn't like, but what other choice did we really have? It was either this or fight all the way to Yriell's place—or, more likely, fight part of the way to Yriell's place and get cut down on the way.

"Save your breath for running," she advised tightly.

The Hawk grabbed my hand and took off after Sage and the king, dragging me with him, so I did as I was told and ran like the hounds of hell were after me.

28

The bush looked very different in the dark, more ominous and alien. I saw trolls and swordsmen in every hulking shadow as I ran, but no one jumped out at us. We soon caught up with Sage and the king, who was flagging badly. The Hawk said nothing, merely sheathed his sword, picked up his monarch, and kept running. The knight's determination knew no bounds. He ran with long, easy strides, as if his burden weighed nothing at all.

By the time we reached the lightning-blasted stump that marked the turn-off to Yriell's house, my breath was coming in deep gasps that tore all the way from the bottom of my lungs. I'd thought I was pretty fit, but tonight's events were proving otherwise. Or maybe there was just something about long-distance sprints in the featureless black of the bush that stole my breath away. This was *not* my idea of a fun night out.

A branch tore at my hair as I passed, twiggy fingers grasping. The straight silver trunks of the gums loomed from the dark like ghosts, and a feeling of dread caught hold of me. We would never get away with this. We'd die here, cut down by unseen opponents, and my dreams of returning to Autumn would die with me. My name would be reviled throughout the Realms as the person responsible for the ultimate death of the king. I should turn back now, while there was still a chance—

Sage grabbed my hand. "Come on, we're nearly there."

The Hawk, carrying the king, had already disappeared through the illusory brambles. Only Sage and I still lingered here, just outside the safety of Yriell's property.

And just where the Aversion was strongest. It had caught me again. Sage's touch lessened its hold on my mind, though a whimpering child crouched somewhere deep inside me insisted I was about to be torn to shreds by those wicked thorns. I closed my eyes and let her drag me through.

It was such a relief to break through the Aversion and feel my terrors slip away. Well, not all of them, of course. It still seemed a fairly even chance that we would die tonight, but that was because I knew Willow wouldn't be able to hold up our pursuers forever, not because of a spell that was messing with my head. I drew a steadying breath, then jogged the last stretch to Yriell's front door.

It opened as I arrived.

"Did I forget to tick a box somewhere to say I didn't want to become best friends forever, fly-boy?" Yriell said, her exasperated gaze running over the Hawk and the man cradled in his arms like an overgrown baby. "Who the bloody hell is that? One of your drunk friends? If you're looking for a hangover cure, you can piss right off. I'm busy."

"It's the king," he said. "Can you help us? We are pursued by his enemies."

She blinked, and for a moment there was such an expression on her face of hope and astonishment all jumbled up together that she looked like a different person. Then she stood back and held the door wider, her forehead creased into its usual cranky frown. "Right. You'd better come in, then."

The light inside seemed almost blinding after our run through the darkness, though there was only one lamp on. The fire in the hearth lent a warm glow to the room. It looked so calm and peaceful. I wanted to curl up in the armchair in front of the fire and read a book. Or, better yet, fall asleep for about twenty-four hours.

Yriell barred the door by slotting a massive timber into place behind it, reminding me that this night was far from over.

"What's to stop them coming through the window?" I asked. Sure, the door looked pretty solid now, but the big sheet of glass right next to it was a huge vulnerability.

Yriell shot me an impatient glance. "This house has more protections than the ones you see. Bring him over here."

She gestured to a small lounge by the fire, and the Hawk laid the king gently down on it. He didn't quite fit, and his slippered feet hanging over the edge looked absurdly vulnerable.

Yriell knelt by his side and took his weathered old hand in hers. "Rothbold, you stupid bastard." Despite her words, her voice was unusually gentle. "I might have known you'd screw everything up without me. You, girl" —she looked up at me— "put the kettle on."

"We don't have time for tea," I said.

"Dansen Arbre and his minions are on our tail," the Hawk added. He had moved to stand closer to the window now that the king was off his hands, and was keeping a close watch for any sign of the pursuit.

"That pillock," she sniffed. "It's about time someone rid the world of his stench."

"I'd be happy to oblige," the Hawk growled.

"Kettle, girl." She stood up, jerking her head toward the kitchen. "No one's making tea. I can see I'm going to need a stronger brew here. Where did you find the king?"

"In a dementia unit at a nursing home." I gazed at her anxiously. Did she have a potion that could restore the king to himself? "Do you think you'll be able to fix him?"

"Depends what they've done to him." Her hands were busy, pulling jars and boxes down from the shelves that lined her walls. "I'll do my best, but there's no telling. The damage may be permanent."

The king sat up, looking so confused and lost that my heart went out to him. Sage immediately plopped herself down next to him on the couch and took his hand. "This nice lady is going to get you a drink to make you feel better."

Yriell snorted. "*Nice lady*. It's a long while since anyone called me anything so complimentary. Who are you? I like you."

"Sage Domani. I'm a friend of Allegra's."

"Oh, I've heard of you." Yriell shot her a glance from under her craggy eyebrows, though her hands never stilled. She had half a dozen bits and pieces combined in a mortar already, and was busily grinding away with the pestle. "You're Fallon Domani's daughter."

"That's right." Sage kept her smile on, but it was a little strained. She hated talking about her father.

"Well, you're still welcome, especially if you'll sit there and keep poor Rothy calm. I'm not the kind of person who judges someone on their bad luck in parents."

Sage nodded, apparently unsure what to say to this. I was diverted by the old woman calling the king of all the Realms "Rothy". Just as well he wasn't himself, since I couldn't imagine that kind of disrespect going down well with him under normal circumstances.

Still, these weren't normal circumstances by any means.

I moved to the Hawk's side, since Yriell seemed to have things well in hand. "Any sign of them?"

"Not yet."

That meant Willow still had them trapped, perhaps. Or maybe they were already on their way here. I hoped she'd had the sense to get out of their way if they had managed to break free of her enchantments. She wouldn't have the strength left to protect herself. I told myself that they'd be far too eager to continue their pursuit of the king to bother playing hide and seek in the bushes with a worn-out spellcaster and tried to feel better.

"Don't worry," Yriell said as she added some foul-smelling liquid to the ingredients in her mortar. It could have been swamp water, from the smell of it. Or maybe raw sewage. I was bloody glad I wouldn't be the one drinking it. "I'll know when they cross my borders."

"Will your potion restore the king's powers as well as his memory?" I asked. Surely the king had power enough to save us all from Summer's minions?

"One thing at a time, girl. I don't even know if I can bring his mind back yet."

"Lady Yriell," the Hawk said, glancing away from his vigil now he knew he'd have some prior warning of danger, "is there any way you can hide the king, or get a message to my fellow knights? I fear that Summer will not give up the chase, but we are vulnerable until we can get the king to the palace."

"And we can't get through the Wilds," I said. "The Greenways will be watched."

"There are more ways to kill a cat than drowning it in cream." She poured her concoction into a glass and hurled a blast of dark green Earth magic at it. She winked at me. "No time for microwaves tonight, eh?"

The liquid bubbled and frothed, then clung to the sides, thick and viscous, and once again, I was glad that I wouldn't have to drink it myself. That stuff she'd whipped up to protect us from the green mist had been gross enough.

And speaking of which ...

"Dansen Arbre used the green mist against us," I told her. "Your potion worked perfectly."

"Excellent." She knelt in front of the king and offered

him the glass. He took it hesitantly, but she didn't let go completely, helping to guide it to his lips. "I'm sorry about the side effects."

"What side effects?"

The king spluttered, and tried to draw away from the foul concoction, but Yriell insisted, pressing the glass firmly against his mouth while Sage held his head. Between the two of them, they got most of it into him, though some of it ended up on his face and clothes.

"Didn't I mention those? You'll probably have raging diarrhoea tomorrow."

Seriously? "It might have been nice if you'd mentioned that."

"Why? Would you rather have fallen into a coma and been hacked to death by our friends from Summer while you slept?"

Well, when she put it like that …

I said nothing, and she nodded, satisfied. We all watched the king for any change. He screwed his face up and swallowed hard, his eyes wide.

"I think he's going to throw up," Sage said.

Yriell took the king's chin in her hand and glared into his eyes. "No, Rothy. Focus. Look at me."

The king stared back, pinned helplessly under her commanding gaze, though he swallowed convulsively a couple more times. He looked like a cat trying to bring up a hairball.

When nothing further happened, Sage said, "What did you mean, there are more ways to kill a cat than drowning it in cream?" From the gleam in her eyes as she spoke, I knew she'd added the expression to her list of fun slang. She was probably storing it away with glee, ready to tell Willow.

"Do you have another way to get to the palace?" I asked, my anxiety spiking again at the thought of Willow. I almost wished the trolls would get here so the waiting would be over. I hated not knowing what was happening out there.

She sighed, releasing the king's chin and standing up. "I'd rather go almost anywhere else in the Realms, but yes. From here, the Realms are only a little trip downstairs away."

I cocked my head to the side, confused. Downstairs was her dark and creepy basement. The things she had on the shelves down there made upstairs look like a chocolate shop. "Isn't downstairs a sith?"

That's what I'd assumed when I'd seen it, last time we'd been here. Although there had been that opening, covered by greenery, that looked as though it might lead somewhere.

"No. I have direct access to the Realms down there."

"Then we don't have to go through the Wilds?" My heart leapt with hope. This was the best news I'd had since discovering the king's whereabouts.

"You think I'm made of magic? You don't see them giving any magic gate-opening swords to me, do you? No, we'll still have to go through the Wilds."

"But the Greenways—"

"Will be watched, I know. Who said anything about using the Greenways?"

"Then it's true? You can lead us through the Wilds themselves, and not get lost?"

"I believe I told you so once. I've got better things to do with my time than make up shit to impress pretty changelings, you know."

The king coughed, drawing all eyes to him.

"I feel … funny." He raised a hand to wipe his forehead and looked around at each of us. "Who are you people?" His voice was stronger. He was even sitting up straighter, his gaze a little keener.

"Look at his hand," Sage hissed.

Even the king looked. The wrinkles were fading from it before our eyes, the sagging skin firming and filling out again. He held both hands out in front of himself, turning them in wonder.

"Sire." The Hawk left his post at the window and fell to his knees before the king.

"I … know you," Rothbold said, as a wave of colour swept down his limp hair, leaving it brown and curly. His face seemed to emerge from under a cobweb of wrinkles, the gaunt features of the elderly man subsiding back into the face of a man in his prime, with sharp blue eyes that suddenly seemed more alert than I would ever have thought possible of that confused old man.

But that man was gone.

"Kyrrim?" The king reached for the Hawk's hands, and the Hawk stared up at him in wonder.

There were tears in his gold-flecked eyes, and my own prickled a little in sympathy. He had been waiting for this moment for so many years.

"Where are we?" The king's glance swept around the room, taking it all in. "What is happening?"

He stood up, and the Hawk leapt to his feet. "We freed you from your captors, sire, but they are still chasing us. I brought you here to the Lady Yriell, and she has released you from the spell that kept you confused."

"So confused," the king said softly. He raised a hand to his forehead again. "I still don't feel right. I can barely remember anything. How long was I captive?"

A deathly hush fell on the room. The fae lived a long time, but no one wanted to be the first to tell the king that he'd just lost twenty years of his life.

"Rothbold." Yriell stepped back into the king's line of vision. "It may take some time for all your memories to return. Now is probably not the time to give you a full update. We need to get you away from here before your enemies arrive."

He frowned at her. "Do I know you? I feel as if I do." He took a few steps towards her, then stopped, a look of surprise on his face. "I feel so weak."

He tottered and looked around, as if for a place to sit. The Hawk stepped up and took his arm. The poor man had been living as an old man for so long, he was probably dreadfully unfit. He might feel like an old man, regardless of how he looked, until we could get the palace healers to take a look at him.

Yriell's gaze turned to the window, though nothing moved in the dark outside. "They're here. Just coming through the Aversion now."

"How many?" the Hawk asked urgently.

"I can't tell exactly. More than one, less than ten. We'd better go."

She opened the discreet little door that hid the stairs to the basement, gesturing impatiently.

The Hawk steered the king toward them. "Take him. I'll stay here and hold them off."

"No need for heroic last stands quite yet," Yriell said, shooing Sage and I toward the stairs. "This house is not without its protections."

A dark shape leapt onto the small porch of the house and crashed up against the window. I flinched away, expecting the glass to shatter, but it held. Outside, the face of a troll leered in at me. I gave him the bird and followed the others down the stairs.

Somewhere at the bottom, a light bloomed, showing the king staring into Yriell's face. Behind us, the walls shook as someone hammered on the front door, and something heavy landed on the roof.

"I know your magic," the king said dazedly. "I've tasted it before. You're my sister."

Yriell patted his shoulder. "Of course I am."

29

Okay, the poor guy was still confused. Yriell looked old enough to be his mother, but he was still staring at her with a kind of wonder in his eyes. Well, we could get this straightened out later, assuming we all lived through the rest of the night.

The sound of shattering glass chased us down the stairs. So much for the house having protections. But Yriell didn't seem perturbed. She didn't even hurry as she led the way across the chamber of horrors that was her basement and into the shorter tunnel, toward where I thought I'd caught a glimpse of daylight last time I'd been down here, filtered through a curtain of trailing leaves.

Of course, there was no sunlight now. Our only light was a small ball of faelight bobbing in the air above Yriell's head.

A hissing sound in the room behind us was the only warning before the tunnel filled with green mist. Shit. I hoped Yriell didn't breathe in any of that. She hadn't drunk the potion with the rest of us. She moved faster, so maybe she was thinking the same thing.

For that matter, I had no idea how long the potion's effect lasted. It hadn't seemed as important a question on that sunny afternoon when she'd given it to us as it did now, trapped in a black tunnel with the mist writhing all around us. I held my breath and forged onward. It couldn't be far now. I didn't remember this tunnel being very long.

Right in front of me, the others disappeared. I let out a cry of alarm, inadvertently inhaling a lungful of mist. Coughing, I staggered forward in the sudden blackness, disoriented.

Then Yriell's head reappeared, the bobbing light behind her. The curtain of leaves fell around her, obscuring her body. Passing through the gateway must have cut off the light. "Hurry up, girl. We haven't got all night."

A footstep scraped on the stone behind me.

Dansen Arbre was bearing down on me, his sword out, silver hair flying behind him, and his eyes lit up at the sight of his quarry so near. For a moment, I froze, my gaze locked on that blade. All I could think was that he hadn't even taken the time to clean it.

Why was there blood on it? Where was Willow?

Yriell's hand closed around my bicep and yanked me through the curtain, so hard I stumbled and would have fallen if the Hawk hadn't been there to catch me. We stood in a little hollow between large rocks, the shadows of tall trees looming all around. The gate we'd come through was the opening of a small cave mouth, almost hidden by a tangle of vines and hanging branches.

"Dansen—" I gasped. The Hawk didn't even have his sword out. We'd be slaughtered. But he only closed his arms around me and dragged me away from the gate.

I struggled against him, looking back in horror at Yriell, who was just standing there, right in front of the gateway, practically begging to be cut down.

The sword burst through, its bloody edge catching the moonlight, followed by Dansen's arm.

I lunged toward her, fighting against the Hawk's embrace, just as his face appeared, framed by the dripping greenery.

And then Yriell spoke a single word, and the sword clattered to the rocky ground.

For a moment, I stood there, blinking, unable to understand what had just happened. Dansen's head bounced on the rocks with a splat.

Or half of it, anyway. I stared at it, watching the blood, black in the moonlight, drip from the open back of his skull. It had been sheared in half, as if a giant had brought down a massive axe on the top of his head and cut clean through. I dragged my gaze away, fighting the urge to gag, and looked at the sword, but that wasn't much better. His hand still clutched the sword's hilt, but his forearm ended abruptly in another neat and bloody cut.

I looked up at Yriell at last and shivered as realisation dawned, grateful for the warmth of the Hawk's arms around me. "You closed the gateway when he was partway through."

"Couldn't have happened to a nicer fella," she said,

looking down on her bloody handiwork with evident satisfaction.

I swallowed. The smell of blood made my stomach roil. Though I had no love for the guy, the savage efficiency of his death had shaken me. "And the trolls who were with him?"

"Will probably live," she said, clearly unconcerned. "As long as they leave the house quick smart." She paused. "Not that trolls are usually either quick or smart. Oh, well. I may have a mess to clean up when I get home."

I eyed her with new respect. When the glass of the front window had broken so easily, allowing our pursuers into the house, I'd thought it meant her protections had failed. Clearly, I'd underestimated her. She'd only lured them to follow us, just so that she could do this.

"Well, then." Her eyes gleamed as she looked around at our little group. One of us, at least, was enjoying her evening. "Let's see about getting Rothbold home."

Rothbold was standing straighter, now, as if merely being back in the Realms had revitalised him. He offered her a slight bow, then held out his arm, slightly bent. She moved to his side and slipped her hand into the crook of his elbow and, as she did so, a strange transformation came over her.

The wild grey curls softened into light brown waves, tumbling down over shoulders which had grown thinner and straighter. She was still ridiculously short, but now she seemed petite and delicate rather than rough and rounded. She smiled up at the king, and her face was as unlined as his, though I could still see it was her face. Just more youthful and beautiful than I could have imagined possible.

"Home for you, too, Orina," the king said, bending down from his considerable height to brush a soft kiss on her rosy cheek.

The Hawk drew in a sudden breath. "Your Highness! I didn't recognise you."

"That was the whole idea, fly-boy. It'd be a pretty bloody useless disguise if you could."

Sage also looked shaken, but I was still lost.

"Am I the only one here who doesn't know what's going on?" I hissed in an undertone to the Hawk.

He glanced down at me, bemused, then seemed to realise that he still had his arms around me. Was it my imagination, or did he seem a little reluctant as he released me? "Princess Orina is the king's sister," he said.

Truly? I looked harder at the now-beautiful woman on the king's arm. I guess there was a certain resemblance there. They both had the same narrow face and pointed chin, and the delicate arch of Yriell's eyebrows was echoed in a slightly thicker form on the king.

"Guilty as charged," Yriell said. "Got sick of all that Court malarky years ago. Bootlickers fawning all over me, trying to curry favour with the king's sister. All I wanted to do was tramp around in the forests, minding my own business, not go to their stupid balls and hunts and what have you."

"So you've been hiding out in the mortal world?"

She bristled a little. "Not *hiding*. Just removing the

temptation to turn a few of those Court toadies into toads for real." Then she glanced at Rothbold and sighed. "Living virtually right next door to my lost brother, too. I wish I'd known. You won't like some of the things that silly bitch you married has been up to these last twenty years."

The king glanced down at the remains of Dansen Arbre. "It seems some things haven't changed. Summer is still manoeuvring for power."

Yriell rolled her eyes. "Yes, and the sun still rises in the east, too. Kellith won't be happy until he is king. You know that."

The king nodded, looking grim. It must suck to know that your own brother-in-law was working against you. Probably your wife, too. Politics was the pits, and I was glad I had no part in it. "I can deal with Kellith."

Privately, I doubted that. He'd probably thought he was dealing with Kellith before, and look where that had got him—twenty years in a dementia unit. But I kept my mouth shut. It was nothing to do with me.

"And who are these lovely ladies?" the king asked, smiling at Sage and me. "I suspect I have you to thank for my deliverance."

"This is Sage Domani of the Spring Court, sire," the Hawk said. "And this is Allegra Brooks, an Autumn changeling."

I bobbed a weird little half-curtsey, unsure what to do in the presence of royalty. I mean, I'd been in royalty's presence for some time, but it seemed different now the king was more himself.

The king raised an eyebrow. "A changeling? You look a little old to be in the Realms."

Yes, thanks to you and your bigotry. It had been the king's edict that forced all changelings to leave the Realms for good by the age of eighteen unless their parents donated enough power to turn them fae. I'd always thought the main motivator for the rule was simply a dislike of seeing old people—which made his incarceration in a nursing home more than a little ironic.

"Special circumstances, sire," the Hawk said.

"I am in your debt, both of you," the king said. He smiled at the Hawk. "And you, too, of course, Kyr." He clasped the Hawk's forearm, and they stood for a moment, their joy at being reunited evident.

My own feelings were a little less joyful. Being presented with such clear evidence that the king's prejudice against changelings was still alive and well made my chance of gaining the reward I most desired look slim indeed.

Yriell cleared her throat. "I hate to break up the party, but we'd probably better get you home. You're not out of the woods yet, you know."

"Is the palace safe?" the king asked.

He'd been out of the loop a long time, so it was a valid question, but again, I was struck at how awful his situation was. Imagine having to ask if your own home was safe, because your family would sooner harm you than see you retake your throne. He should be getting down on his knees and thanking the Lady for the curse of the Brenfells, or Kellith would have killed him twenty years ago. My mother may have kicked me out of the Realms, but at least she hadn't tried to kill me.

"It will be with me there," Yriell said.

"Once the news of your return becomes public," the Hawk said, "they won't dare move openly against you. And your knights are still loyal. But first, we have to get you there."

I could see the king was bursting to ask questions. He'd missed so much. But he nodded. "Then I am in your hands."

"Well, strictly speaking, you're in mine, brother dear," Yriell said. "Fly-boy, there, is worse than useless out here in the Wilds."

She tugged him into motion and led the way from our rocky dell. It was a beautiful, clear night, and the setting moon still cast enough light for our fae and changeling eyes. Yriell moved with confidence toward the encircling trees, and I thought we were in for a night of forcing our way through the undergrowth, but branches swept themselves out of her way as she approached, and thick bushes miraculously cleared a path for her.

The rest of us hurried to keep up with her as the path closed again behind her just as quickly, the branches trailing almost fondly across her head or caressing her skirts. Flowers which had closed for the night sprang open again as she neared, and a heady perfume followed us. It was as if the Wilds welcomed her, even worshipped her.

"I see you've lost none of your touch," Rothbold said.

"This is my home," she said simply. "More than any four walls could ever be."

She never faltered or looked lost in the trackless wilderness. In her company, the Wilds no longer seemed as terrifying as usual, though I couldn't help feeling uneasy over the lack of a path. The rules for survival were deeply ingrained in me. But I trusted Yriell, so I followed where she led—if not gladly, at least resolutely.

Several times, we stopped to rest, and soft grass formed a carpet for us. Strawberries appeared as if from nowhere, ripe and ready to be plucked. The king ate some with evident enjoyment, though his exhaustion was also evident. He was the reason for the frequent stops, his muscles nowhere near up to an extended hike through the woods, no matter how easy Yriell's power made the way.

I was starting to wonder if the Hawk would have to carry him again when the trees abruptly thinned, and a silver archway appeared before us. Mist hung beneath the arch—not green this time, but real mist that swirled silver and grey—blocking the view through the archway.

The king stopped at the sight of it and stood still, looking down at his feet. We had arrived at our exit from the Wilds, it seemed.

"Rothbold?" Yriell's voice was gentle. "Are you well?"

"Just … preparing myself." He took a deep breath, then nodded to the Hawk.

"Allow me," the Hawk said, and stepped through.

Once he'd gone through, we could no longer see him.

Yriell patted the king's arm. "Shall we join him?"

"Yes." The king straightened his shoulders and stepped through with her at his side.

Left behind, Sage and I looked at each other.

"Do you think Willow's all right?" I asked.

"Absolutely. Willow's not stupid. She wouldn't have stuck around once her magic failed."

"But there was blood on Dansen Arbre's sword."

"That was there before. I think he nicked the Hawk's arm when they were fighting."

I breathed a sigh of relief. "Good."

She raised her eyebrow at me. "You wanted the Hawk to get hurt?"

"No! I mean, good that Willow's okay. Shall we go through?"

"I guess we have to. There's no going back the way we came."

True. The Wilds wouldn't be so gentle without Yriell. Princess Orina. Whatever she was calling herself now. I held out my hand to Sage—I kind of needed the moral support, and I suspected she did, too. "Let's go."

Together, we stepped through the silver arch. On the other side, the swirling mist cleared, and a whole new world awaited.

Whitehaven sat atop a cliff above the vast, whispering darkness of the sea, buffeted by every wind that blew in from the ocean. On the seaward side, there was nothing but cliff beneath the white walls that shone like a beacon even at night. On the landward side, we approached massive gates that had obviously not been designed to face any kind of siege. They were purely decorative, as white as the walls and encrusted with jewels. Dragons danced across them, and the leaping dolphins that were the sigil of the king's House, and over it all, the great branches of the Lady's silver tree spread their shade.

Nevertheless, there were guards at the gate, though their weapons looked more ceremonial than practical. They stopped our little group and demanded to know our business at the palace.

"Your king has returned, you fools," the Hawk barked at them. "How dare you challenge him?"

The guards' faces blanched, and they stared at the king.

"Forgive me, Sir Knight," one faltered. "Our orders …"

And he all but bolted into the small guardhouse just inside the gates. In a moment, he returned with another man, obviously more senior, who took one look at the king and fell to his knees.

"Your Majesty! Welcome home."

"Not much of a welcome, Adain, with us standing around out here," Yriell pointed out in an acid tone.

"Princess Orina!" The poor man looked as if he wished the earth to swallow him up. Who knew—if he annoyed Yriell too much, that might even become an option. He scrambled back to his feet and roared at the hapless guards to let the king pass.

After that, everything started happening much faster. A messenger ran ahead to the palace, while we walked a path of shining white pebbles through the gardens, heavy with the perfume of night-blooming flowers. The towers of the palace rose above the trees, gleaming softly against the night sky. It was supposed to be impossible to look directly at them in the full sun, because they shone so bright. Whitehaven was renowned as the most splendid residence in all of the Realms, with its walls of pure white and its gleaming marble floors. At night, it was lit by hundreds of crystal chandeliers, which chimed and made unearthly music when the ocean breezes entered through the arched windows.

As we approached the wide marble steps leading up to the palace, two men appeared at the top, one tall and solid with a mane of russet hair, the other thinner and dark-haired. Both wore courtly dress, with swords buckled at their sides.

The king's face lit up as they hurried down the steps to meet us. When they reached him, they dropped as one man to their knees, and he offered his hand to each of them in turn.

"The Lion and the Dragon," the Hawk whispered into my ear.

"Sire, can it really be true?" The Lion's eyes glistened with happy tears as he kissed his king's hand. "I had given up hope of ever seeing you again."

Both men nodded to the Hawk as they fell in with our party. He nodded back, but said nothing, and I remembered him telling me how everyone had turned against him after the king disappeared, even his fellow knights. He still seemed separate from them, even though his faith had managed to bring the king back. It would take time to heal the rifts of the last twenty years.

A third knight joined us just inside the palace doors, a

lean man with a shock of silver in his otherwise dark hair who'd managed to button his shirt with the buttons aligned in the wrong holes. He must have been in bed when he got word of the king's return. He moved with the same lethal grace as the Hawk did as he, too, bent his knee to the king and kissed his hand.

"The Wolf," whispered the Hawk, his breath tickling my ear.

The knights fell in around the king in a tight, protective circle, even the Hawk. The tramp of their booted feet on the marble floors as they hustled him down the wide hallways echoed off the glittering walls. Whispers followed us, and now and then, as we passed a corridor, I would catch a glimpse of servants and palace officials hurrying along as word spread of the king's return. Several times, the king called pages to him as we moved, then sent them scurrying off to do his bidding.

We entered an enormous room where light reflected off the thousands of crystal drops in the chandeliers. A strip of white carpet led from the door, across the wide acres of marble floor, to a dais where the golden throne of the Realms stood.

Sage and I hung back with Yriell, as the knights marched the king across the room and delivered him to his throne. Then they took up stations in a menacing row behind him. I noticed the Wolf had taken a moment at some stage to rebutton his shirt, so he didn't look quite so disreputable anymore.

Yriell leaned against a pillar beside us, arms folded across her chest.

"What's happening now?" I whispered. Whispering seemed appropriate in such a place.

"They've sent for the queen," she growled. "So Rothbold's presenting her with a fait accompli. Got his arse back on the throne and there's nothing she can do about it."

"Would she want to—" I began, but the gilded doors to the throne room opened again, and a woman glided in, dressed in white.

Effortlessly beautiful, her long, fair hair was piled in an elaborate style on top of her head, and a small circlet perched there, studded with diamonds. Everything about her was pale and perfect, but no smile lit her face at the sight of her husband safely home again. This one could have given the ice queen a run for her money.

The Hawk stepped forward from the line of knights as the queen approached and bowed. "I have returned something far more precious than your drake skin dress, madam."

I couldn't see her face, but her voice was cool as she said, "So I see. You are to be commended, Sir Knight."

The king rose from his throne and came down the steps to meet her. She made him a very proper curtsey as he took her hand.

"Ceinwen. Are you well?"

"Very well, my lord." She smiled up into his face. "All the better for seeing you."

Seriously? That was the best she could do, having not seen her husband for twenty years? Not even a peck on the cheek? There was no way that smile was genuine. The king's answering smile wasn't exactly enthusiastic either. I felt a little sympathy for him. Maybe he didn't have such a great opinion of changelings, but it must suck to be married to someone who clearly didn't care for you.

Yriell suddenly stood up straight as a man hurried in. "Ooh, this should be good."

He had the same almost white-blond hair as the queen, braided back from his face, and the same icy blue eyes. With such a family resemblance, it wasn't hard to guess that this must be Kellith, Lord of Summer. He stopped at the foot of the dais but ignored the king completely.

"Sister, before you throw away your daughter's birthright, beware. What proof is there that this man is indeed our beloved King Rothbold returned to us?"

"Beloved king, my arse," Yriell muttered beside me.

"You think me an imposter, Kellith?" the king asked, with remarkable calmness under the circumstances.

Still, Kellith ignored him. "How can we be sure this man is not an Illusionist? It seems unlikely in the extreme that our dear Rothbold would return after all this time."

"Why, brother," the king said, "I thought you had killed all the Illusionists. Your zeal to protect the throne is commendable, but I'm sure my lady can vouch for me."

He bent and whispered in the queen's ear. That pale and icy lady flushed red, then cleared her throat.

"It's him," she said simply.

Yriell snorted. "Wonder what he said to her?"

I would have loved to know, too, but I contented myself

with watching Kellith. He bowed low to the king, acknowledging him at last.

"Welcome home, brother."

His smile was polite, but I could see the effort it cost him. He was *not* happy with the change in his station.

As Yriell might have said, it couldn't have happened to a nicer fella.

At Yriell's request, the king sent the Dragon to the mortal world to make sure Willow was okay. The queen took the king to meet their daughter, and suddenly, everyone had things to do, so Sage and I slipped out of the room and found a window seat tucked into a little nook further down the echoing hallway.

"What now?" Sage asked.

I leaned back against the wall and sighed, exhaustion surging through my whole body now that the crisis was over. The king might soon wish he was back in the nursing home rather than putting up with his bitch of a wife, but I'd done my bit. His fate was out of my hands now. "I guess we go home."

Sage glanced around, though the corridor was empty. "It would be kind of rude to just disappear."

"Since when have you cared about offending people?" I didn't even open my eyes. My eyelids felt so heavy, and it was nice to sit down and relax, though the wall wasn't all that comfy as a pillow. Still, I'd take what I could get.

"Since the person in question was the King of all the

Realms. Pissing him off seems like it could be a career-limiting move, you know?"

"We don't have careers in the Realms. We're just outcasts."

"True. Still, we can't get home unless someone helps us."

That was true, too, now that the gate glyph was broken. I hoped Eldric wasn't going to be awkward about that, since I had such a good excuse. Surely the king would put in a good word for me? I'd given up on the hope that the king might reward me with access to the Realms—he'd certainly made his views on changelings clear enough—but surely that wouldn't be too much to ask?

"Yeah." I'd be happy to sit here for hours—and it might be hours before someone remembered us in all the excitement. "Yriell will probably take us home eventually."

Or maybe the Hawk. I wouldn't say no, even if in my heart I half-despised myself for my interest in the gorgeous knight. Might as well fall in love with the king himself as set my sights on a man like Kyrrim. We moved in such different circles that they weren't even in the same world. Literally. Just because, at times, it felt as though he was stealing every opportunity to touch me, it didn't mean he was truly interested. Probably it was all just wishful thinking on my part, and I'd misinterpreted his natural courtesy as something completely different.

Well, that wasn't a depressing thought *at all.* I sighed and cracked an eyelid to check on Sage, but she was staring out the window at the garden. It must be nearly sunrise;

there was enough light to make out the forms of ornamental bushes cut into the shapes of birds and animals. They were kind of creepy, actually. A giant leafy peacock seemed to be staring straight at me, so I shut my eyes again and thought rather longingly of the comfortable bed waiting for me back at Willow's place.

Willow. Dammit, I needed to make sure she was all right. How long before we could get out of here? I shifted uncomfortably against the hard stone wall.

A familiar voice laughed. "You've picked an odd place for a nap, girl. There must be a hundred beds in this draughty old castle—couldn't you have found one for yourself?"

I opened my eyes and frowned at Yriell. She might look young and pretty now, but her take-no-prisoners attitude hadn't changed. "I'm sure the palace guards wouldn't mind me wandering around, making myself at home."

She sat down on the window seat between me and Sage and surprised me by patting my knee in an almost motherly gesture. "As if anyone should deny you anything after what you've done for this kingdom. My brother will be showering you with gifts as soon as he gets his head on straight."

"Really? Because it didn't sound as if he cared much for changelings."

"Crap, girl, is that why you're hiding here with a face as long as a wet week? His opinion of changelings in general has nothing to do with his feelings about *you*. My brother may be a bit of an idiot, but he's a decent man. He'll show the proper gratitude. Just give him time."

"Is he fully recovered, yet, do you think?" Sage asked.

Yriell sighed. "I wouldn't be telling this to anyone else, but his access to his power is limited. The king's power comes from the Realms themselves, you know, and he's been kept in the mortal world for so long. It will take time to re-establish that connection. Plus, I think there might be a few screws loose upstairs, too, if you know what I mean."

"Oh." Sage digested this. "He seemed very … kingly."

Yriell snorted. "Kingly. Yes, he puts on a good show. By the Lady, I hope he gets it all back quickly. He'll need it. At least now we know what they wanted the drake skins for."

"We do?" I had no idea what she was talking about, or what the missing drake skins had to do with the king's present state of confusion.

"Yes. Drake skin is a key component of a very nasty spell that will fog the mind—permanently, if you take it long enough. We're lucky Rothy only took it for a short time."

Only a fae could consider years a "short time". But he'd probably been asleep for a good part of it, at least. The Hawk had slept for seven years after inhaling only a small amount of the green mist, and the king had got a much larger dose. Possibly, he'd only been conscious in that nursing home for a couple of years.

"It also helped weaken his connection to the magic of the Realms," she continued. "And this is not a good time to be vulnerable to his enemies." She sighed. "Hopefully, this experience will at least have taught him not to trust the bastards."

"Summer, you mean?" I asked. The Realms were full of bastards, of course, but Kellith was one of the biggest, by all accounts. And he was the queen's brother. It wasn't as though he was someone the king could avoid. "Surely the king will do something about Kellith now?"

"Like what? Stop inviting him for afternoon tea? There's no proof that Kellith had anything to do with this."

"But Dansen Arbre's from Summer," Sage objected. "And he's close to Kellith."

"Which proves absolutely nothing. If I know Kellith, he will have made sure that there are no trails leading back to him, even if Arbre was dancing to his tune. That man knows how to keep his nose clean. No, poor Rothbold will have to play happy families with him, all the while keeping one eye out for the knife in the back."

He would need all his loyal knights to keep him safe—especially if he wasn't quite himself yet. The Hawk would have his work cut out for him. At least now the queen couldn't send him off on stupid quests to distract him from that work.

It was ironic how that had turned out—obviously, the queen hadn't known what her brother was using the drake skins for, or she wouldn't have made such a fuss about her stolen dress. Did she even realise that her own brother was behind her husband's disappearance? I'd taken an instant dislike to her, but I had to admit, it was possible that she didn't. If he hadn't taken her into his confidence about the drake skin, he may not have revealed his role in the affair at all.

Thinking about the drake skin made me recall a last, lingering question.

"Why do you think Arbre gave the drake skin to Peter? Do you think it was payment for something?" That had never made any sense to me—why had the fae paid off their human helpers with something as valuable as drake skin? Particularly as it seemed they needed it themselves to keep the king docile?

"Who the heck is Peter?" Yriell asked.

Quickly, I explained about Edgar's son, where he worked, and how he'd gone crazy while high on drake skin. How he'd supposedly died from its use.

Yriell shook her head. "I doubt they gave it to him at all. More likely, he saw poor Rothbold all blissed out on it and decided to nick some and try it for himself. Stupid boy."

And then he'd passed it on to a few friends, to make a quick buck. Edgar had said his son was short of money. That would explain the sudden rash of users.

"Do you think he really died of an overdose?" Sage asked. "Or did Arbre find out he was stealing the drake skin and kill him?"

I shrugged. "We'll probably never know."

"Do you girls need anything? A bed? A stiff drink?"

"I could do with a bathroom break," Sage admitted.

Yriell stood up. "I'll show you where the nearest one is."

They'd barely left when quick steps sounded on the marble floor and the Hawk appeared. I stood up as he approached and tugged my shirt straight, wishing I looked less wrinkled and blood-spattered.

Not that he wasn't blood-spattered, too. My gaze was drawn to his arm, where half his sleeve was soaked through with red. Sage was right; he had been struck in his duel with Dansen Arbre. The night had been so hectic that I hadn't even noticed.

He grinned at the sight of me. I'd never seen such a carefree expression on his normally serious face. I was even more surprised when he caught me by the waist and hoisted me into the air, spinning me around. "We did it!"

I laughed down at him, giddy with the feel of his strong hands clamped on my waist, the muscles of his shoulders moving beneath my palms. His tawny eyes smiled back at me, his whole face transformed by the lifting of the worry that had hung over him like a dark cloud. I liked this more relaxed version of the knight. Hell, who was I kidding? I liked all the versions. My heart pounded with the thrill of being in his arms as he set me down at last.

"The Dragon has returned," he said. "Willow is unharmed. She had a message for you."

"Oh? What's that?"

He grinned again. "She said to remind you that you had the early shift at work tomorrow, and not to stay out partying all night."

I laughed, and he joined in. He was so close that I could feel his chest rising and falling against my breasts.

"You know, I think that's the first time I've ever heard you laugh."

A shadow crossed his face. "I haven't had much to laugh about until I met you."

My breath caught at the intensity in his eyes, and my world narrowed until he was the only thing in it.

"Allegra." His deep voice was husky, and I thrilled to the sound of my name on his lips. "My time will not be my own now that the king has returned. I may not be able to spend as much time in the mortal world as I would like."

I was so engrossed with his lips that it took a minute to register what he was saying. Right. He was trying to let me down easy.

I pulled myself together and dragged my gaze away from that oh-so-kissable mouth. "You don't have to make excuses. I know you're a knight. I'm not expecting to see you again after this."

"Not expecting, or not wanting?" His tawny gaze pinned me, refusing to let me look away. "Because *I* want to see *you*."

My heart stuttered in my chest, my hopes leaping wildly as he snugged me more firmly against him.

And then a childish voice piped up, "Sir Knight, Lady Allegra—you're wanted in the throne room."

A page stood right next to us. With obvious reluctance, the Hawk released me, then offered his arm with a slight bow. Courtly manners firmly back in place, he escorted me back to the throne room on his arm.

The king rose as we entered, and a hush fell over the room. Despite its enormous size, it was half full, and all eyes turned to the door. Where had all these people sprung from? Half the Realms must be here.

The king came down the steps of the dais to meet us.

Before I could drop into a curtsey, he took my hand and kissed me on the cheek. He looked better even than he had an hour ago, his face smooth and unlined, his posture upright. Hopefully, that meant his return to full strength wouldn't take long.

"Allegra, the Hawk has told me of all you have done in my service these last few weeks. This kingdom, and I, personally, owe you a great debt. Though I can never fully repay it, I have a gift for you."

At my side, the Hawk smiled approvingly and stepped back as the king took both of my hands between his. A sudden tingle in my fingers made me gasp. When I looked down, a golden glow had risen in the king's hands and was now enveloping mine. A strange warmth travelled from my hands, up my arms, and filled my whole body. The room seemed to come into sharper focus, and suddenly, I could hear every creak as someone shifted their weight from foot to foot, every tiny whisper of fabric against skin. My senses had heightened, and the light from the sparkling chandeliers overhead pierced my eyes.

I gasped at the flood of new information—the sound of so many people breathing, the intensely felt pressure of the king's hands on mine, the bright lights. I staggered, and suddenly the Hawk was at my side, his strong arm around my waist. The golden glow faded, and gradually, the world became manageable again.

"I have gifted you the ability that every fae child is born with: to gate into and out of the Realms," the king said.

Did that answer my question about the strength of his

own powers? I wasn't sure. Foolish of him, perhaps, to share his power with me if he wasn't at full strength, but maybe this largesse made him look strong to his enemies, who would assume he must be completely recovered if he was prepared to waste power on a lowly changeling. I could hardly think, reeling at the immensity of the gift he'd given me.

"You are free to come and go as you wish."

"Thank you, Your Majesty," I stammered. "You are very generous."

"It's no more than you deserve," he said, still smiling, and then he signalled to the Hawk, who drew me away.

Suddenly, dozens of people I'd never met were crowding around to congratulate me, and servants appeared with food and wine. All of a sudden, Willow's crack about not staying out all night partying didn't sound so odd as the throne room took on a festive atmosphere. Through it all, the Hawk stayed at my side, introducing me to people and fending off the most inquisitive ones with courteous yet firm words.

Finally, the Hawk was called away, and the king and his knights left the room. The party showed signs of winding down by then. It was full daylight, after all—past time for most fae to be in bed. Yriell appeared out of the thinning crowd with Sage in tow.

"Time to get this show on the road," Yriell said.

"Are you drunk?" I asked, getting a whiff of her breath.

"Of course I am. There was free beer. Do I look stupid?"

I shook my head, laughing, as we left the palace and

wandered back through the gardens. They were even more beautiful in daylight.

"Want to do the honours?" she asked as we passed back out through the palace gates.

I shook my head, a little overwhelmed at the thought. There would be plenty of time later to experiment with my new powers. "Not this time."

"All right, ladies, hold onto your hats. Next stop, home sweet home."

And as she waved goodbye to us at Willow's sith a little later, it struck me that this really was home. It was ironic, really. I finally had the means to go back, right when I realised I didn't need to.

All these years, I'd been longing to return to the Realms, thinking that was my home, when really, the Hawk had been right all along. Home was where the people you loved were.

THE END

Don't miss the next book, *Changeling Magic*, coming soon! For news on its release, plus special deals and other book news, sign up for my newsletter at www.marinafinlayson.com.

Reviews and word of mouth are vital for any author's success. If you enjoyed *Changeling Exile*, please take a moment to leave a short review at Amazon.com. Just a few words sharing your thoughts on the book would be extremely helpful in spreading the word to other readers (and this author would be immensely grateful!).

ALSO BY MARINA FINLAYSON

MAGIC'S RETURN SERIES
The Fairytale Curse
The Cauldron's Gift

THE PROVING SERIES
Moonborn
Twiceborn
The Twiceborn Queen
Twiceborn Endgame

SHADOWS OF THE IMMORTALS SERIES
Stolen Magic
Murdered Gods
Rivers of Hell
Hidden Goddess
Caged Lightning

THIRTEEN REALMS SERIES
Changeling Exile

ACKNOWLEDGEMENTS

I'm always thanking my family in my books, and this time is no exception. Thank you to my husband and daughters for cooking multiple dinners when I was stuck in revision hell, and to Mal and Jen for beta reading. Thanks to Connor for helping me nut out plot problems—it's great to have another writer in the family. Love you guys! Your support means a lot to me.

Also a big thanks to my sprinting partner, Melanie, who cheered me on and helped me focus. Without her this book probably still wouldn't be finished!

ABOUT THE AUTHOR

Marina Finlayson is a reformed wedding organist who now writes fantasy. She is married and shares her Sydney home with three kids, a large collection of dragon statues and one very stupid dog with a death wish.

Her idea of heaven is lying in the bath with a cup of tea and a good book until she goes wrinkly.

www.ingramcontent.com/pod-product-compliance
Lightning Source LLC
Chambersburg PA
CBHW032208180726
48284CB00001B/245